Praise for J.D. Austin's *The Last Huck*

"*The Last Huck* stands out as one of the most impressive debut novels of this decade. The characters, sardonic, clever, and intensely authentic, efficaciously propel Austin's masterful narrative through the backdrop of Michigan's Upper Peninsula like skate blades cutting Lake Superior ice in late winter. With this splendid, unforgettable, first effort, J.D. Austin proves himself a name to watch out for in American letters."

—Joseph D. Haske, author, *North Dixie Highway*

"*The Last Huck* tells a tale all-too-familiar for Yoopers: whether or not to sell family property that has been handed down over generations. It's a bittersweet tale of mourning the past, accepting harsh economic realities that cause people to leave the U.P. and the continual dream to return to the land they consider home. J.D. Austin's tear-jerker about family and a sense of place will speak to readers on many levels."

—Tyler R. Tichelaar, award-winning author of *My Marquette* and *Kawbawgam: The Chief, The Legend, The Man*

"If *The Last Huck* is any indication, J.D. Austin is a young author who will have a long and successful career. The story of a Finnish family caught between holding on to tradition and the need for ready cash is told with raw language and emotion. Memories of a happy childhood on the family farm clash with the reality of a four-day weekend when adult brothers and cousins confront their demons. Austin's attention to detail and description is both gripping and tender as he probes into the past and how it affects the future."

—Sharon M. Kennedy, author *The SideRoad* series

D1447322

"A deep love of land and the sorrow of losing it are the emotions underlying this powerful account of two cousins journeying to Michigan's Keweenaw Peninsula to sell property they share so that one may pay the medical expenses of a young child. In his first novel, J.D. Austin vividly captures the painful conflicts between the young men as they spend one last weekend in places that were the scenes of their happiest childhood memories."

—Jon C. Stott, author of *Summers at the Lake: Upper Michigan Moments and Memories*

"J.D. Austin's storytelling resonates with the discovery of identity for three boys, one of whom is incarcerated. Each one is a Yooper who, like Huckleberry Finn, loves the outdoors and have acquired their self-knowledge and experiences from their grandfathers, Finnish miners in the early 20th century. We are a large country with diverse literature. I find the analogy between the 19th century regional novel and this first book from Austin provocative and literate."

—Donald M. Hassler, Professor Emeritus of English, Kent State University

"In *The Last Huck*, young U.P. writer J.D. Austin picks a topic that is familiar to almost every family with aging or recently deceased members. Here, Nik (Niklas), his brother Jakob and cousin Peter, have taken possession of a farm passed down to them at the death of their Uncle Jussi. And Peter, who is in dire need of some quick cash, wants to sell the farm—even, if need be, via a Quit Claim Deed. However, the other two are not so much interested in dispatching the family property, much less doing it rapidly. The adventure that ensues not only immediately draws the reader in, but does so in a fashion that makes it virtually impossible to put the book down. Austin further provides many additional surprises along the way. It is always a joy for seasoned sojourners to witness young talent blossom and flourish as we pass through this life. You've done a great job here, Mr. Austin. Congratulations!"

—Michael Carrier (MA NYU), author of 17 *Jack Handler* Murder Mysteries / Hardboiled Thrillers

The Last Huck

A Novel

[signature]

J.D. Austin

Modern History Press

Ann Arbor, MI

The Last Huck: A Novel.
Copyright © by J.D. Austin. All Rights Reserved.

Learn more at JDAustinStories.com

ISBN 978-1-61599-805-0 paperback
ISBN 978-1-61599-806-7 hardcover
ISBN 978-1-61599-807-4 eBook

Published by
Modern History Press   Phone 888-761-6268
5145 Pontiac Trail   Fax: 734-663-6861
Ann Arbor, MI 48105

www.ModernHistoryPress.com
info@ModernHistoryPress.com

Distributed by Ingram Group (USA, CAN, EU, UK, AU)

Author photo: Jake R. Bartz
Cover art: Frankie Mayfield
Cover design: Doug West

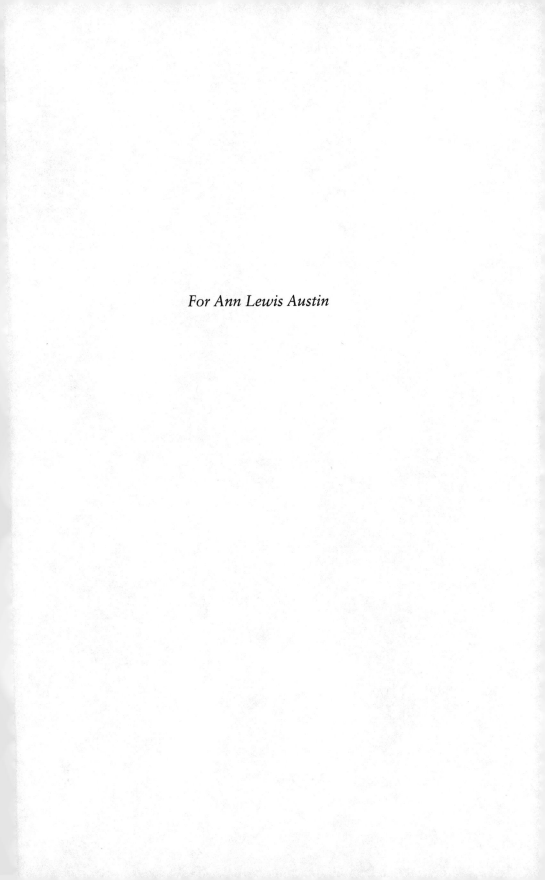

For Ann Lewis Austin

"Thy life is not thine own to govern, Danny, for it controls other lives. See how thy friends suffer! Spring to life, Danny, that thy friends may live again!"

– John Steinbeck, *Tortilla Flat*

"Everything I've ever let go of has claw marks on it."

– David Foster Wallace, *Infinite Jest*

❧ 1 ❧

Late August, 2009

Halfway between Houghton and Baraga, Niklas noticed a cluster of wooden crosses in a patch of wildflowers on the outside edge of a tight curve. For a second, he wondered why. And then, a second later, he remembered why. And then they were gone.

Peter Kinnunen arrived at his wits' end on the third Friday of August. His son had just returned from the doctor's office. His wife, who'd driven to the appointment, was crying in the bedroom.

He took out his cell phone and stared sightlessly at his cousin Niklas' name on the screen. He flipped the phone shut and went into the bathroom. After a few seconds he came out without a flush. Face twitching, he took out his phone again and called Niklas. While it rang he gritted his teeth and prepared lines in his head. Nik picked up after three rings.

"What up?"

Like a deer in the headlights, Peter froze against his own best interest. "Uh, Nik, I... do you have a moment?"

"Yeah, sure, what's up? I don't want to go to Shakers tonight or probably ever again, if that's what you're asking. I thought I was going to die last time."

"No, I, uh... no, it's not that."

"Thank goodness. What's up?"

Peter, frozen, was unsure of how to proceed. "Well, man, look. I'm running out of money, literally, I think... I want to huck it up to Uncle Jussi's farm and stay for a weekend and see about maybe, uh... selling it."

Niklas let a sinister silence hang. "You mean our farm?"

"Yes. Yes, I know, and I know this sounds bad." The words tumbled out of Peter's mouth like rubber balls on concrete. "I know how special it is to us, to you especially. But we haven't even been up there together since the funeral, since the place became ours. Our lives have gone in different directions. And I'm broke, man, I've thought about this a long while." The idea had occurred to Peter two nights ago, which, in his current state of mind, was a long while. "Look," he continued, "Of course you and Jakob would get your share. But let's be for real. He will need the money, too."

Terrifyingly calm, Niklas asked, "Do you hear yourself?"

"I'm serious, dude. We're all broke and we all live south of Crivitz. This just makes sense."

"There is zero chance in hell you will get my signature on anything. Won't be able to get a Quit Claim. Not from Jakob either."

Peter felt himself heating up. "Dammit, Nik, my back's against the wall. Tina's hands are full with our kid 'cause we can't afford daycare and I'm on furlough. Again. I'm going to lose my family if we don't do something."

"Well," Niklas said, "You and everybody else. This won't put out the national economic dumpster fire."

"Dude, I have bills. Selling Jussi's place would pay a good number of them."

"Sure," said Niklas, growing vindictive, "But think about what you'd actually get. It's not even worth selling. A third would barely cover two months of your life."

Peter ignored the jab. "That's not true. I bet we—"

"You."

"Sure. I bet I could find a neighbor interested in splitting it up into lots or logging it or something. Who knows? But I'm pretty sure."

"Look," said Niklas, voice atremble, "I'll huck it up there with you. I miss that place like hell. But we can't sell it, you know that. Especially not without Jakob here to sign off. Again, not even sure about the whole Quit Claim thing."

"Jakob would want me to be abl—"

"You don't give a shit about what he would want."

"That's not fair."

"Have you called him yet?" Nik demanded. "Written him a letter?"

"Come on, dude, I—"

"That's what I thought." Niklas was warming up. "So, what, you're gonna call him up and say 'Hey, Jakob, been a few years, mind if I rob you blind for the sake of bailing myself out?' He'd be less insulted if we just sold the place and apologized to him afterward."

"Well… so why don't we do that?"

"You're making a terrible case for yourself, Pete."

"Nik, man, all I'm saying is come up with me. We don't have to decide on anything," Peter lied. "Just talk things over. Up there. Who knows, we might do all right if we find the right guy? We could leave aside a portion for a smaller lot somewhere, maybe."

"Yeah," Niklas said, "Go fuck yourself. Not a chance. That's Uncle Jussi's land. I wouldn't take a million for my portion."

Peter bit his tongue and waited. He knew Niklas wouldn't be able to resist the trip north. Niklas had always been that way. "I'll cover gas," Peter added. A long moment passed.

"When do we leave?"

"Next Friday. That gives us two nights up there. All I'm saying is think it over. That's all I'm saying." Even though it wasn't, and Peter knew it even as he said otherwise.

"I hear you," Niklas said. "And I suspect you're full of shit."

"We could write Jakob a letter. Up there, around the fire, from both of us. He'd like that, wouldn't he?"

"I just call him these days. He wrote me a few letters the first few months. I never wrote back because we just got to calling every few weeks."

"Why didn't you write back?"

"I don't know. The letters were really intense. And we got to calling."

"Do you still have the letters?" Peter asked.

"I carry them with me everywhere."

"Geez, Nik."

"Yeah, well. He's up for parole in November."

"Shit, really?"

"Yeah. My dad's got his hopes up for a family Thanksgiving. I think he's setting himself up for a letdown."

"Huh. Well. Maybe we should write to him."

"Maybe," Nik sighed. "Sure."

A moment passed. Peter hesitated. "Well, just swing by my place after work next Friday when you're packed."

"Yeah," Niklas replied acidly. "Try to be ready when I come by, huh? I don't want to sit in your ridiculous living room getting dirty looks from Tina about the sawdust on my clothes."

"Oh, relax. I'll be ready. You can toss the football with Olly, yeah? He loves that."

Shamefully, this was a tactic, and the missing edge in Niklas' voice as he responded said so. "Yeah, sure. How is the little stud? Last time I came by Tina was fussing over him asking if he felt up to playing, or needed his meds or something, I forget. He told me he hadn't been to school in a week. He was real stoked about that, but, you know. He doing OK?"

Peter took a breath. "Yeah, he's good. Just been a little under the weather and the doctors wanted to run some tests. The tests took him out of school for a few days."

"Ah. Well. I hope the results are good. I'm sorry, dude."

"Thanks."

Silence hung, then broke with Niklas' words.

"So we gotta call Chris, right? And Mike?" Peter cracked a smile on the other end of the phone.

"Sure, we'll call Chris and Mike. I'm sure we'll see that whole crew at Schmidt's. Bonfire might happen too." As Peter said so, he wondered if that one pretty bartender was still working at Schmidt's. "Nik, who was that bartender—"

"Hayley," Nik said, answering before Peter finished.

"Damn right. Hopefully she's still working."

"Fingers crossed. Hopefully she remembers us."

"I suppose she would remember Jakob best."

Niklas laughed, a real full laugh this time. "I guess I should call Jim to open the cabin up. I think he's got the keys. I can't wait to see Jim."

"Me neither. Good call, I'd forgotten he's been keeping up the place."

"Yeah. Wonder how he's holding up."

"Me too." Peter looked out the window at a bird feasting on little mayflies gathered on the sill.

"Should I bring the bong?" Niklas asked. "Would that be disrespectful?"

"If you want," Peter said. "That's all you though."

"Maybe I won't. We never did when Uncle Jussi was around. Hmm. Yeah. I'll just bring a bowl."

"All right. I'll have the bag."

"Sounds good. When do we have to be back?"

"Monday for work, I figured."

"Yeah, all right. Shit." Both Niklas and Peter knew that this was the end of the call. The planning had begun. At the last second,

Niklas spoke up again. His voice was soft, and there was a desperate edge. He sounded like he was about to throw a Hail Mary, and hoped Peter would be there to receive it.

"Say, Pete. Uh. You ever thought about, uh...?"

"About what?" Peter had no idea.

"Nothing. Never mind. I'll see you Friday."

⚡ 2 ⚡

The Beginning

As the story goes, pieced together with as little conjecture as possible in the mind of his grandson, Hannu, young Olli decided to leave Finland for Upper Michigan in the spring of 1901. He was excited at first but grew nervous as the date of his departure approached. Numerous as his friends were, he fretted all the last weeks up until his departure about his goodbyes. The longest-standing friendships of course deserved a goodbye dinner, a long house call, a parting gift. But what of the friends whose surnames he didn't know, of the intimately familiar faces at this tavern or that inn, the lovely girls he'd danced with over long winter evenings? In the end he called on all of his close friends and said a prayer that his acquaintances would remember him fondly and take no offense at a noticeless departure.

The ship sailed from Hanko in June; the mood aboard was one of cautious optimism. Cramped together in the hold mere hours after departing, Olli got to talking to a few of those next to him and learned that his countrymen were a great deal more nervous for what awaited them on the other side of the Atlantic than he was. Going around the circle, more like a clump in the dark and musty hold each shared what they were leaving behind and why. When it was Olli's turn, he shrugged.

"My mom says she don't want me to be poor like we've been since grandfather. Her cousin has a son who got work in the copper mines. He wrote her these letters about the great forests, and the Indians, and it's all snowy and near a great big sea of a lake. It sounded close enough to home. I thought it might be fun, or at least an adventure."

An older man beside Olli roared with unkind laughter. "Well, son, perhaps your grandchildren will be happy. Or maybe their children will be. The mines will swallow you up if you're not careful. You ought to be a little more desperate, like us. Gives you an edge. Keeps you honest."

The man laughed at himself and Olli smiled back, wondering who was responsible for the axe handle up the guy's ass.

Much later, after he'd worked in the mines for twenty-odd years, after acquiring a small farm, getting married, shepherding his children through school—after just about every one of his neighbors had caved to various pressures and purchased a car, after the doctors said his cholesterol would kill him if he didn't ease up on the fried meat and potatoes—after all that, Olli Kinnunen's kids and grandkids knew of only one subject that would raise his voice and the hairs on the back of his neck. That subject was strike-breakers, and it drew from Olli a venom and the suggestion of violence, which was strange and a little bit scary. By that time his belly was wide and round and he'd achieved the age where you no longer care if your reading glasses are crooked. He could talk to anybody, of any age. He joked with everybody, all the time. His grandkids remember stories about how he used to sing to the cows he took care of. During summer, he regularly and patiently opened windows and fanned blackflies from the living room back outside where they belonged. So it was strange that what seemed like old politics could still inspire rage over an unavenged transgression.

⚡ 3 ⚡

Friday, August 27, 2009 5:37 p.m.

There comes a time during summer in the Midwest when everyone sort of looks around and agrees that summer ought not to let the door hit its ass on the way out. A time of sweaty palms around the morning coffee, of bedsheets laundered thrice weekly, of hot pavement in the morning echoing with the meaty slap of flip-flops. A time of cold showers when even the rain won't cool you off.

It had stopped raining when Niklas left his apartment on Milwaukee's east side. The hot kind of rain, the kind that riles people up when it thickens the air and wafts upward from the concrete in an odor that might be pleasant if it ever came at a time when your underclothes were dry. At five in the afternoon the sun was well on its way back down, and the light came shallow from the west; the light was a haunting blend of yellow-amber, breaking through the pregnant clouds, somehow simultaneously dark and golden. Niklas nearly missed his bus drinking in the sky with closed eyes, his haste forgotten, head cocked as though photosynthesis were really possible if only you tried hard enough.

The hiss and sigh of the Green Line's air brakes brought him back to earth. He slung a backpack over his left shoulder and his guitar case over his right. Three people got off the bus; one massively obese old woman with a walker, one flinty-eyed guy with a garbage bag full of empty cans, and an elderly lady who stopped to chat with the driver. Niklas waited for a moment on the concrete for the woman in front of him to finish. Once he'd fed two bills into the machine, his hands were empty but for a single soiled envelope stuffed with three letters. Filthy untied boot laces danced around the ankles of his paint-splattered jeans as he made for the rear of the bus. He took his blue backpack off and set it on the seat next to him, put the letters in the breast pocket of his damp t-shirt, and rested his guitar against his knees. He looked out the window and saw himself in the plexiglass. He was six feet tall and trim, with thin, straight blond hair that was shaggy around the ears, a thin, fuzzy beard, and perennially ratty clothes. His manner reminded people in some indirect way of a puppy.

8

Immediately after sitting he began to feel around and unzip his backpack to make sure he hadn't forgotten anything: the hard cylindrical lump of his water bottle; a hardcover and a paperback, both novels; his knife, sharpened last week; a glass pipe, a cold metal grinder, a lighter, and a double zip-lock with a few grams of pot (procured from a coworker at the lumberyard, actually the same one who'd sharpened his knife); a few Clif bars; a phone charger; glasses that he sometimes wore, but usually not, preferring to just squint; his orange bottle of antidepressants. He sniffed the area of the bag where the pot was—barely a whiff, all clear. Once satisfied that everything was there, that what was forgotten was truly forgotten, he zipped everything up tight and took a deep breath.

Out the window, a decrepit Brady Street slid by. Torn awnings, unrepaired from the previous winter's damage; patio tables and chairs that were fully occupied perhaps twice a week during this peak summer season; neon signs in the windows of the barrooms which were flickering or almost out of juice. Niklas wondered how much of this was normal Brady Street grittiness, and how much was actual damage done by the recession. An abandoned newspaper on the bus floor sat face up. The date read Friday August 27, 2009. Niklas took the letters out of his breast pocket and thumbed through them to make sure they were all there. He caught a glimpse of the corner of the last one. The date read March 2009. Niklas rubbed at a raised lump of dirt next to the return address on the envelope. He worked it long after it was obvious the spot wasn't coming all the way out.

The bus driver chatted with a bent old man up front. Niklas couldn't hear much beyond their tone, which was familiar. The bus driver had a thick Northwoods accent, which reminded him of old Jim Markham, their neighbor and friend over in Liminga, not five minutes from Uncle Jussi's farm.

Niklas' chest and gut clenched as he remembered what he'd forgotten—not an item, fortunately, but one of the most important things nonetheless. He flipped open his phone and found the name in his contacts. As the bus crawled down Brady Street the phone rang in his ear and his pulse quickened. He prayed he would say the right things.

"Hullo?"

"Jim! Niklas Kinnunen."

"Nik! How are ya bud?"

"I'm real well, Jim," he lied. "You holding up OK?"

"Oh yah, I'm fine."

"Cynthia doing well?"

"Oh yah, she's good. Wit da kids in town now. They're having dinner at Gino's." The recorded bus voice announced Brady and Water Street, Niklas' stop. He pulled the cord and cast around for a question that would buy him some time to get away from the noisy street corner.

"Any plans for the evening alone?"

"Oh no, I was just out back finishing da rafters on da extension. Going to a meeting with Randy in a while. He was supposed ta..." The bus pulled up and Niklas hopped off, laden with guitar and backpack. He walked quickly toward an alley to talk. The clouds had burned off. The afternoon was all the way golden now, casting crisp shadows on the pavement. In the cool shade, Niklas brought his attention back to the voice in his ear: "...hopefully gonna help me wit dose rafters and da ceiling. Could probably do 'em myself. Not da ceiling, though. One of you boys used to be da one holding up da plywood for me."

"Well Jim, maybe we can come by and do some work with you. Peter and I are coming up tonight for the weekend. We're really excited."

"Oh! We weren't sure you'd make it back before we croaked! Ha!"

"Could you—"

"You want me to open her up for ya?"

"Yes, please. Thank you, Jim."

"I gotta remember where I put da key. I remember your dad gave it to me after da funeral... hmm. When are you guys gonna be here?"

"I'll try and hustle Peter so... hopefully midnight?"

"Sure. I'll open her up."

"Thanks, Jim."

"Oh, sure. You guys going to come by for a sauna?"

"Sure, we'll help you with that ceiling, though, yeah?"

"Oh yah! That's good."

"Well, excellent. Thank you so much."

"Oh, sure. See you soon."

Niklas hung up and walked with the river on his right along Water Street toward Peter's condo. He always felt like a rat in this part of town—paint on his jeans, sawdust in his hair, hands dirty, shoes torn—generally a zit on the otherwise unblemished sidewalks. The crowd today was either jogging after work or already refreshed and on their way to an overpriced dinner. Subtle spray tans and Ray-Bans and hair beat to submission with an iron along with regular dye jobs—the inhabitants of the Water Street condos that lined the river mystified Niklas with their cosmetic discipline. Just like the cars in their heated garages or the labels intentionally left on their clothes, it was all a carefully curated "dick-measuring contest," as Jim used to say. But Peter had always been like that, or perhaps he'd merely aspired to that kind of crowd. It can be hard to make the distinction, and Niklas' faith in his cousin was entirely reliant on the latter being true, though he wasn't sure.

At the bottom of the short flight of steps leading to Peter's building, a blond girl in a black Nike bra and spandex jogged past him breathing heavily up the steps. Niklas hesitated, then followed her straight into the lobby without buzzing up. He was reminded afresh that wealth and taste are often not on speaking terms; the tacky modern chrome and pastel of the lobby and elevator put Niklas in the mind of a fancy therapist's office. He followed the jogger girl into the elevator.

"What floor?" she asked, after pressing three for herself.

"Four. Thanks." She smiled at him with bright brown eyes. She reminded him of one of Jakob's old girlfriends, a soccer player from California who'd cruelly left him in Chicago. Niklas felt a blush rising; he was relieved when the elevator arrived at the third floor, though he craned his neck to retain the view for as long as possible when she left.

He exhaled with relief when the elevator spat him out on the fourth floor into a world of chrome, except the carpet, which was a hideous orange patterned with abstract purple blocks trimmed in green. Peter's place was about five doors down on the right, he could never remember exactly which. He overshot and had to double back a few doors when he heard the aggrieved voice of Peter's wife, Tina, from behind one of them. After a second's hesitation he knocked.

11

At first he couldn't tell who had opened the door for him. A giggle escaped from down below. He looked down, and there was Peter's seven-year-old son Olly in all his gap-toothed glory, smiling up at him as if to brandish his remarkable milk mustache.

"Heyyy buddy!" said Niklas.

"Hi Uncle Nik! Can you give me a piggyback ride?"

"Sure bud. Where to?"

"Pleaseeeee!!"

Niklas laughed and set down his bags and slung the kid up onto his shoulders. They walked down the hallway into the kitchen, where Tina and Peter were going back and forth in savage whispers that weren't very quiet at all. They looked up in unison as Nik and the boy came in, eyes like some insolent puppies' who'd been caught raiding the cupboard. Tina, though rail thin and only five feet tall, had the commanding presence of a football coach. Her dark hair swung across her face as she took in the situation, and her expression twisted with outrage.

"Hello Niklas. Put him down, please." She wheeled on Peter. "What's going on?"

Peter tried to smile in Nik's direction, and grimaced. He wore a t-shirt and khaki pants, his dirty blond hair cropped short and face patchy from a few days without a shave. His face was more angular, eyes more restless, though he was about the same height as Niklas. If you looked at their faces together, you would be certain that Niklas was the more generous, patient, earnest, gullible. Peter's eyes were flighty and suspicious, his nose sharp, while Niklas' steady, upturned visage and rounded nose put people at ease. He nodded shiftily at Nik. "Hey, bud. Aren't you a little early?"

"Dude, you said six. It's, like, quarter of. Please tell me you've packed."

Tina looked like she was about to blow a gasket. "Packed? *Packed*, Peter? Packed for what?"

"Sweetie, Nik and I—"

"Don't 'sweetie' me!" She seemed to suddenly wake up to the fact that Olly was in the room. She marched over to him and corralled him by the shoulders into his room. In a moment she reappeared, eyes shining with rage.

"Peter, tell me you'll be here tomorrow for Olly's appointment."

Peter blanched. "I thought it was next week. That's what you said last week, right?"

"Yes! Yes I did. *Last* week I said it was *next weekend*, which makes it this one!"

Niklas raised an eyebrow at Peter. Peter looked at his feet for a while then gingerly met his wife's eye. "Christina, I know you want me there. But if we have to go through with… with things, we're gonna need more funds than we have. Nik and I have some family business up on the Keweenaw this weekend that should lighten the load significantly. Please trust me on this."

Tina was shaking her head, nearly mute. She started several quick sentences without finishing them. When she finally got a grip on language, she spoke slowly, her gaze shifting from one to the other of the men. Tears leaked from the corners of her eyes and her voice was wobbly.

"I know better than to ask you two not to do this, if your minds are made up. Peter, you promised about tomorrow. I'll spare Niklas the scene but I can't believe you're hanging me, hanging us, out to dry like this. I hope you guys get whatever you want up there." And she marched out the door.

"What *we* want, hon—" Peter started to say, but then their bedroom door slammed and he and Niklas were alone. He took a couple of breaths and looked around to get his bearings. "All right Nik, why don't you take a lap and I'll pack a ditty bag. I'll be ready in fifteen minutes." The term 'ditty bag' gave Niklas a start. It was one of his dad's, instead of 'duffel bag'. He hadn't heard it in years and it tugged at his heart.

"OK, hustle up then," Niklas said. "We're burning daylight and I told Jim that we'd be there by midnight. He's going to open up the cabin for us."

"All right. I'll be glad to see Jim."

"So will I, so hustle up. I'll be back in fifteen." Niklas left Peter to pack a bag and salvage what goodwill he could with his wife before hitting the road. He strode toward the elevator as Tina's strained, pleading voice once again floated out into the hallway.

* * *

On his way out of the lobby, Niklas passed a beanpole skinny boy in ripped jeans and heavy makeup with a beautiful black lab puppy on a leash. The puppy bounded up to him; he sank down to receive and return the embrace.

"His name's Baxter," the boy said. Baxter slobbered all over Niklas hands and face. His owner smiled faintly. Niklas had made a habit of spending extra affection on dogs ever since his own childhood dog, Poppy, had died unexpectedly—the memory of her face out the living room window as he'd left the house as a child had haunted him terribly. She'd died in the summer when he was eleven, just before Peter's family left for New York.

The day Poppy died, the boys were camped at their spot down by the creek, about a ten-minute walk along the creek through the woods from Uncle Jussi's cabin. Niklas and Jakob's father, Hannu, was home in Marquette at a conference. They'd been camping for four days, and hoped to stay another three nights, helping their Uncle Jussi mend a section of the orchard fence and weed the lingonberry patch which Hannu had planted in honor of his wife's Swedish heritage, and pick turnips when they weren't off on some adventure. A few of the tart red pellet-sized berries were visible on the bushes already. On the fifth morning, Niklas rose at sunrise to soothe his parched lips and take a shit. The clouds were dark and fat with rain, the air thick with moisture. Jakob and Peter were awake by the time he got back. They decided to play euchre in the tent for a while on account of the weather, but gave it up because Niklas insisted on Jakob as a partner and Peter didn't want to walk all the way to the cabin to ask Uncle Jussi to play with them. They drifted off for about an hour and then Uncle Jussi came tumbling out of the woods, unzipped the tent, jostled their shoulders and insisted they rouse themselves.

Jussi barely met their eyes all throughout his story. Their sweet dog. Poppy, was dead. Her illness was not entirely clear and completely beside the point. She'd been healthy one night, slow the next, then immobile, and finally dead four nights after she first fell ill. She was tender and skittish, fiercely loyal and slow to become so; people loved her extra, once they got to know her.

Jakob lost it and sprinted from the campsite with Niklas on his heels. Jakob drove ninety the whole way back to Marquette from Atlantic Mine. Their father, Hannu, was rocking Pernilla, their mother, but his beard was damp with sweat and tears. Poppy was wrapped in her favorite quilt on the back porch. Fistfuls of lilacs sat atop the crest in the blanket that must have been over the dog's heart. Jakob threw himself down beside her and wept. Niklas went back inside and tactlessly grilled his parents about her final hours.

Had she been comfortable? Did they feed her the carrot heavy chicken and rice dish that was her unlikely favorite? Had she any final messages for them, however flimsy the conjecture surrounding the message might be?

The answer to the first two questions was "Of course" and his mom started to answer the third, "but a fresh salvo of tears silenced her. His dad finished what his mom had started. On Poppy's last night, after an hour of vomiting and quiet whimpers she was doped up on pain meds from the vet. Just before she dropped off to sleep in the front room below her favorite window, two neighborhood tabbies she'd grown friendly with came crying to the front door. When she didn't leap up and bound over to bark her greeting, the cats' cries persisted and increased in volume. Pernilla let the cats in for the first time ever. They slowly walked up to the old dog who raised her head slightly, fighting the meds. Each cat in turn stepped gave her a nuzzle and left the house with their heads bowed, tails stiff in mourning. Pernilla went to stroke Poppy. The dog let out one last feeble bark, licked her outstretched hand, and died.

Two years later, Niklas' buddy, Drake from high school, went to jail for selling meth. His dog, Berkeley, had finally succumbed to some long festering illness and Gwen, Drake's mom, called Niklas up one day and asked if he could come spread Berkeley's ashes with her, since she didn't have anyone else. Drake was in jail, her other sons were out of town. Niklas readily agreed. It was a wretched day all around with the most fabulous weather. They parked and walked all the way out to the end of Presque Isle and spread Berkeley's ashes under a massive spruce tree near the water.

Niklas was stroking Baxter's head, lost in memory, when the skinny guy's voice brought him back to earth. He had to eat dinner, he said, and then he had to rush out to a drag show. Just as quickly as Niklas had forgotten the warring family he'd left upstairs, as quickly as the guy and his dog had appeared, so quickly did the elevator swallow them up. Alone again, Niklas walked outside for a lap around the block to wait for Peter, fingers crossed for the advent of other dogs.

He was sitting on the curb lost in thought when Peter called. He'd been watching three ants coordinate the dragging of crumbs from a half-eaten roast beef sandwich that was rotting on the sidewalk. The lead ant paused, and Niklas brought down a fingernail, severing the ant's head from its thorax. A fellow ant came along and began dragging his buddy along, minus a head. Niklas wondered whether he was being dragged to safety or added to the food supply, and a wave of remorse passed over him just as Peter called to summon him back upstairs.

Tina answered the door. She was sniffling, and she spoke to the floor in barely a whisper: "Please be safe. Call me if anything happens. Watch out for deer, and please get him home in a few days. It's always the second deer, you know. The one that jumps out after you think you've dodged the first one." She paced quickly into the apartment and disappeared down the hallway to the bedroom.

Peter stood in the kitchen with a backpack and a ditty bag at his feet, wiping a tumbler at the sink. He turned around and looked at Niklas with wild eyes. After a second the flames died, and he seemed to realize what was happening. "Give me a second," he said. "Bathroom." He set the glass upside down in a cabinet above the sink and disappeared.

Niklas waited on the couch, tapping his foot on the living room carpet. He had to knock twice to get Peter out of the bathroom, and when he finally opened up he was all ready to go (Niklas heard no flush), stumbling over himself to get out of Niklas' way. He grabbed his bags and the two boys took off out the door.

* * *

They headed north on I-43, the sun blasting in from their left, the fields of farmland north of Sheboygan glowing in the late afternoon sun. Farmhouse roofs, the domes atop silos, little bits of machinery strewn about all caught bits of the setting sun and flashed at the cars that whizzed by. The hills began to undulate gently; the trees beside the road were still mostly hardwoods, and the brush was firm-soiled and not yet bogged with swamps. Niklas ached for the last three hours of the drive on the two-lane way through the swampy foothills and forest of the Upper Peninsula, and especially for the last hour; the first sight of Lake Superior coming down and around Keweenaw Bay was always triumphant.

Peter had remained silent for the first twenty minutes but warmed to conversation as the familiar road passed beneath their wheels. The country seemed to loosen his tongue. Niklas treaded carefully, unsure of Peter's exact state of mind. He was eager to keep Peter in a good mood and tingling with anticipation at this first adventure in quite a while. They lingered on the subject of fantasy football, though only Peter was actually playing this year.

"You want to huck it the Big House this fall?" Niklas asked, hopeful. "I got a buddy from Chicago that invited me for the Wisconsin game in September."

"I wish," Peter said. "Tina gave me a really hard time after the debacle at the Northwestern game. Even my dad heard about it all the way in New York."

Niklas suppressed a laugh, but the memory was a sad one too. "I still feel bad about that. I remember I'd forgotten at the time you had a kid. Jakob reminded me like six hours into the drive north after the game." A burst of laughter. "And that motel room in Dunbar! With the heart shaped hot tub. I remember losing my mind 'cause I thought the wallpaper was moving like a bunch of vines to swallow me up."

Peter cracked a smile. "When I think about that weekend I can remember most of it, but not *why*. Why did I think it was a good idea to drive to Jussi's place after a football game. After the game it all just…"

"Went insane, like, to a different dimension. I can't believe we're nostalgic about it now. I remember sitting in the motel parking lot in Dunbar at like four in the morning, coming down, thinking, *Shit, not only am I gonna be sober tomorrow, we're all way too beat to make it to Uncle Jussi's.* I legit cried at the thought of work on Monday."

"We were so close," Peter said, with uncharacteristic wistfulness. "We almost made it. I remember, I was pissed when you guys woke me up outside the motel."

"I tried so hard to keep Jakob driving. We were about to hit that stretch after Crystal Falls where it's like a hundred miles without any real place to stop. He'd been hitting rumble strips for half an hour. He was probably right to stop, but I was still high enough to pull hard for the alternative."

Outside, the rim of the sky began to turn pink, and the rumpled hills grew slightly less shallow. Niklas zipped open the pack at his feet and made sure the envelope with Jakob's letters was safe and uncrumpled. Peter gazed with glazed eyes sightlessly out the window.

"Man," he said. "I guess that really was the last time I was up. Three years ago, almost."

"Three years. Forever ago, and nearer than yesterday."

"You went up last Christmas though, right?" Peter asked.

"Yeah. No, two Christmases ago. This last one I was in Marquette."

"Ah, right. It was right after the funeral you went up though, right?"

"Sort of. A few months later." Niklas paused. "Jakob had just, you know, gotten in trouble."

"Right, yeah. The Northwestern game was in September, and Jakob's trial was over in, what, November?"

"Yeah. It was after that I went up to the farm with Dad. It was right after I got out of the hospital, actually. I was in for ten days, right after the trial. Dad thought I needed a sort of halfway house situation, or at least company, when they let me out."

"You were moving to Milwaukee around then, I remember," Peter said. "You came over for dinner a few times that winter. Olly loved it."

"Yeah. And Dad just called me one day in mid-December and picked me up and we just drove north. I think he was going through it to, you know—of course he was. We kind of cleaned up the cabin and collected Uncle Jussi's stuff into boxes. Dad drank more than I ever saw him drink, and at night we played the guitar and sang around the fire even when it snowed. Music was the only thing that helped Dad's mood. It felt so weird being there, knowing the land was ours and not his anymore. He said he's glad for that, that he wouldn't know what to do with the place without Uncle Jussi. It still feels weird to me, and even weirder that we three never stood together on the land that's now ours. We found some awesome bits and pieces cleaning out the cabin, though. This old skinning knife that I got sharpened on the way home. I can't find it now. It's really bumming me out."

Peter nodded. Niklas grew sentimental about almost everything, which made their current predicament that much more fraught, though to Peter, Nik didn't really appear to have processed it yet, or perhaps hadn't taken him seriously on the phone.

"I'm sure you'll find it," Peter said. "You take it home?"

"No, it's in Marquette. I think it is, at least."

"Huh." Peter had the cruise control set at seventy-six. They passed cars steadily as the sun sunk low into the western sky. Their long shadow flew across the gravel and brush ditches beside the highway. The asphalt of the road looked a bloody beige, the fields and roadside brush a rich amber-green.

"The smokestack, too," Niklas said, in the middle of a thought.

"What?"

"We got to go by the smokestack out in Freda. You know, the old crushing plant, right on the lake?"

"I think that was mostly you and Jakob. I was gone by then."

"No, you came out with us a couple of times."

Peter squinted. "Maybe."

"It's just a massive stretch of concrete ruins. Dad told me that Grandpa Teemu worked there with Jim's father. They were both on the crusher. You remember that giant circle in the concrete? Some of the infrastructure is still intact. We'd always climb up into the old smokestack by the lake and make fires. You could see stars out the top at night. You could walk out a hundred yards onto Superior in the winter. The ice froze in these massive mounds. Some of them were caves. We gotta go," he said again. Peter stared straight ahead, stone-faced. Niklas wondered at his ill temper. It was something more than stress at his own situation—beneath the surface, Niklas could smell resentment.

"I need a piss," Peter suddenly announced. "Cool if we stop soon?"

"We been on the road barely an hour." Niklas was champing at the bit, annoyed at this interruption.

"I'm just hydrated."

"Bullshit," spat Nik.

"Come on."

"We just got on the road. I want to hustle up there. Let's wait till we switch drivers."

"OK, but I actually need to piss. Please."

Niklas felt a surge of suspicion. Peter usually just went ahead and did things. There was something vulnerable in his *Please*.

"Fine. You gotta cover gas though."

"All right."

Once again, Niklas was surprised at the lack of protest. He forgot about it as they passed a sign announcing Green Bay in twenty-nine miles. To the east the sky was a deep indigo, which paled around the silhouettes of trees on the horizon. In a few minutes Peter pulled off the highway and made for a Kwik Trip.

Niklas bit his tongue in frustration as Peter pulled into a parking spot instead of beside a pump. He leapt out right away and Niklas watched him make a beeline for the bathroom. He followed Peter inside, stretching his legs on the way in, and grabbed a chocolate milk and a thing of chicken tenders. On the way out the door, it occurred to Niklas it'd be late by the time they got up north. He turned back and got a case of Miller and a fifth of Kessler, and a box of oatmeal raisin cookies for Jim—his favorite. His father had always impressed upon him the duty of never arriving anywhere empty-handed, and indeed many a time had brought these exact cookies for Jim.

Outside, Niklas leaned on Peter's car using the roof as a table, wolfing his tenders. He watched blue-jeaned men stop to fill up and stock up after a day's work, their shirts and hands dirty, their boots creased, hunger and thirst in their eyes. As Niklas finished his chocolate milk, he watched a family of five negotiate the rearrangement of a tightly packed pickup. Peter had been in the bathroom for fifteen minutes. Niklas decided to go check on him.

The girl behind the counter was whispering something to an older lady in an apron. Both were looking at the bathroom. Niklas' heart sank. He headed through the aisles and looked around before he opened the bathroom door, hoping it was someone else being whispered about in nervous tones.

Peter was leaning over the sink. Blood was streaming from his nose past the already drenched wad of tissue in his hands. He was so preoccupied, he failed to look up when Niklas entered, rushed up, and patted his back.

"Jesus, man. What happened?"

"Bloody nose." Peter wouldn't look up.

"Yeah, man, and the Pope is Catholic. I mean *what happened?*"

"Not sure. I get these all the time these days. It's the dry air according to Tina."

"Not today it's not."

"Huh?"

"Dude, it rained all morning."

Peter looked like he was just now finding this out. "That's right. Huh. Who knows."

Niklas gave him a hard, searching look. "All right. Well, clean up and hurry back. I'll drive the rest of the way if you want."

Peter nodded and shrugged. Niklas left him to clean up the bloody sink, knowing he probably wouldn't and some poor Kwik Trip employee would get stuck with it. He waited at the car for another five minutes. Finally Peter came out with both nostrils plugged, talking at a hundred miles an hour.

"Man, that was fucked. You ready to go? Got the keys? Sweet. Oh, hell yeah, you got beer! I hate these bloody noses, man. They never catch you at a good time." And on like that, rapid-fire, as they got back on the highway.

⸱ 4 ⸱

The Rags of Time

Jakob Kinnunen and his cousin, Peter, had played a lot of hockey as boys, and when they did they always made Jakob's little brother, Niklas, play goalie. Niklas bore this curse of youth well—in fact, he grew up to start in goal at Marquette High all four years, making All State his junior and senior seasons—but the truth was he'd always wanted a shot at "skating out." He'd begged for a chance all growing up, and they'd never quite said no, but still he never ended up anywhere but between the pipes. Often, at homemade rinks in their friends' backyards, the exchange went something like this:

"Guys! Hey, guys!" Niklas yipped. "Can one of you play goalie this time?"

"I have to practice," Jakob always said. "I've got games coming up." Niklas looked at Peter.

"I have to practice, too," said Peter.

"You play house league," Niklas replied indignantly. "Let me skate out. For once. Please?"

"I don't know how to play goalie."

"Come on! Dad said to let me swap with you guys this time!" Jakob, feeling for his little brother, would sometimes begin to capitulate, but never did he go all the way.

"All right, Nik, he did, you're right. Why don't you and Peter switch off? He'll play for an hour then you guys switch."

"What?!" Peter never could stand the fact that Jakob was well and truly the top dog, not even decades later as grown men. "Why don't *you* swap? He's a goalie in real life."

"Because we promised. Dad said. He's right."

"He doesn't get to make me play goalie!"

"Dude, come on. Just for a little while."

"No! He's the goalie. I'm not a goalie."

Despite the fact that Jakob was defending him, Niklas always felt shame boiling in his stomach whenever they spoke over top of him like this, looking at each other as though they were the parents and he the child. He reared up into the picture and

22

snapped: "Hey. Remember? Last time you guys said I could play out."

"I know, Nik. Come on Peter, just play for an hour. I have to practice. The high school coaches are coming to games now. Just for a while."

"No! Why do I have to? Why don't you?" Peter could never stand drawing the short straw.

This would go on for a little while until they all got sick of arguing and laced up their skates to play. Inevitably Niklas was always promised, as collateral for giving in and putting on the big pads, that *next* time they would surely take turns in goal, Peter and Jakob, and that he could skate out the whole time. And, inevitably, whenever the next time was, Jakob had a game coming up, or tryouts or the playoffs or whatever, and Peter couldn't stoop to a task that Jakub refused, and Niklas ended up donning the mask once again.

Such was their childhood: Jakob, the proud, passionate leader; Peter, the ever-resentful first mate, quick to imitate Jakob, quick to exclude others; and Niklas, who loved his older brother and cousin above all, who adored life in spite of its crimes against him, whose wide eyes filled quickly with both wonder and tears at the slightest of provocations.

The three boys were raised as brothers, in spite of the fact that one of them wasn't. Their fathers were in fact brothers, but were it not for certain turns of phrase and common edges of a sensitive temperament, no one would ever know. When the boys were born, all three uncles lived within a mile or two of each other in Marquette, MI—Hannu, Jakob and Niklas' father, who lived with his family by the university; Uncle Olli, Peter's father, who lived in a modern apartment downtown; and Uncle Jussi, their little brother, who lived part time with Hannu in town and part time two hours away on his little farm. Jussi was developmentally disabled, but as far as farm work was concerned he was as able as any of them physically, you just couldn't give him real complicated instructions.

Everyone loved Jussi a little bit extra, and thought of him as their guardian angel. He took a special liking to the boys from the first, and they loved him right back, tenderly and vulnerably. Jussi was named after his grandfather Olli's best friend, Jussi, who died tragically and very young, though it was more common among miners in those days to die young.

The farm was two hours west of Marquette, a fifteen-minute drive west along the canal from Houghton to Liminga. It was a section of forty acres atop a gentle rise, wooded densely with pine, spruce, hemlock, and maple. There were no swamps, though snowmelt bogs were common enough. A creek ran from the southern end of the property almost due north, through the forest, winding around the orchard and the vegetable patch about fifty yards east of the cabin. The cabin had already been there when Hannu had gotten the property; everything else he built with the help of Uncle Jussi, and, when they were old enough to swing a hammer and wield a drill, Jakob, Peter, and Niklas.

The boys' earliest memories were of playing in the long grass beside the orchard or along the creek in the woods while their fathers worked with Jussi, building or clearing or tending to some part of the land. The boys made swords and spears and bows and arrows out of chokecherry limbs and fresh roots with their pocket knives. They begged their fathers to teach them to fish, and their fathers sent them out one day with Uncle Jussi, who was brilliant with a fly-rod. The boys took to fishing, and did so with relish for the rest of their lives. They climbed every tree they could, though once Peter fell and broke his arm thanks to a poorly placed boot on a rotted branch, and he refused to climb after that. They dammed up the creek, just to see if they could. Jakub always led the charge through the woods with Peter close behind, Niklas hustling to keep up with the rapid pace of their stride and conversation. Soon enough the boys were putting up and mending fences on their own, weeding and watering the blueberries and lingonberries, pruning the apple and cherry trees, making mulch with the woodchipper and dumping it in wheelbarrow loads beside the potatoes and the vegetable patch for Hannu and Jussi to spread later.

In the winters they snowshoed and, as they grew older, cross country skied around the property, on the track of rabbits and deer and foxes and numerous other things in the snow that was almost always fresh. Hannu played the guitar well and sung even better (he sang tenor in the choir at church), and so the boys soon learned guitar and three-part harmony, or their best imitation of it. Music and reading by the fire, punctuated by skiing off the porch and into the woods to loosen their limbs and set the blood flowing again—that was how the short winter afternoons and long winter evenings passed with ease, at least in the beginning. Later there was hockey, endless hours at the Dodgeville rink, whose surface they maintained with buckets of warm water every evening. Jussi and Hannu would pick them up in the truck after many hours in the dark and hand them a thermos full of hot cocoa. It was a life so pleasant that Niklas couldn't remember ever being cold.

Spring was always an awful tease, still cold and blustery and utterly tiresome; when summer finally came, the collective shout of relief rode up on a gust of wind all the way to the sun. June was everybody's favorite month, not because it was nicer than July, but because it came first.

When he was sixteen, Jakob discovered the old ruins of the crushing plant out in Freda by the lake, and asked his father about it afterward. He was stoked to learn that his grandfather, Teemu and their neighbor Jim Markham's father, Jim Sr., had worked together there in the forties and fifties before the plant closed down in the sixties. Pernilla, Hannu's delightful and staunch wife of Swedish descent, was shocked that Hannu had neglected to tell the boys their family story, especially since so much of it took place on the very ground they were growing up on. So, one afternoon, she called up Jim and asked him to come over and take the boys out to the plant with Hannu and tell them about their grandfathers. The boys all remembered that afternoon vividly, Jim's voice echoing off the torn concrete and getting mixed up with the roar of Lake Superior as he told stories of his father and their Grandpa Teemu, who had been great friends. As the day wore on he told as well of Teemu's father, their great-grandpa Olli and his dear friend Jussi, who came over from Finland in 1901, ten years before Jim's father came from Cornwall, all of them coming for work in the mines. When Hannu said they had to go home for dinner there was nearly a mutiny.

From then on, the boys hung close whenever Jim Markham was around helping out on the farm or visiting, and bugged him and Hannu for stories wherever they were together. It wasn't that Hannu didn't tell stories on his own, quite the contrary in fact (he read to Jakob and Niklas every night well into middle school), it was just that when the two of them got going, riffing off of each other and filling in the gaps in each other's histories, there was something open that was otherwise shut, some emotional valve, some old blend of stage presence and nostalgia that infused the stories with life and sadness; the bone-deep memory of the men of the Northwoods for whom oral tradition is perhaps the most celebrated of traditions, though nobody would tell you that straight out.

All throughout their childhoods, Uncle Jussi was the boys' most gentle companion and, as they blossomed like squash plants in July, their biggest fan. After he taught them to fish, he racked his brains for other things they might want to learn, because he felt really good answering their questions about line and bait, awash in their admiration as he tied a fly with grace and precision that their imaginations could barely quantify. When they grew a little older, he showed them how to use fencing pliers, and Hannu was delighted when one late spring day after the snow had melted they all mended a saggy spot in the fence around the apple trees while he was off at Jim Markham's place, finally learning how to sharpen a chainsaw blade.

Jussi was proudly in the stands at all of Jakub and Niklas' hockey games, all growing up, and made many of Peter's too, though later when Peter moved away Jussi saw very little of anyone besides Hannu, Jakob, and Niklas. His favorite thing in the world was to be an uncle, second only to being Hannu's brother. He loved his brother, Olli, too; they both did, he and Hannu, but when Olli moved his family out east when Peter was sixteen, no one was surprised, and when Olli only came back for alternating Christmases and Easters, no one but Niklas was upset.

⸗ **5** ⸗

With a twist of his thumb and forefinger, Jim Markham killed the engine of his skid steer. The high hollow drone of the engine died slowly, then came to rest, leaving Jim alone with his rattly breath and the sound of the wind in the trees. He sat for a while. Eventually he got out and walked around the corner of the old barn where he kept his in-use tools and parked his machines. Machine parts and bits of hardware and tools that had fallen out of favor all lay in rusty piles on the ground, growing now dense and now sparse as Jim made his way up the hill toward his house. The grass grew long in the places where it wasn't beaten flat by the tread of his boots. He walked past the old but pretty sailboat derigged on a trailer, its fiberglass cloudy with age. An old tractor parked beside a partially disassembled sawmill sat permanently beside the abandoned trailer on the other side of the parking lot. Most of the property was like this. It was only toward the northern perimeter that the woods grew too dense to walk through.

The house used to be a trailer. Now it had a peaked roof and rough but thorough extensions on all four sides. Inside it was really only the kitchen and the living room, separated by the back of one long couch. But it was cozy, and appropriately tacky and messy in the manner of modern country homes.

He climbed the steps to his front door slowly, and gently opened the screen door, so as not to disturb anyone who might be napping on the couch. He walked into the kitchen, where his wife, Cynthia, was washing some dishes. An old western blared on the TV beyond the couch, like always.

"Hey, hun."

"Huh!" Cynthia started, or pretended to. "What are you sneaking up on me for?"

"I'm not sneaking."

"Well." She smiled her grimace of a smile, and he grinned back.

"I'm headed over to Hannu and Jussi's old place. Hannu's boy, Niklas, called me while I was out on da skid steer this afternoon.

He's coming up, and da other one, da cousin, Peter, he's coming with him."

"The other one still locked up?"

"Supposed to be out by Thanksgiving."

"Oh."

"I'll be back in a while."

"OK. Are dose boys going to come by while dey're here?"

"Oh yah. Coming by for a sauna dis weekend."

"Oh!" Cynthia turned back to the sink.

"You're eyes just lit up! Ha!"

"Oh you go open up."

"Ha! I think dey're a bit green for you, hun!" He cackled as he turned back out the door and walked with new energy toward his great red F-150. Gravel crackled and dust swirled in clouds as he backed up and headed east toward the canal road in the direction of Hannu and Jussi's place.

As the road grew smooth beneath his tires and the hills opened up before him, Jim wondered to himself what had happened with the Kinnunen family he'd known. He'd last heard from Hannu back in May, when Jim had reached out with questions about the farm.

"What do ya want me to do with it? Nearly all da fruit just rotted on da ground last year. You want me to pick it for ya, freeze it or something?"

"No, Jim," Hannu had said wearily. "That land is the boys' land now. Jussi was clear about that, though I would've done the same had he not been."

"It's too bad," said Jim. "Even if ya don't plant nothing, that land'll give you fruit for a few years. Sure you don't want to come up and pick your berries and your apples and your cherries? Come on, bud…"

"I know, Jim. I'm tired, and I'm getting on toward being an old man like yourself. Surely you know what I'm saying."

"Oh, sure. You're not fat like me though yet, so watch it! Ha!"

"I'm getting there, too. Tell you what, next time the boys come up, you have my full permission to bug them about the fruit. But that's it. It's their land, now."

"All right," Jim said, more than a little sad at the gulf that had grown between them since Jussi's death. Jim could hear the hurt in Hannu's voice when he spoke about his dead brother—caring for

Jussi and working on the farm in the summers had been his life's chief joy, beyond his children. Jussi's deficiencies hadn't made him any less delightful a comrade, in fact, quite the opposite. Since people had had to take extra care of him, the void he left in passing was doubly large. The first few weeks after his death, Hannu had come out to Jim's place all confused, babbling about forgetting something important and lapsing mid-sentence into a thousand-yard stare. It made perfect sense to Jim when he'd called and said he passed on the land to his two sons and their cousin, who played there all the time in the summer and functioned as brothers all growing up.

Jim swung his truck into the Kinnunen place and turned off the engine. He sat still in the driver's seat for a minute as was his custom.

The truck door closed with a slam; the woods were quiet, the air rustling gently in the grass, as though late afternoon was waiting restlessly for evening. He could see the shed through the trees off to the right, and the edges of the sixty-gallon rain barrels set up behind it, the whole lot of it painted dark green. His first step into the long grass sent grasshoppers hopping off in several directions. He walked down the sandy driveway and through the trees toward the little cabin that sat about thirty yards off by the edge of the woods. A breeze kicked up and cooled his sweaty torso. As he marched along the edge of the woods, the rich odor of pine and spruce lay heavy upon his nostrils, and a thick, soft bed of dead pine needles lay beneath his feet. The cabin came slowly into focus as he approached. It looked more frail than he remembered, and as he got closer he saw that several porch boards had been warped or weathered away. He pulled the squealing, rusted screen door open, lifting it so its bottom didn't scrape the porch, twisted the old brass key in the lock till it clicked, then pushed through the heavy front door.

The one room of the cabin was spacious and very dark. Jim's eyes first rested on the cots stacked against the eastern wall, bedding piled on top of the stack. The ribbed log walls stained dark and cracked with age looked vulnerable in the fading light. Small windows on the east and west walls were cobwebbed and blurry. In the southwest corner was the woodstove, a potbelly, its chimney angling up past the rafters through the roof. A frying pan, pot, spatula, and kitchen knife sat on top of the rusty iron stove.

On the southern wall hung three pairs of snowshoes from separate nails. Two were the modern, metal and plastic kind, the third the traditional, wood and rawhide variety. Jim's gaze lingered on the old pair. The youngest one, Niklas, always used to want that pair, even though the bindings were flimsy.

The shelves on the western wall, merely two-by-sixes on brackets, were bare of the things they once held: photographs, guns, tools, instruments, cans and bottles of this and that, unlaminated maps with rings left by coffee cups or beer cans, sport equipment, pens, pencils, and of course all kinds of books. The boards sat empty now except for a few thin candles and candlesticks and a lantern. Jim ran his hand across the bottom-most shelf and it came away with a thick lace of dust. The candles were still in their plastic wrapping.

In the northwest corner was the cooking area, the only intact piece of the old farmhouse. There was a ceramic basin sat on a wooden box; inside the basin were stacked three white plastic plates and three red plastic cups on top of a frying pan. Inside the cups were three sets of utensils. Four wooden chairs were stacked beside a table on its end leaning against the wall. An old rug still covered much of the central floor space.

The room felt barren. Hannu wanted it to be theirs, he'd said, to make what they wished of it. The place had given him and Jussi more than he could ever have asked for, and he couldn't bear keeping it up himself without the original reason for doing so. Jim wondered at the time whether Hannu wasn't throwing out some baby with all that bathwater, but he wasn't a fool, and his intentions were surely good.

Jim started back to his truck, then turned back and trudged east up the rise toward the orchard. After seeing the cabin, he wanted to take a look at the orchard. He strode to the gate and unwound the bit of chain that kept it latched. He walked carefully through the orchard to the spot where the blueberry bushes stopped and the apple trees began.

Though several small green apples lingered from the trees, the rest of the orchard was dying from neglect. The leaves on the blueberry bushes were curled at the edges and cracked under the slightest pressure. Every bud and leaf with any life left in it below chest height had been eaten by the rabbits and the deer. At a distance, Jim could see sprigs of chokecherry sprouted up in the lingonberry patch, boxing out the blueberries as it continued to spread outward. The fence sagged in several places where the snow had weighed it down, and there were little holes dug by rabbits that had burrowed under it.

Jim had seen what he'd come to see. He rewound the chain around the orchard gate and walked slowly down the hill. An evening wind kicked up. Briefly, head cocked, Jim thought he could make out the sound. He remembered the first time he'd ever heard it, standing out by the driveway with Hannu, talking over the truck bed about the price of sand, or maybe it was ammunition. A gust of wind raked over the trees and Hannu had held up a hand to silence him.

"Listen... you hear that?"

"Huh?"

"The wind, Jim, the wind. It sounds like flutes when it scrapes the tops of the trees."

"Does it?" Jim listened intently. At first there was only the wind, but then... quiet at first, the thin, haunting sound reached his ears. It came in breaths, but just before the wind died down there was a long note, a whole note of sorts, that died slowly as the gust moved on. Hannu had his eyes closed in rapture.

"Isn't that something?"

"Sure is. Makes me want to take a nap! Ha!"

Jim leaned now against his truck bed, in the exact spot where he'd stood with Hannu all those years ago. Many a lingering chat had occurred right here, after the work was done but they weren't ready to say goodbye. They never were, but eventually it was always time to leave. Jim looked for one long moment at the spot where Hannu had always stood. The green shed and rain barrels through the trees had always been a place to rest the eyes when he wasn't looking across at Hannu, whose gaze was intense. The rain barrels had been Jim's idea.

He closed his eyes and said a prayer and got back into his truck to drive home.

⚡ **6** ⚡

Early Summer, 1901

The boat from Hanko had stopped in Copenhagen, then in Hull on the west coast of England. There everyone piled into trains to Liverpool and then into ships across the Atlantic.

On a late afternoon in early June, Olli Kinnunen stumbled wearily from the Copper Range Railway train when it stopped in Houghton. The journey had taken four days, through Chicago all the way from Boston. He was eager to find the Finns the recruiters had promised back home. He found a room in town, but a few nights made it clear that his countrymen were elsewhere.

After a week of sleeping rough to "look things over," he went to work as a trammer in the Atlantic Mine south of the canal on the west side of the Keweenaw Peninsula. He was a formidable laborer and built like a linebacker, but had struggled in school and now refused to learn English for his first six years in America. He began having second thoughts when he discovered that most of the women, even the full-blooded Finnish ones, spoke English with an easy fluency that silenced him at social gatherings.

Just as he was settling into a difficult and somewhat lonely but reliable groove, the Atlantic Mine went under, putting Olli out of work. That winter of 1906, Olli followed a group of miners north to Calumet and found work with the Hecla Mining Company. Stoic and Lutheran though he was, the stability and prosperity of Calumet rekindled his fraternal spirit and after some personal mining of his own, Olli discovered that he loved to dance.

One day he was waiting for a drink in a crowded bar. Bodies jostled this way and that. Olli didn't feel the man tapping on his shoulder until the taps were frustrated claps on the back. Olli turned and noticed a man with a big brown beard. The man barked angrily in English. Olli stared back blankly. The man set down his drink, spat on the ground, and busted Olli's nose.

Olli stopped seeing stars after a minute or two and noticed a second man, a great slab of a man, helping him to his feet.

"Here you go fella, up you go." The man introduced himself as Jussi, also a miner, and offered him a drink. "God knows I know what that feels like," he said, his grin revealing missing teeth.

If Jussi hadn't become a friend, Olli would have thought him a loudmouth. Jussi was in many ways still a boy, which accounted for his state of perpetual bachelorhood. He was an excellent angler and hunter, showing Olli his best fishing spots and teaching him to shoot with a twelve-gauge. The two spent many spring and summer days rising before dawn to fish for hours, then make a smudge fire, frying the trout with bacon grease, and eating it with bread. Jussi was a ruthless prankster, often waiting, jowls quivering and eyes leaking with mirth, for everyone else to get the joke and roar with laughter, which they inevitably did. His sense of humor was very un-Finnish in its raunchy, high-volume persistence and, therefore, during winter days when the sun barely made it above the tops of the trees, Olli felt it almost salubrious.

Friendship made the long days as a trammer pass with surprising haste and after a couple of months, Olli was beginning to come out of his shell. Jussi drank and worked and danced and fought with the relish of the perennially robust, and soon Olli had a healthy number of bar fights under his belt merely by way of being Jussi's friend. Olli acquired a taste for winning these fights and by the end of that first winter together he was doing just as much of the fighting as Jussi was. They fell into an older brother/younger brother dynamic. It was Jussi who told him open-handed blows will save you many a broken hand, Jussi that first took him to the Italian Hall for a night of dancing, Jussi who taught him how to tie his flies for trout, Jussi who made him feel like he actually belonged somewhere.

On a Friday night in April, Olli went to the dance hall with Jussi. They'd been friends for long enough that Olli no longer got annoyed when Jussi disappeared for long portions of the evening. Olli found a friend from work and proceeded to get much drunker than he'd planned on getting.

When it was almost time to leave Olli excused himself to find Jussi. After fifteen minutes of fruitless searching he gave up and made for the door. On his way out, he spotted a short blond girl craning her neck and scanning the floor. He approached her and spoke to her in Finnish.

"What?" she said. "Speak up, I can't hear you."

Olli blanched. "Sorry, please. No English," he said.

The girl switched to Finnish. "Are you looking for someone?"

"Yes. I came with my friend but he always disappears. It's all right, he'll be okay. Never mind."

"Well, good for you," she said. "Have you seen a girl that looks like me except much prettier?"

Olli paused for a moment, wondering what exactly she was asking. "No, ma'am."

"My little sister," she clarified.

"I'm sorry."

"Never mind. Could you walk me home?"

"Um. Sure."

They made their way out the door.

"I'm Ana."

"I'm Olli.

A second later, Jussi stumbled outside, drunk, looking for Olli. "Buddy, hey, you ready to go—oh, I'm sorry." He noticed Ana. "I'll, uh… I'll see you at work." And Jussi stumbled home.

That summer, Ana patiently taught him English on his day off, and soon enough was leaving a steaming pasty on his doorstep each morning before work. Nearly all of his fellow miners had wives who made them pasties or sandwiches but he couldn't very well do the work of a two-person household himself, could he? Ana suspected that he could and that his dismissal of a proper lunch came from some deeply rooted male instinct to try your hand only where you are sure you will succeed, or else with stunts that will impress your buddies. He was terrible in the kitchen and his few friends were not the kind to be impressed by anything, much less an uglier pasty than the ones their wives sent them off to work with every day. Whatever the truth, Ana's pasties exposed the error of Olli's bachelor ways and they were married on a crisp September afternoon at St. Paul Lutheran Church, the leaves quilted orange and yellow and red and everything in between. Olli's side of the church was nearly empty but for Jussi and a small handful of others. As a wedding present, Jussi gave him a "half breed," a hunk of float copper that was part silver, found down in the mines and smuggled away in his lunch box.

They honeymooned in Marquette and even went to a hockey game, Olli proudly answering her questions about the game in far more detail than she desired. They had a daughter a year later and named her Sofia. Things were happy for quite a while. With Ana's help, their social circle broadened. Sofia was a bright kid and soon she was showing off to a degree that made the other mothers in Ana's circle ask if she could tutor their children, which she did until Sofia was of school age and Ana ran out of patience with children not nearly as bright as hers.

Olli nearly lost an eye in a mining accident in 1912, just months before their first and only son, Teemu, was born.

⋇ 7 ⋇

August 2009, Friday, 7:41 p.m.

Niklas and Peter zoomed north, through the crisscrossed suspension of the bridge high over the riffled water of Green Bay, toward the woods and lakes of northeast Wisconsin, past gas stations and fireworks shops and towns of decreasing size. Many of the trucks towing boats pulled off, leaving the darkening stretch of highway almost exclusively to the boys. Soon the trees changed mostly to evergreens and the road from four lanes to two. Maples remained, and a few oaks, but now mostly hemlock, spruce, and pine flanked the road. The land grew subtly jagged and as they crossed the border into Michigan, Niklas sensed the ridges of the copper country just beyond the horizon. Their phones changed to Eastern Time just past a place where the road bored through a Pleistocene slice of blasted shale that rose up thirty feet on either side of the road for a hundred yards. Immediately after this temporal gateway, a blanket of evergreens stretched out before them into the distance. Niklas felt his foot stamp down on the gas, seemingly of its own accord. The forest looked endless and they hadn't seen another car for twenty miles.

Meanwhile, Peter had started on the beer. He drank slowly, and after two beers put on a Neil Young CD. They crossed the Net River and crested a hill just as the last of the residual pink and orange was dying in the west. The talk turned back to sports. They complained about the Brewers but remained optimistic about the Packers. Signs advertising berry stands and deer feed and trails for ATVs and snowmobiles began to crop up everywhere. Peter began to doze before they got to L'Anse. Niklas turned off the music and found a high school football game, deep along the AM dial. He let his brain pleasantly empty itself and felt the muscles in his back and shoulders slowly come loose.

He was thinking of camping out tonight, or maybe just crashing on the rickety cabin porch. In the old days, Peter had liked to piss Jakob off by pretending to masturbate at night in their tent. Jakob's mistake was getting so angry about it. Surely Peter would like to call Tina, too, and sort out whatever they'd fought about earlier that afternoon. Finally, the hills fell away to the right and the Keweenaw Bay spread out before them, its glittering edges lacing around a deep lake of twilight blue. The water looked choppy as they came around L'Anse and up the bay. Up through Baraga, Niklas realized he was doing seventy-five, and slowed to sixty. More logging trucks barreled past, headed south, each uniformly overstacked with logs like a coal train car whose load reaches above the edges of its walls. The bay receded as they turned inland, heading northwest up the Keweenaw Peninsula.

Niklas pulled off at The Pines, fished a ten out of the sleeping Peter's pocket for gas and walked in. He filled up ten dollars' worth of cheap reservation gas and got back on the road for the final stretch.

Pretty soon they passed a couple of trailers that belonged to Rich, the chainsaw carver. His place was always easy to find even in the dark because he had an eight-foot-tall carving of Bigfoot out front, so fine in detail as to include individual wisps of body hair and the veins protruding from beneath his loincloth. Niklas remembered when he and Jakob had been inside his shop when they were teenagers because one year Hannu had the idea to get their mother a carving for Mother's Day. They'd had to remove Pernilla's favorite oak tree from their backyard in Marquette for fear of storm damage. She'd loved watching the squirrels that congregated around the tree at all hours of the day. Hannu thought that if they got her a carving large enough, using wood of the oak that had been removed, the squirrels might stick around. The boys were all over the idea and took great pleasure in visiting the shop with Hannu and asking Rich, a gruff but pleasant chainsaw guy in his thirties, questions about everything they could see. It wasn't much: a garage with a few sawhorses, all his tools, and about a dozen unfinished projects. The boys went away determined to convince Hannu to let them try carving with their chainsaw the next time they went out to Uncle Jussi's. When they finally got the carving, which was a four-foot-tall squirrel with an armful of nuts and a white bit of painted glint in his eye, even Hannu was giddy at the craftsmanship. It had only been two hundred bucks, and Pernilla was delighted, and they all felt that something had been accomplished in their dealings with Rich. They certainly bragged about it enough afterward, and Hannu did eventually let them try carving unsplit logs out behind the cabin, but it was way too hard and they decided to go play by the creek in the woods instead.

Just minutes away, Niklas found himself reminiscing about the land that would surely be different than how he remembered it. In the old days, many a summer afternoon found Jakob leading the charge through the woods to the creek, Peter striding importantly at his side, trying in vain to look as old or as tough, Niklas scrambling to keep up but delighted to be included.

On Niklas' seventh birthday, Hannu took the three boys out to Uncle Jussi's to play in the woods. Jakob immediately took charge, announcing that they would march north along the edge of the creek and find a place to build a dam. The three little boys tumbled along through thick woods, past the huge mound of field stones left by some farmer a hundred years ago. Hannu had begun to teach the boys to identify trees and Niklas insisted, because it was his birthday, on stopping and building their dam next to a pretty grove of aspens that made the world feel quite a bit brighter and more than a little ethereal. Niklas called the spot "Lantern Waste" after the portal between Narnia and England in *The Lion, the Witch, and the Wardrobe* which Hannu had read to him the previous winter. In the winter, you had to hike in on snowshoes and push through thickly knitted pine and spruce boughs, not unlike the old coats of the wardrobe of the story. Jakob generously agreed, and started giving out orders right away, telling Peter to go collect sticks and asking Niklas to help him pack mud and rocks into little bricks to be laid across the creek.

"It's gonna be impossible," complained Niklas, gathering mud in his hands anyway.

"No, it's not," declared Jakob. "How do you think beavers manage it?"

"I don't know. I've never been a beaver. Should I play beaver? Will the dam be stronger then?"

"Sure you can," said Jakob. He knew as the leader he must accommodate his little brother's imagination.

Niklas went on all fours and tucked his bottom lip under his front teeth, scurrying around for a good patch of mud to pack up. Peter came out of the woods, his arms piled high with sticks. He laughed at Niklas when he saw him.

"Can I put you on a leash, Nik?"

"I'm playing beaver, not dog!"

"You're too big to be a beaver."

"Here," Niklas passed him a smooth twig that he'd shorn of all its bark. "Wave the wand and make me small enough to be a beaver."

Niklas, lofty imagination notwithstanding, was not without humor. He knew Peter, and knew that in order to score a point he had to remain on home turf. Peter stood looking confusedly at the wand and looked to Jakob for reassurance. Jakob was hunched over, ankle deep in the creek and laser focused, scouting for the perfect placement for a dam.

Peter decided to use the wand as a switch and brought it whistling through the air down on Niklas' lower back, exposed by a t-shirt rumpled forward by gravity.

"OW! Peter! Gimmie that," and Niklas snatched at Peter's hand to wrestle the stick away.

Peter laughed. "You'll never get it, come on, jump!" and he held out the stick. Niklas jumped for it and at the last second Peter pulled the stick out of arm's reach.

"Jakob. Jakob! Peter hit me with the stick and now he won't let me have it!"

Jakob looked up from his mud brick manufacturing. "So what?"

"So it's my birthday!"

Jakob pondered this for a moment. "Peter, come on. Help me collect sticks. We need to build this dam or else Dad and Uncle Jussi are gonna make us help with dinner."

"He's gonna make you do that anyway," said Peter.

Niklas, meanwhile, had found himself another stick and was winding up to swing for Peter's exposed calves. Hannu had praised Niklas during Little League for his level, consistent swing, and the stick connected painfully with Peter's left calf.

Peter's face twisted with rage and he turned on Niklas, now half-cowering, half-smiling by the creek with Jakob. "You chicken. Come wrestle me if you're not scared."

"I'm not scared, I'm helping Jakob with the dam. See!" and he smirked and held up a handful of mud, which he threw at Peter. Several flecks of mud flew off to his right and hit Jakob in the cheek. Jakob turned angrily on Niklas. "Stop it. You got my face all muddy."

Niklas backed off in contrition. Peter was indignant once again. "Right, only stop him when he gets you muddy, Jakob."

"Can you stop whining and help me with this dam?!"

Peter sullenly obeyed. Niklas sang softly to himself in the creek, picking up handfuls of mud and letting it sift and drip in clumps through his fingers. "*Yankee Doodle went to town, riding on a pony, stuck a feather in his hat and called it macaroni!*"

Peter saw his chance. "That's the little kid version of the song. I know the real version but I'm not gonna tell you."

"You will, too! Tell me! C'mon, Peter, tell me it! Tell me!"

Jakob looked up. "Peter only knows it 'cause I told it to him."

"Nuh-uh! I heard it from Timmy Olson at baseball practice!"

"Yeah and I told Timmy too. Nik, you're too young for it."

Niklas' eyes welled up in frustration. "I am not! I just turned seven! Dad says he's gonna let me watch PG-13 movies next year!"

Peter wheeled on Niklas. "Nuh-uh, you're so lying!"

"No I'm not! You're lying, idiot."

"I'm gonna tell Uncle Hannu you called me that! I'm gonna tell Uncle Jussi."

Jakob's face grew grave with importance. "No Peter, you can't tell Uncle Jussi."

"Why not?"

"'Cause you can't. I'll punch your teeth in if you do."

"But why not?"

"'Cause it's Uncle Jussi. You can't call Uncle Jussi stupid or dumb or anything like that. It's not fair."

Peter looked perplexed at this. "My Dad said Uncle Jussi is touched. What's that mean, Jakob?"

Jakob straightened his back and pulled back his shoulders. "Uncle Jussi's an angel. That's what Dad says. He's an angel from heaven. God doesn't like it if you call his angels stupid or touched. They're his angels."

"But why doesn't he have any kids? My dad's married to my mom and Uncle Hannu's married to Auntie P. Who's Uncle Jussi married to?"

"Angels don't get married," said Jakob. "Angels have more important things to do." Niklas started to speak but Jakob cut him off. "No, Nik, don't bug me about why. Angels are just angels."

"But how is Uncle Jussi all alone? He's got to be touched!" Peter said this last like he was trying to convince himself of it.

Niklas broke in. "I don't think Uncle Jussi's an angel. He's just nervous around girls like me."

"It won't always be like that, Nik. Remember Stacey Hargraves? I got a crush on her after she told me happy birthday when I was eight. That's next year for you. Unless you're touched."

"I'm not touched! I just don't want cooties. Girls are boring. They don't like to play in the mud." And Niklas returned his attention reverently to the mud brick his hands were forming, the mud drying in the waning afternoon sun. A woodpecker beat out a sharp arboreal prestissimo somewhere way up off to the left.

"Well, I bet Uncle Jussi doesn't know the real version of 'Yankee Doodle' like I do," said Peter with a heap of self-satisfaction.

"Sure he does. So does Dad, I bet."

Niklas thought to use this as leverage. "If you don't tell me the real version then I'll just ask Dad."

"He won't tell you. You're too young."

"Am not!"

"Are too!"

"AM NOT!"

"Stop!" said Jakob with an edge in his voice that made the other two clam up in a hurry. "You guys hear that?"

"Hear what?"

"Shh! Wait… there it is. Dad showed me. The wind sounds like a bunch of flutes when it scrapes real fast over the tops of the trees. Listen," Jakob said again as he cocked his head to one side and cupped his hand by his ear.

For a few moments, Niklas only heard the wind and its correspondent rustling. Then, ever so slightly at first, he heard it: a high-pitched hum, sort of like when you blow across the opening of an empty glass bottle. It rose and fell, peeking its head out and then disappearing again in an instant, holding on for a whole note and then fading away so that you could only catch an eighth note here and there. It was gone in a second.

"I bet you'll never guess it," said Peter to Niklas, tiring of the natural beauty.

"Guess what?"

"'Yankee Doodle'. The real version."

"I can't guess that!"

"Why not? I did!"

Jakob intervened. "No you didn't Peter. Even *I* didn't guess it. Nobody could ever guess it."

"I bet my dad could," said Peter. "He could guess it. He's super-smart."

"So is our dad!" said Niklas. "Our dad's a teacher. I bet he's smarter than your dad!"

"Nuh-uh! My dad says soon we're gonna leave for the east. He says folks are smart out there, way smarter than in the U.P."

"Oh yeah? Well our dad says your dad is a real prick sometimes," said Jakob. "That's what he said last Christmas when your dad made Uncle Jussi cry."

"Well my dad says it's just 'cause Uncle Jussi's touched. People that are touched will just cry sometimes because they're weaker than us."

Niklas watched this exchange with rapt attention, head moving back and forth like it was a tennis match. Jakob got to his feet angrily.

"Peter, if you don't stop talking like that about Uncle Jussi I'm gonna have to fight you."

"I'll tell Uncle Hannu."

"If you're a tattle-tale I should fight you anyway. Our dad taught us not to be tattle-tales."

"I'm not a tattle-tale. I'm just gonna tell if you beat me up."

"That's a tattle-tale."

"No it's not! Come fight me if you think it is!" Peter rose to his feet but Niklas couldn't help noticing that his lip quivered. Jakob sensed this too, and rather than risk trouble with the adults he thought of another solution. "I'm not gonna fight you. I'm just gonna tell Nik the real version of 'Yankee Doodle.'"

Nik leapt to his feet in excitement. "Yes, c'mon pleaseeee Jakob! Tell me! I'll work on this dam all night if you tell me! I'll do whatever you say. C'mon, just tell me!"

"You can't do that! He's too young! You said he was too young!" Peter was panicked at the thought of losing this edge of wisdom over Niklas. "C'mon, Jakob. Don't tell him. We'll tell him next year."

"No, I'm gonna tell him." Jakob was having fun now. "Hey, Nik, you wanna hear the real version?"

"Yes, c'mon, tell me Jakob!"

"All right, here it is. Yankee Doodle went to space, riding on a rocket—"

Peter interjected, blurting "LALALALALA" to drown out Jakob's voice. The brothers wheeled on him and in unison barked, "Shut UP!" and Jakob shoved him. Peter backed off and Jakob turned to Niklas again. "*Yankee Doodle went to space, riding on a rocket, stuck a feather up his butt and called it Hershey's chocolate!*"

The three boys instantly forgot their quarrels and doubled over laughing. Peter said, "Jakob! You missed a word!"

"No I didn't! Which word?"

"It's ass, not butt!"

"Hey! Don't swear around my little brother! I changed it on purpose!"

Niklas jumped in. "I'm not little! I'm seven years old! I'll say whatever I want! Ass ass ass dammit shit ass!"

"Hey," said Jakob, peals of laughter subsiding. "Don't say those words around Dad. He'll get mad at me for teaching you."

"But you didn't teach me! You teached me ass, but dammit and shit I learned at the rink from Coach Barnes!"

"Just don't tell him. Little brothers never get blamed, you wouldn't understand."

"I'm not little anymore! I'm seven years old!"

"You'll always be my little brother," said Jakob, and the three boys turned back to the tasks at hand, packing mud and gathering sticks for their dam. The wind gave a brief rush and the sinking sun fell behind a cloud for a moment, the shadow casting a spooky gray light over the boys in their dense grove of aspens, and for one fleeting moment Niklas felt, true to the spirit of Lantern Waste, that just for a glimpse they had all borne witness to something mysterious, something magical, carried off to the east with the clouds as the sun reappeared at the end of a gentle summer breeze.

* * *

Past Rich and his Bigfoot sculpture, Niklas could practically smell Houghton around the corner. Soon the trees fell away and the canal was on their right. Niklas poked Peter awake just before they passed by Michigan Tech. At the sight of the lift bridge, their stomachs both turned, Niklas' with raw excitement, Peter's with tempered excitement and raw guilt. The lights of Houghton had never looked so friendly; it felt like the city's arms were wide open, just for them. They drove down Shelden Avenue slowly, looking around for things that might have changed since they'd last been up. Niklas turned onto the highway briefly, then onto the canal road with the bridge behind them.

Soon the dark water rushed by as they drove through the night and up into the hills, which rose in dark, pine and birch covered ridges on either side of the canal. A deer leapt out and Niklas slammed on the brakes. There was a second and a third; Niklas noted the beginnings of antlers on the first one as it darted into the darkness wide of the headlights.

"Yo, help me watch for deer."

Peter nodded. The abrupt stop had woken him all the way up.

Country roads always take longer than you think they will, perhaps because of the faults of memory, or in this case anticipation. The woods around them were thick and dark. Through the windshield, Niklas began to make out the brightest of the stars. Finally they got to Liminga Road, turned left, around the first curve, around the second, up a hill, a slight left, and they were down the stretch. In the dark they could always spot the mailbox and the sand of the driveway at about the same time.

When they got there, Niklas turned in slowly, unsure of the state of Peter's tires. The headlights swung to the right and lit up the trunks of birch and aspen, settling straight ahead on the clearing and the woods beyond. Peter sat up. They could barely make out the silhouette of the cabin against the trees. Niklas turned off the car and the headlights and they sat still for a minute. They heard the evening breeze whoosh and set the trees to sighing.

Niklas looked across. "Well, shall we drop our stuff and hit Schmidt's?"

"Sure. Yeah, let's do it." Peter's mind was far away. Niklas got his bag and guitar from the back seat, checking again to make sure the letters were safe and his things were in place. Then he walked along the edge of the clearing with the woods on his left toward the dark cabin. The breeze was intermittent. He took several deep breaths of cool, pine-scented air. When he got to the porch, he tipped his head back and drank in the marvelous sky. The diagonal cloud of the milky way was obscured by the tops of the trees, but still, Niklas could see it clearly, with the stars that splashed south across the visible sky, making the inky silhouettes of the trees that much richer. He opened the screen door, which creaked; he suddenly remembered that it was mounted crooked and the bottom scraped the deck when you opened it. He opened the thick oak door that Jim had unlocked several hours earlier.

The familiar smell of the cabin made him choke up. After a long moment, he set down his bags and took out his phone to use what light he could from the screen. He knew the shelves were straight ahead, and they'd left extra candles the last time he'd been there. The glow of his phone screen revealed five white candles, one of which he took and sheared of its plastic wrapping. He retrieved his lighter from the little pocket of his backpack, lit the candle, then placed it in one of the wooden candle sticks.

The door creaked and Peter walked in. "No flashlight?"

"I think we took it with us when Dad and I cleaned the place up."

They both pulled cots from the stack. Niklas got the breakfast table upright in the center of the room. They both shed their clothes and put on clean ones for the bar. Niklas took a while finding a pair of clean socks. He realized with mild frustration he must've only brought one other pair. Peter laced up his shoes, got out a little Ziploc baggie, and sat down at the table. He took out his driver's license and spilled out enough coke for two lines. He took out a five-dollar bill and rolled it up. He cut up the lines as Niklas pulled on a hoodie and a ballcap.

Peter leaned over and did the first line. "That's all you," he said to Niklas, gesturing at the second.

Niklas sat down. "That's huge, dude. I'm only gonna take half." He took the rolled-up bill and did about two thirds of the line. Peter quickly did the rest, licking his finger and gumming the remains.

"Ready to roll?"

"Yeah. Shit, where's my wallet?"

Peter cast around and found it sitting on his cot under the shirt he'd been wearing. The boys stood up, patted their pockets, and headed out the door. Their feet thumped on the porch and snapped softly along the pine needles that lay thick upon the earth. It was silent for a while as they walked to the car.

When they returned, hours later, full of liquor, it was actually cold. After the fire died the night hung thick upon them like the scratchy blankets whose fringe just barely brushed the cabin floor.

Saturday, 5:17 a.m.

The light lay thin and shallow on the yard beyond the cabin porch when Niklas stirred just after dawn. He could feel a pinch in his back and his eyes throbbed and his skull felt heavy with the weight of a hangover. He licked his lips and found that they were dry and cracked. He rubbed his eyes and stared at a grove of chokecherry across the yard at the edge of the woods. Stretching, he felt an ache in his gut. He extracted himself from the sleeping bag and got up to head for the outhouse. He pulled on his boots and jeans, surprised at the bite in the morning breeze. Wrestling a hoodie over his head he winced and gingerly fed his right arm through the sleeve. He reached around with his good arm and felt pine needles still stuck in clumps to his back.

The end of the night came back to him slowly, in pieces. They'd found Chris and Mike at Schmidt's after an hour and a half of waiting. It was twenty minutes till closing time, so they decided to take the bottle of Kessler in Mike's ATV back to the farm to make a fire. Somewhere along the line, Niklas got to talking about how they all used to wrestle each other whenever they drank together in the woods. In five minutes, Peter and Chris had squared off, a gross mismatch in Chris' favor, lit white in the dark by flashlights pointed by the two spectators. Niklas remembered a particularly awkward fall of his own during a bout towards the end when the memories were blurred around the edges. With a smirk he thought of Peter, surely hurting from his winless evening, though he probably didn't remember much.

He walked around behind the cabin down a path through a grove of spruce trees, brushing aside boughs that had been untrimmed for three years now. They'd torn down the other outhouse and built this one with Jim's help when Niklas was twelve. It was hardly a legitimate outhouse. It was essentially a single stall over a tank in the ground with three plywood walls and four by four posts set in concrete. A five-by-five sheet of metal roofing angled back and thankfully didn't leak, and as Niklas examined the state of the place he noticed a bird's nest up in the corner that hadn't been there before. The front was obscured by two overlapping pine trees that provided privacy but always soaked Niklas with dew on the way to his early morning shits.

He recalled working on it with his father and Jim, the first real project he'd been able to really contribute to as a worker. They'd struggled with the wind. The property lay at the top of a hill and on certain high summer days the gusting wind made it impossible to walk two steps with a sheet of plywood. The "throne room" took two days to really finish, days during which Niklas learned to relish the soreness in his back and shoulders and feet, the first sip of water and breeze on a sweaty forehead, the joy of a freezing plunge in Lake Superior and a massive plate of lake trout and wild rice on a stomach emptied by a day's labor. On the windy days at the farm, all Jim and Hannu talked about was how sweet it would be to go for a sail; on the truly blustery days, they just left the tools in the shed, hitched Jim's little boat to the back of his truck and all drove down to Breakers Beach to go out on the canal. Peter had moved east by then. Niklas recalled the heartache of not understanding why, of missing him, and going round and round about it in his mind as he listened to the whine of the drill and the wind in the treetops and held things in place for Jakob to screw in, handing him a hammer that lay in the grass when he needed to force something into place.

As he emptied his bowels, Niklas watched the light grow slowly behind the trees in front of him. His right arm rested on the board that used to serve as a little bookshelf; Hannu always kept a dozen books by the "throne," a couple of titles each from Orwell, Chekhov, Steinbeck, Twain, Jim Harrison. Niklas hadn't read on the toilet in years, but the empty board signified an abandonment by his father that stung to a surprising extent. He wondered about Jakob, what he was doing at this exact moment, whether they allowed you to bring books to the bathroom in prison.

Niklas finished up and dumped compost from a bag down into the putrid cavern beneath his feet. He felt light and awake now. He pushed briskly through the dewy branches and back on to the path. He stopped at the woodpile, strategically set between two massive birches whose limbs kept it dry, and grabbed an armful for coffee.

Back in the cabin he quietly built a fire in the stove. Peter snored softly. As Niklas walked to the corner of the cabin he could smell last night's vomit somewhere on his clothes. Back outside he gathered kindling. Once the wood had caught, he realized that instead of grocery shopping last night they'd gotten hammered at Schmidt's, caught up with some old buddies, and banished everything that wasn't right in front of them from their minds. Tomorrow hadn't existed then, but here it was, and there wasn't any coffee. He realized, too, that he was quite hungry.

Niklas looked over at Peter. He had yet to stir, despite Niklas' having accidentally let the screen door slam on the way in from getting kindling. All of a sudden, his eyes snapped open. Niklas almost pitied the pained look on his face. They were quite a long way from the comforts of Water Street.

"No coffee," Niklas said, taking a gulp of water from his Nalgene. "We gotta get groceries."

Peter sniffed and twisted around slowly. "What time is it?"

"I don't know. Morning."

"Dawn."

"Come on, dude."

Peter rubbed his eyes. "I don't know how Uncle Jussi slept on one of these all those years. Shit it hurts my back. I'm not built for this."

"You're fine." Niklas went back to the fire and Peter went outside. Niklas heard piss splattering against the ground right outside; he rose and went to the door.

"Dude, can you, like, walk ten feet into the woods?"

"Are you serious?"

"We gotta be here for a few days. I don't want to be smelling piss when we sleep and cook and stuff. This is routine stuff, Pete. Don't piss off the porch."

Peter started walking up the hill. Niklas barked at him. "Don't go up and piss downhill, you idiot. Seriously?"

Peter looked back, miffed, and muttered, "Ok, Jakob," under his breath. Gone was the wide-eyed follower, or perhaps he would return if the three of them were all together. Grudgingly, rather than risk an argument this early, he padded off into the woods and pissed on a tree. He felt a pang of anger, and wondered whether to feed it, whether it would be a useful tool in overruling Niklas this weekend. It was easier to screw somebody over when you bore a grudge against them. And then suddenly he grew unbearably sad at himself. His head pounded fiercely.

Peter glanced at the lightening sky on his way back to the cabin—it was going to be a cloudy day. Back inside the gloomy room, Niklas was sullenly feeding the fire. Peter pulled a chair back to sit down at the table and sent swirls and eddies of dust spiraling into the air. Gentle light from the window caught the dust in beams and fell upon the dark floor. Peter stared hard at the edge of a shadow on the floor and tried to catch it moving. He rubbed crust from his eyes, wondering where to begin.

"So, uh," Peter said. "I guess I'm gonna start asking around the neighbors. Might hit Roy's beforehand. You coming?"

Niklas looked over his shoulder from his spot by the woodstove. "I'm getting coffee with Coach Klingberg at the Suomi."

"When?"

"Nine. He's got work at ten. Can you drop me off?"

"I guess, but we should go soon so I can get started on the neighbors. I gotta call Tina. She's been on me about this so hard lately, and then the whole mix up with Olly's appointment. I really hope this works out."

Niklas gave him a hard look but said nothing. His eyes drifted to the window. "So, are we going soon or what?"

"Sure. Let's go." Peter pulled on his sneakers and fresh khaki pants. On the way out, the screen door got stuck again, the bottom catching on a seam in the boards of the porch. Niklas looked at it with a frown and squatted down beside it. Peter waited a moment, then hit the unlock button on his key fob to try and get Niklas' attention. The car's quiet beep seemed to wake him up. Peter walked to the car, Niklas following him distractedly. When he'd sat down beside Peter in the passenger seat, he wore the same frown.

"That door's all fucked up. We should fix it. I'm tired of lifting it up every time and explaining it to new people so they don't break it."

"Well, soon enough it'll be someone else's problem."

"I'm serious, though," Niklas insisted. "We should fix that before the next time we come up here."

"Do you not think I'm gonna be able to sell the place?"

"Fuck off. We're definitely not selling it this quickly."

"Goddammit, dude, I told you why I needed to come up here. I told you I was in a fucking corner. Why else are we here?"

49

Niklas looked at him, half confused, half disgusted. "Why were we ever?"

"If your heart's too wrapped up here, I shouldn't have brought you."

"You don't have a choice! This is just as much mine as it is yours!"

They were breathing hard. Peter started the car.

"I'm fixing that door today," Niklas said, staring forward. "Take it off, remount it half an inch higher and it won't scrape the bottom. Then, *next time*, we don't have to deal with it."

Peter pulled out onto Liminga Road and let a minute pass in silence. "I'm asking you, dude, to hear me when I say I wouldn't ask this of you if I weren't desperate."

"And I'm asking you to respect my choice. Which is that you can shop around, but that I'm not signing away shit until Jakob gets out and we can talk about it."

"Well, just don't get too worried about stuff like fixing doors, huh? It'll only make it harder."

"You're talking like the decision's already been made," Niklas said coolly.

"It's not like we come up here, ever."

"I would if I had a car. I would come and camp in the summers and visit Uncle Jussi in the winters."

"Visit his headstone, you mean."

"You're a fucking asshole."

"Come on, Nik."

They passed the rest of the ride to Houghton in silence. The car turned right onto the canal road and began the steep descent down to the canal's edge and into Houghton from the west. The houses along the canal rushed by. The sun slipped out momentarily from behind the clouds and the water sparkled, and the great bridge to Hancock loomed in the distance, and the breeze kicked up again, tossing the leaves. It was utterly cruel to think of leaving for good, and both boys in their own ways were keenly aware of this. Peter sped down the hill into town, pausing at a stop sign, then passing with the bridge on their left into Houghton proper.

Peter pulled up and parked across the street from the Suomi. A line of trucks drove past as Niklas opened the passenger door. "Say hey to coach for me," Peter said.

"Sure. Meet back at the farm this afternoon?"

"All right." Peter winced, feeling his shoulder. "Hey, did we wrestle last night?"

Niklas laughed. "Yeah, I told the story of when I finally pinned Jakob the night of my eighteenth birthday. Chris was there and he said he could pin either of us. You were blacked out at that point. You got tossed around a bit."

"Huh. I feel like it."

Niklas chuckled, slammed the door and headed across the street into the Suomi.

Peter parked by the canal. Inside the library, on one of the public computers, he checked his email, sent a few responses, then spent half an hour creating a listing: forty acres near Liminga, a creek, a bare cabin, asking price thirty thousand dollars. He posted the listing and left the library, feeling the chill bite of wind on his face as he stepped out into the sun. He saw a woman he thought he recognized, and almost called out to her across the street, but she looked too old and too pregnant to be the person he knew. He got in his car and sat in the driver's seat staring at the canal and across to Hancock until a car drove in front of him and shook him out of his daze. The needle on the gas gauge barely rose beyond the red E, which annoyed him a lot more than it should have. He had to get gas, then groceries, then call his angry wife while Niklas was off getting breakfast with his old coach. He punched the gas, headed up the hill toward the grocery store. His right shoulder ached dully and screamed whenever he flexed it in certain ways. He felt the engines of resentment cranking up inside his chest. At the last minute he swerved right across two lanes of traffic onto the canal road.

He drove along the canal road for ten minutes, trying in vain to take pleasure in the water rushing by and the familiar string of houses with boats on trailers in their driveways on the lake side of the road. Soon he hooked a right and pulled into Schmidt's Corner. There were only three trucks parked in the dirt behind the tavern, nothing else. Peter parked in the corner by the back door. Just as he shut his door with a slam, his phone rang, cutting abrasively through the quiet. It was Tina.

"Hey, baby."

"Hey, how's it going out there?"

A truck roared by, paused at the stop sign, then growled off. "All right. My back's stiff from sleeping on a cot. I can already feel

51

the fried food balling up in my gut." He knew she would warm to these words of complaint.

"Well, that's just incentive to hurry up, right."

"I know. How's Olly? How're you holding up?"

"Oh, I'm fine, Peter."

"Ok. I'm glad. What's—"

"I know you're trying to do the right thing but you know how hard these trips always are. You get in a car with Niklas and Jakob—"

"You know it's just me and Niklas." An edge had come into his voice.

"And it's honestly a relief that it's not the three of you together. Nothing would ever get sold."

"Right, well, maybe there's a reason for that."

"It's because those two don't know when to stop! Life is not one big crazy adventure, Peter. You're not meant to follow your heart everywhere. Look where it got Jakob. Look where it's getting Niklas."

"What's wrong with Niklas?"

"No career, no interests except keeping you three stuck in the past and romping around in the woods. He's the worst of all."

"That's not fair. You know that's not fair. Jakob is his hero. So was Jussi. You can't blame him for dealing with everything that's in the past by pining for the best of it."

"How? The bills need to get paid somehow."

"What do you think I'm doing? What more—"

"I'm just trying to make sure nothing up there gets in your head. I'm your family now, not Niklas and Jakob."

Peter was stunned. "OK, Tina. Loud and clear."

"I'm sorry. That was the wrong way of saying it."

"You don't say."

"I'm... Peter, I... I just want things to be OK for us. OK?"

"Yeah. Well. Twisting the knife is not helping your case. Tell Olly I love him. I'll call you tomorrow." And he hung up without waiting for a response.

The weathered boards of Schmidt's stairs creaked as he climbed them and pushed the door open. He walked past the pool table up to the bar, where two men in jeans and camo ball caps sat drinking Labatt's. Peter ordered a shot of Kessler and a High Life from the butch bartender, who squinted at him but said nothing as he tossed the shot. Warmth radiating outward from his gut, he thought he saw one of the men smirking at him and saying something to his buddy.

"Didn't think we'd see you back so soon, bud," the guy said, his buddy chuckling.

Peter felt his face grow hot. This had been happening more and more lately, trying to remember what he'd done or said during the hours of a binge. He wondered if they'd seen the wrestling.

"Yeah, well, here I am."

"Want a shot?"

"What the hell. Kessler."

The guy closest to him, the thinner of the two though the distinction was marginal, asked him what the deal was. Peter swigged his High Life and considered the question and his audience.

"My wife is trying to pull one over on me."

"Get outta town before you end up at the bottom of da canal!" The one on the outside motioned for another round of shots.

"I wish it were that simple."

"Well, why's she doing that?"

They all three shot the shot. Peter got up. "I'll tell you all about it after I take a piss," reaching shamelessly into his jacket pocket as he pushed into the bathroom.

❦ 9 ❦

Summer, 1913

Hard times fell upon the Keweenaw in the years before the Great War. The city planners had jumped the gun, overzealously building Calumet to handle a boom that never quite came. To compensate, the companies leaned extra hard on their labor and the labor responded in kind. The workers for Hecla, along with those from the Quincy and Copper Range Mines, rallied under the Western Federation of Miners and struck at the beginning of July. It was the first real union mounted offensive and it lasted nine months.

Olli was among the mob that forced the mines to close. There were organized marches. Many were hurling stones and hunting down bosses and though Olli was tempted, he confined his violence to his mind and soul, using his Olympic frame to carry the wounded to the tented field hospitals at the edges of the conflict. When two men got shot down in Seberville, Ana insisted that he step back and help her at home with Teemu and Sofia. Olli was a man of action and was deeply uncomfortable with leaving the fight for miners' rights, and Ana, always a pillar of compromise, began volunteering in the evenings for the Women's Auxiliary of the Western Federation of Miners (WFM). Olli would build a big fire and, with Sofia and little Teemu on his lap, tell old stories, family stories, folk tales, and sing softly until only embers remained, tickling the walls with gentle orange kisses. That fall Ana would often return home after volunteering to her husband snoring in his great blue armchair, with their two children flopped like sleepy cats on his bulky torso. Both Olli and Ana, in their own ways, were the happiest they'd ever been.

One cold afternoon in early December, after fighting her way home through a gathering snowstorm, Ana rushed into the kitchen, cheeks flushed, a rare instance of her emotions untethered from their typically short leash. There was going to be a Christmas party, she said. The WFM was losing steam and many families had packed up and headed south to find work elsewhere. She had lost some sleep wondering if their life in the Keweenaw would survive the winter, and though the WFM's coffers were frighteningly light

Ana felt that this Christmas gathering would stoke the spiritual hearths of the miners and weary wives and children. It was to be held at the Italian Hall on Christmas Eve.

Unfortunately, or so they thought, both Teemu and Sofia fell quite ill a week before the party. Olli dutifully offered to handle the kids himself, knowing his wife had poured a portion of her soul into planning this party, but Teemu's temperature was still frighteningly high on the morning of Christmas Eve. Ana loved her husband dearly and part of that was knowing that he wasn't the brightest bulb in the chandelier, so she sent a note with her friend Aino apologizing to her friends at the Women's Auxiliary, explaining the situation and wishing them the best of luck as hosts of the evening.

Teemu's fever broke in the afternoon, thank goodness, and Sofia looked to be on the come down from something like the flu. As night fell, Ana was flustered and began pacing the living room wondering aloud if she could make it to the Italian Hall in time to be a help and not a burden. Olli, who'd been in the other room caressing foreheads and telling stories, heard the note of stress in her voice, gave each child a kiss on the forehead, and went to the other room to investigate. Ana was in a heap of anxiety on the ground talking nonsense to herself. Olli picked her up easily and rocked her as he'd rocked his children just moments before. Eventually, she calmed down and told him that the ladies left in charge were too fond of the drink for her comfort, that they'd gone over budget, and the WFA's pockets were nearly empty with four more winter months on the horizon, that there were supposed to be lots of children at the hall, that she knew that bodies and minds needed to be rallied for the cause, but what if the men got too hot? Olli stroked her hair and assured her that Jussi and the other working people of Calumet had no intention of getting so worked up that the children got dragged into it.

You never really understand God's twisted sense of humor until you're on the wrong side of it. The miners were civil, the wives stayed off the booze, the kids kept their shirts tucked and their fingers out of their noses. Over a hundred families from the surrounding area attended and by all accounts for several hours things were warmly jubilant.

An unaccompanied man (who many later alleged was wearing a Citizen's Alliance jacket) came up the stairs and walked several paces into the crowded hall. He took off his hat, shouted "Fire!" and promptly left. There ensued a rush down the stairs that left seventy-three souls—more than half of them children— trampled to death.

Ana and Olli heard cries ring out across the town and Olli had to restrain a distraught Ana before going to investigate himself. It took too long to cut through all the chaos and get a coherent timeline together in his head but once Olli did, his eyes came alive with the same burning rage that would be found in Jakob nearly a hundred years later. Olli searched and questioned passers by, and when the other stricken men decided it was fruitless and went home, he wept. Jussi was nowhere to be seen, and not at his house, either. Olli ran around looking late into the night, far beyond the hour where he couldn't ignore that his Jussi was likely among the dead. This was confirmed the following week after an overwrought Women's Auxiliary meeting in which death tolls were tallied and the strike leaders essentially decided to admit defeat. It took weeks for Ana to recover from this meeting. Had they not been sick, Ana was sure her children would have been among the dead. Olli did all he could to ease her grief while he wallowed in his own, but something between her third and fourth ribs had broken. Forever after she was gun-shy with the children and tended to act as though if things were up to her they would be kept inside little glass boxes like reptile enclosures in a menagerie.

⚞ 10 ⚟

Saturday, Midday

Jim Markham, arms loaded with two by sixes, stood up straight with a straining back and lumbered over to the edge of his house's extension. He set down the last load of lumber and the drill under the edge of the roof in case it rained later. The sky was blue, and the leaves quivered all together in the breeze that chilled the sweat on Jim's forehead and neck as he walked inside. Cynthia sat at the kitchen table with her glasses on the end of her nose, going over some bills. She looked up as he walked in and retrieved a mug for coffee. The TV played an old Western, like always, with the volume at a medium level. She watched him fill the cup and sit down at the table next to her.

"Pretty out dere, isn't it?" she said.

"Oh yeah. Real nice day." He settled into the chair across the table.

"I walked through da woods this morning. Da leaves are already starting to turn. It's early."

"Oh no it's not. You say dat every year, and every year, it's da same time. Same time, every year."

"No I don't. Middle of August? I never—"

"Yes you do. Every year, same time." Jim smiled at her, and she smiled back.

"You got a call while you were out working," she said.

"Oh yeah?"

"It was Hannu Kinnunen. He sounded upset."

"Well, gimmie da phone. I'll see what's going on." Jim, in spite of the fact that just yesterday he'd been missing Hannu and wishing he would call, took the phone from Cynthia and dialed his number with a dash of apprehension. He was curious as to why the boys had suddenly appeared after almost three years absent and plenty of grief to keep them away. The phone rang in his ear and he listened to his own rattly breath.

"Hello?"

"Hannu! Jim Markham."

"Jim! Glad you got my message. How's things?"

"Oh dere fine. Just working on da house. Dis fella down in Baraga's moving away, wants me to sell his boat. I met him doing a porch job at dat church. He's moving away and he wants me to sell it for him."

"Oh, well. You take it out yourself yet?"

"Oh, no. Been to lazy to look at it."

"Yeah?"

"Got the other one. No need."

"Really? Well, I'm sure you won't have to keep it for too long. You advertising anywhere?"

"I might put up some flyers."

A pause lingered. Jim broke the silence. "So, Cynthia tells me you called a little bit ago?"

Hannu paused on the other end of the line. "Well I got a call from Don Klingberg this morning. He said Niklas and Peter are in town."

"Oh, ya. Niklas called me to open up da place for 'em. Dey said dey'd come by for a sauna at some point."

"Don seemed worried about Niklas. Apparently Peter and him are thinking about selling the place."

"Huh! Really? Didn't say nothing to me about it."

"Hmm. I'll be honest, Jim, I am surprised." And, Jim gleaned from the tone of his voice, disappointed too.

"I'm not sure. You talk to them yet?"

"No, I haven't. I wanted to talk to you first."

"Oh, well. I don't know. I'll ask 'em when I see 'em next. Should be next day or two."

"All right. Thank you, Jim."

"Sure."

Each man cast around for something to say, not wanting to hang up just yet. "How's Pernilla?" Jim asked.

"Oh, she's getting along. She's got her group that goes out climbing and kayaking and all that. She could kick my ass, probably."

"You better watch your back! Don't say nothing sarcastic! Ha!"

"Oh, I won't, don't you worry. How's Cynthia and the kids?"

"Oh, dey're fine. Went out to Gino's last week with Jason. He on one of dose phones texting the whole time."

"I'm sorry to hear that. You keeping busy yourself?"

"Oh, ya, was out with my skid steer over in Atlantic Mine, had to dig a bunch of holes for this woman's orchard. She's moving up from Illinois, called me to dig the holes a week ago. Got to take my grandson's bike over to my brother Floyd's. He's got my jack, borrowed it last week. Gotta get new tires on dat bike. Runs great, though, I rode it over. Tires are almost bald, though."

"Well good. This woman's got a whole mature orchard coming in?"

"Oh ya."

"Well I have a special fondness for orchards, as you know."

"Da lingonberry king, dey call you!"

"Once, but not anymore, Jim. That's the boys, though perhaps not for much longer it sounds like."

"Oh I'll talk to 'em. Knock some sense into 'em if I have to."

"I appreciate it."

"Oh ya."

"Take care, now. Tell Cynthia I send my love."

"Oh ya."

"Bye, Jim."

"Bye-bye!" Jim clicked the red button on the house phone as he looked up at Cynthia, who'd finished with the bills, removed her glasses, and now sat at the table watching him. As he hung up she started to speak but he cut her off.

"They're coming the same time as every year. End of August. And you're always calling it early when it's the same time every year."

"Well," Cynthia said with her smile-grimace. "I was walking outside earlier. The temperature is dropping. It's early for that, isn't it?"

Outside, the leaves on the trees had stopped shimmering. The wind had died for a moment. It picked up again seconds later and set them quivering once more.

"Oh, here we go," said Jim.

≈ 11 ≈

Winter, 1937

Ana and Olli learned quickly as parents do that Sofia and Teemu, their children, would sooner lose fingers or get hypothermia than be trapped inside even in the depths of Michigan's winters. Sofia grew up tall, broad, and tough, playing with the boys and physically dominating them until she was well into her teens. She married a pulp cutter from Iron Mountain and had a quartet of big boned, blue-eyed kids almost right away. That her life was repetitive and entirely family oriented never occurred to her; she delighted in her children's successes, commiserated in their failures, and bragged about both to the other mothers in town who heard in her complaints the comfortable foibles of a well-made life.

Her little brother, Teemu, was blessed or cursed for inheriting all the excitement his older sister shied away from. He was accident prone from day one, always coming home with cuts or bruises or resentments boiling over at having been blamed for something he didn't do. When he was seven his dad took him out ice fishing, and because he didn't complain, all his dad's buddies told him he was a champ and gave him the first piece of trout on toast they cooked over a huge smudge fire in bacon grease. By the time they returned home and Teemu was sufficiently defrosted to speak in full sentences, he was full of such glowing warmth from the fish and the approval that he couldn't bring himself to say anything but "When can we go next?" And so it was that all the world or at least his parents and his parents' friends (and even some of his friends' parents) came to think of little Teemu as the toughest kid around. By the time he was ten and playing hockey, Teemu was well past the point where he could've called for a tack and turned his personality in a different direction.

Adolescence came like a thief in the night and now Teemu was putting opposing forwards on their asses as a freshly minted and no longer scrawny high schooler. In modern times he would've made the perfect checking third-line forward. As it was, in the late twenties he dropped his gloves and fought quite a bit though his mother forbade him from bringing his fists off the ice with him.

Olli, on the other hand, loved the fighting and cackled with pleasure every time his son's gloves fell to the ice and his knuckles bloodied some poor kid's nose. There was a kind of domestic harmony, a yin and yang, in their opinions of Teemu's on ice violence: reliably his mother would tut and sniff and talk about the skill and finesse that Jimmy this or Jarmo that or David whomever had exhibited while Teemu had made himself out to be such a *thug*. And his dad would laugh and say something along the lines of "Look, bud, your teammates love you and, between you and me, you're the only kid in the U.P. whom the opposing team's mothers fret about by name before their sons have to play you." Back in those days fighting, both on and off the ice, was a much more common affair, and in addition to being a tough son of a bitch, Olli's son's antics on the ice were an insurance policy off it.

As Teemu aged, he grew ever closer to his father. By the time he was a teenager fighting his way through the toughest kids in U.P. high school hockey, Olli had taken to regaling him with stories from the old days with Jussi. Olli grew misty-eyed the first few times his old friend came up. On several occasions, he devolved into a teary rage and railed against the Citizens Alliance and the scabs who'd killed his friend. Soon, though, the thrill of recalling their joyous tumbles with fellow ruffians and the law became too sweet to be sad. And Teemu loved these stories, clung to every embellished anecdote. Olli made a big deal out of passing on Jussi's first commandment of street fighting: strike with an open hand and save your knuckles. Of course, Teemu couldn't do this on the ice, but his knuckles weren't threatened as much by hockey fights, and he was under strict orders from Ana to solve his off-ice problems with words, a sickly sweet phrase of hers that made him crazy. "I spent far too much time patching your father and Jussi up before you came along," she said. "No son of mine will brawl his way into prison or the hospital." And Olli qualified every trip down memory lane with the fact that the best and only good part about fighting was telling about it after you won. Sometimes you get your ass kicked.

Worse, in a sense, was kicking someone else's ass harder than you'd intended. As a cautionary tale Olli threw in one about a bunch of guys who'd spilled beer on one of their buddies and ended up with Olli and his friends curb stomping them outside until teeth in numbers ran in the muddy, bloody late spring gutter.

That he was capable of such cruelty, Olli said, had shocked and horrified him afterward. Those guys probably had brain damage, would maybe have to eat wet food through a straw. Keep your fighting on the ice, Olli told Teemu, and you won't ever hurt anyone or get hurt all that badly.

Teemu took this advice and only ever threw two punches in street clothes. They were thrown a minute apart and had almost diametrically opposed results. It was at once his finest and darkest hour.

He was nineteen when it happened, possibly the stupidest of all ages, especially in men. He'd been rejected earlier that afternoon by a gorgeous Irish girl from downstate who'd laughed him away when he'd asked her for a date. He was in a bar with a buddy from his job at the stamp mill, Jim Markham Sr., already soupy with booze when they spotted what looked like a Citizens Alliance patch sloppily sewn onto the shoulder of a black leather jacket worn by an older guy a few seats down the bar. The guy was bragging loudly about something to his friend when Teemu, who'd served as audience for too many of his dad's anti-Alliance rants not to take notice, poked the guy in the back of the head.

"Piece of shit scab," said Teemu, remembering his father's slur, liking how it sounded on his lips, standing at the ready. Then two guys who Teemu had somehow missed fanned out behind the fellow he'd poked, who turned around with a cheap grin that might as well have been a snarl. They were on the upper floor and it was December, so the balcony was empty. All five men headed for the balcony doors, Teemu feeling sick to his stomach about being outnumbered and endangering Jim Sr. who thankfully joined him in what looked for all the world like an inbound ass-kicking.

The man on the left caught Jim by surprise the second they were out the door with a sucker punch to the temple. Jim went down limp as Teemu looked on, horrified and guilty. The Alliance guy with fire in his eyes grabbed Teemu by the collar while he was distracted and hoisted him over the railing. Teemu thought he was getting thrown off until the man's friends came and braced the man's legs so that he could dangle Teemu over the edge without dropping him. It was fifteen or twenty feet down, and unless the snow was fresh he was bound to break at least an ankle. He looked up into the man's face as spit flew into his.

"Tell me why I shouldn't drop you right here, you red piece of shit," the man screamed through a wild grin.

Teemu whispered something.

"What, asshole?"

Teemu, again, whispered something.

The man signaled his friends and hoisted Teemu back up, slugging him hard in the stomach twice. He leaned over Teemu, who was doubled over, and spoke in his ear. "I said, what was that, you piece of shit red?"

Teemu, who was embellishing, noticed Jim on the ground had opened his eyes. Teemu caught his eye and winked. He whispered again in a mumble. The man screamed, "I will throw you off this fucking balcony."

Teemu turned abruptly to look the man in the face. "I said you should've dropped me motherfucker," and threw a devastating left hook that connected with a crunch. The man pitched over and lay still. Jim, still obviously shaken but back in the game, returned the sucker punch favor into one of the henchmen's kidneys. Teemu followed him up with a savage uppercut and the last man, rather than square up against Jim and Teemu, fled the bar.

Sofia had married off and moved to Iron Mountain two years prior so the filial duty of attending family dinners rested solely on Teemu's shoulders. The following evening his knuckles were so bruised and painful that he didn't even bother wrapping them up or hiding them. He was setting the table with Ana when she noticed.

"Sweetheart, my goodness, when did you get in a fight?"

Teemu balked, having planned on saying his hand got smashed at the mill. He said stupidly: "Oh. Um. Well, uh, yesterday, uh, actually."

Ana escaped to the kitchen and returned with a handful of bandages and wraps. "I haven't had to use these for years. I'd hoped their days were done. Silly me." And she wrested Teemu's colorful hand painfully into her lap as she examined its bruising and the extent of its cuts.

"Wait, Mom. How'd you know?"

She rolled her eyes and answered without looking at him. "I really thought you just got like that on the ice. You really can't be fighting. I'm surprised these bandages were all I ever needed. Your father came home with knuckles like that too many times. You'll get laid up or end up in prison. It's a miracle your father didn't."

"My hands never get this bad during games."

Ana huffed and finished wrapping the hand without a word.

Half an hour later the three of them, Olli, Ana, and Teemu, sat down together for a dinner of pork chops and fried onions and potatoes and a beer. Teemu's left hand, his dominant hand, lay fetal and defeated in his lap.

He looked at the pork chop and tried in vain to draw up a battle plan that allowed him to eat the pork chop without using his busted hand. The pain wasn't an issue; Olli would ask about the fight and chide him for using a closed fist, whereupon Ana would scathingly remind Olli that fighting had nearly cost him his wits and his freedom and that if he wasn't careful his son would pay doubly for the sins of them both. Teemu had gotten his job at the stamp mill three months before and along with it quite a few brownie points with Olli. Starting a quarrel at the dinner table would surely spend some hard-won goodwill.

And yet, as he neared the end of the pile of fried potatoes and started in on his onions, he saw no possible way forward. He might as well just get it over with. He lifted his wrapped hand with a wince from his lap and gingerly picked up his fork to stabilize the meat. His uncoordinated right hand dragged the knife awkwardly across the pork chop, working slowly, finally separating a bite by tearing through the last quarter of the cut like you do when your hatchet can't get all the way through a tree limb. His father watched his progress.

"Get in a scrap?" asked Olli, cautiously optimistic and hoping it didn't show.

"He did," snapped Ana. "And I stitched and wrapped him up." She began cutting her pork chop with pointed ferocity as if it was the one that had gotten in a fight. Teemu, throughout the exchange, had laboriously managed to cut another three bites of pork. He rewarded himself with a bite of onions.

Olli's eyes were lively with amusement but he kept them on his plate. "Well. Didn't I ever tell you about my old friend Jussi's first rule of—"

"Yes, I'm sure you did," said Ana, still attacking her pork chop, her knife scraping with a bone-chilling screech against her plate.

Olli started to speak but stopped himself. He swallowed a bite of potatoes and suppressed a grin. "Jussi never bruised his knuckles."

"Horseshit," spat Ana.

Beyond the veil of his father's facetiousness, Teemu could sense vast quantities of admiration. In all the stories Jussi was always the one with the clever quip, the knockout blow, the crazy scheme and the big brass balls to pull it off. The man had attained legendary status in Teemu's imagination, and he regretfully remembered the advice about striking with an open hand.

"Will you be able to work?" asked Ana, suddenly worried.

"I'm off tomorrow and it might be better by Monday," said Teemu, partially ducking the question. Both of his parents reacted immediately; Ana rolled her eyes and huffed while Olli snorted sympathetically.

"Thing's gonna sting for a while," said Olli.

"How long?" asked Teemu.

"Two or three weeks, though I can't see under the bandage, so."

Teemu was miserable. The glow of victory had worn off and left the physical and occupational consequences all to themselves. Olli took note and, after swallowing his last bite of onions and glancing furtively over at a distracted Ana, offered one of Jussi's favorite post scrap condolences: "Sure hate to be on the other end of that one, huh, bud?" Ana looked up in exasperation as Olli clapped his beaming son on the shoulder and escaped to the kitchen for another beer.

Fortunately for Teemu, his hand healed up nicely in just shy of two weeks. It was a painful two weeks at the plant—his knuckles pulsed with swollen heat every time he flexed his hand in a few particular ways, and pain shot up his arm and made him drop whatever he was carrying. Fortunately, he was a tough kid and a good worker; his foreman and coworkers at the plant didn't mind him slowing down for a week or two, especially after he regaled them with the tale of the brawl, polished with gentle embellishment, since typically he did the work of two or three men at once.

Soon enough he was back to hustling with the biggest and strongest guys on the job and if not for the story of the fight, told and retold until it became the stuff of legend, people would have forgotten it had ever happened.

⚡ 12 ⚡

1999, Marquette

Jakob's imprisonment was even more heartbreaking for the family because he'd been a brawler from day one and many of the neighbors had thought it inevitable. Hannu and Pernilla didn't, of course. They only saw their sweet little boy and his beautiful drawings, heard not his thirst for vengeance but only his sweet tenor in the second row of the choir at church, sensed not his desperate obsessions and acknowledged only the products of his manic moments of productivity. His life screamed up toward the sky and then plummeted and then screamed and plummeted again, a roller coaster of sequential heartache. He knew no middle ground, and treated all moderation with contempt. He was up for parole in November.

His path to the pen was rife with coincidence—one or two adjusted details and he'd never have gotten popped (although most people, upon hearing the news of his incarceration, were shocked but not surprised). It began, as these things often do, with frustration in love.

Jakob began his senior year of high school as social royalty. He was six foot three and lean from hours in the gym and practice for the wrestling team, of which he was the captain. His dirty blond hair was buzzed in a way that only certain men with forgivingly shaped heads could call fashionable. Judging by the stubble on his chin, he was already a man. He was the first in his grade to acquire a fake ID, and the first to receive a ticket for underage drinking, which he proudly passed around study hall one February morning when the snow was four feet thick and the only thing to keep you warm was boasting. He was ruggedly handsome and the senior girls who typically surfed the local bars for guys from Northern decided he was desirable. After a string of one-night stands that soon assumed the status of legend among the student body, especially the boys, Jakob was reported to be dating someone. The girls at his school were mutinous.

As it turns out, Jakob had flipped the script on the senior girls and taken up with a soccer player in her senior year at Northern.

Her name was Tallie Rosenbaum and she was the picture in the dictionary next to "California girl." She was five-eleven with light brown hair dyed blond except for the roots, broad shoulders, slender hips and legs perennially tanned and smooth despite the winter.

At the end of September, her senior year, Tallie was considering relaxing her ferocious work ethic on the pitch for the sake of some partying, for making up lost time after a decade of training, dieting, traveling, and refusing booze and cigarettes and pot. Around the time these thoughts were brewing in Tallie's head, Jakob was flagging in his efforts to sleep with every attractive girl in his school. He'd gotten into a few emotional scrapes and was sensing other needs buoyantly forcing their way to the top of his mind.

Hannu had promised he would match whatever Jakob could save toward the purchase of a car. Jakob decided to make some money and take a trip the following summer.

In this situation, most seventeen-year-olds would find a job at a restaurant or store and save up little by little, but Jakob was far too impatient for that. The previous summer his buddy, Blake, a defensive end on the football team and fellow POI for the ladies, had taken him way out onto Presque Isle and given him his first marijuana. Jakob didn't mind it but was baffled by the fervor of his classmates' desire for it. He bought an eighth for himself in June but barely touched it and ended up selling off the last two grams.

The general lust for the drug and the confusion at his ambivalence toward it stuck in Jakob's craw. The phone in his room blew up for two days with buddies of increasingly tenuous connection calling to inquire about the two available grams. He was only asking for ten bucks and Blake's response to that was, "I mean, Jesus dude. You could get three times that. People think you must have the best shit around." Jakob sold it to the girlfriend of a hockey teammate for twenty-five bucks and the effusiveness of her gratitude once again confused him. Apparently the rumor had spread that he was something of a dealer. This pissed him off, and at first he ignored all related inquiries. But then Hannu made the car offer and Jakob had an idea.

He called Blake and asked a few questions. He walked downstairs from his room and asked his mother how much she thought he had in his savings account. He went back upstairs, called Blake again, then left the house and drove, in the beat up old Corolla that he and Niklas shared, first to the bank and then down to the ore dock. He returned with a vacuum-sealed package containing an ounce of hydroponic marijuana that allegedly originated in Humboldt County.

And Jakob went to work. He'd told Blake of his intentions so the word could get around and that weekend showed up to a party with the intention of selling every last crumb of the ounce. He was wiped out before midnight. By virtue of his social status, the male athletes immediately began hitting him up in droves. Girls now had an excuse to corner the studly Jakob Kinnunen and many, despite the overlap of friend groups, sought him out individually. He scaled up his operation, refusing to sell small amounts, middle-manning anything from half an ounce to half a pound. He was polite when doing business but didn't linger, and certainly didn't cut unsavory deals despite the surprisingly large number of girls who thought a blow job would earn them a couple of grams. (He'd unwittingly accepted one and then afterward had to explain to a naked, righteous stoner girl that he wasn't that kind of plug.) He refrained from sexual relations with customers for exactly two months, until the week before Thanksgiving when he met Tallie.

She was headed home for Thanksgiving break and had gotten Jakob's number from a soccer teammate whose boyfriend was on the Nordic ski team. "The kid's in high school, but Pat and the team swear by him," the friend had said. Tallie, frankly, didn't care if the kid had two heads as long as he sold her enough pot to endure a brutal week with her family back in Oakland.

She didn't know what she'd expected, but it certainly wasn't a ruggedly handsome man in a clean flannel shirt and jeans flecked with muddy filth that on anyone else would have been repellent but on Jakob were rugged and charming. He looked a little like Tallie's father had when she was very young, blond hair trimmed short with a number three on the razor and several days of stubble on his cheeks. She was sitting in the passenger seat of his car in front of her house, staring like a fool and forgetting what she'd come for.

"You're in high school? Seriously?"

"Yup," he said, eyes narrowing in suspicion. "You wanted an eighth, right?"

"No, yeah, for sure," she said. "How much?"

"Forty."

She dug around in her purse and retrieved several crumpled bills. "Should be forty right there."

Jakob licked his finger and peeled off the bills one by one, counting. When he was done he handed her back five singles.

"Did I give you forty-five?"

"No, I just don't take singles."

"Oh, shoot, let me run inside then. I'm sure one of my roommates has a five."

She opened the door but Jakob caught her arm. A pulse of electricity traveled up through his wrist. "Not what I meant. Ones are just clutter. You're good to go."

She, too, had felt the pulse and after searching Jakob's face for the creases of trickery slumped back into the passenger seat and closed the door. "You must be loaded if singles are more trouble than they're worth."

He blushed and deflected like a good Midwesterner. "Most people just pay me in twenties and tens. Don't have a place for the singles in the piggy bank."

She burst out laughing, laughing harder than the joke deserved. "What's your name?"

"Jakob."

"Jakob."

"Last time I checked."

"Well, Jakob, if I give you a call once Thanksgiving's done with, do you think you could hook me up again?" She looked him right in the eye, mouth open slightly, and put a hand on his arm.

Jakob was tongue-tied. "Uh, well, sure, yeah. 'Course. Just let me know."

Tallie smiled. "Thank you, Jakob." And she gave his arm a squeeze, opened the door and walked back up through her snowy front yard. He watched her go, marveling at the wonder of her rear. When she got inside, her roommate, Lauren, was waiting in the front room having seen the whole thing. Lauren was smirking at her with a knowing look.

"You better not have paid for that weed, slut," said Lauren. "You look like you have scoliosis."

Tallie managed to get through the week in one piece, though not without chemical assistance from Jakob's little sandwich

69

baggie. She called him up when she got back and he said he'd be happy to sell her more. She put on her nicest pair of jeans and a figure-hugging sweater under her coat, made sure her eyeliner wasn't smudged in the bathroom mirror, checked her purse for a condom, and went out to meet him.

It wasn't as easy as she'd thought. They chatted a little in his car and he awkwardly tried to steer the conversation around to weed, confused and refusing to believe that a college girl, no, a *woman*, was flirting with him. He twisted nervously in his seat and listened to her babble about her week in Oakland and how much she hated the cold weather. She asked him a few questions but he was too flustered to answer at length like you do when you're trying to flirt. After twenty minutes of this, things were at a relative standstill and so she went for his zipper.

Motive and action were now utterly on their heads. In Tallie's twenty-two years on the earth, no man had ever refused a blow-job. The fact that a high school pot dealer just pushed her away was baffling. How much more obvious could she be? But Jakob gently took her hand away, apologizing, saying he wasn't that kind of dealer, saying he was saving up for a car and couldn't take sexual favors. When he said this, she was utterly embarrassed and hastened to explain her true motives. He took some convincing but eventually broke down. The next week they had a drink at the brewery on Third Street, after which they retired to Tallie's room.

In a week they were dating, and they happily spent eight months holed up in Tallie's room or hiking in the woods or at various bars around Marquette. She taught him how to make fresh pasta. He taught her how to ice skate. They grew quite fond of each other, especially after Tallie told Jakob she loved him, and he told her that he loved her too. They said it a lot to each other, those last three months in the spring of their senior years.

"You're so earnest," she said to him one day, watching him watch hockey on TV.

"What do you mean?" he frowned.

"I don't think there's an ounce of irony in anything you do."

"What do you mean? We laugh all the time about, like, how Lauren is more tan in the winter because she likes tanning beds more than being outside, or how my dad still reads to me before bed sometimes."

Tallie smiled. "Well, sure, but those are all such earnestly observed ironies. Irony is a part of your life because it's a part of everyone's life. But it's not how you deal with people. And your dad reading to you before bed is sweet and only aesthetically ironic."

Jakob shrugged. "Is that all good? Or?"

"It's refreshing," she said, beginning to tire a little of his neediness. "Everyone's always hiding under a thick layer of irony. Especially back home. Once I figured out that you were just a serious person and not upset at me all the time, it became one of my favorite things about you."

Jakob furrowed his brow.

"Baby, hey, it's a good thing. I love you."

He smiled. "I love *you*."

Tallie graduated on time in May and moved to Chicago, with the understanding that Jakob would follow in August, to Loyola. His choice of school surprised his friends and coaches but not his teachers or Hannu, who had firsthand experience of his voracious curiosity and knew him as a closeted intellectual, having seen his excellent report cards all these years.

Tallie got a small apartment in Uptown and an entry level job at her father's logistics company in the city. Whether she arrived in Chicago with the intention of shedding Jakob from her life is unclear, but that's certainly what happened. He called her the morning of his scheduled move-in at the Loyola dormitories. After five rings she picked up.

"Hello?"

"Tal. It's me."

"Oh. Hey."

"I'm just about all packed up. Should be moved in by seven or eight tonight."

"That's exciting. Are you in touch with your roommates?"

"Not really. So what do you wanna do tonight? I'm sure you've scouted out the best spots. I've got some acid too but I figured we'd wait for daytime on that one."

"Maybe on the beach sometime."

"Sure. So, uh, tonight?"

"Don't you think you'll want to be with your new friends?"

"They're not new friends yet. Either way I can't see how some dorm party would be better than the bars with you."

"Well, but then all the freshman whores won't get their shot at you."

"Um. But they wouldn't anyway, uh, right?"

"I'm sure they would."

"... but so, uh, Tal. You want to give me your address and I'll swing by this evening when I'm done?"

"Are you sure you don't want to go out at school? Welcome week is fucking insane, I think I was blacked out for five days straight back at Northern and didn't drink again until I met you. You should kick it with your roommates."

"Um, OK. But, like, I haven't seen you since the Fourth of July. And even that was—"

"Yeah yeah, I know. How about tomorrow night?"

Jakob felt the first stirrings of jealousy and distrust stirring in his gut.

"So, but can I at least swing by for a bit? I'm sure shit won't heat up at school till later... I've missed you."

"I'll see you tomorrow night, Jakob. Come on, it's one day."

"Well, what are you doing tonight?"

"Just going out with some friends."

"Since when did you have friends? Last time we talked you were striking out in the friend department."

"Just some girls from work."

"Where are you guys going?"

"Jakob... I'll see you tomorrow."

"Wait, Tallie, hold o—" and the line clicked dead.

They never did go out the following evening. Over the next two weeks, there were several phone conversations like this one, with Jakob growing increasingly nervous and confused about Tallie's social schedule, which was all at once busier than he'd ever known it to be. Her patience on the phone ran out quickly and she snapped at him for asking very reasonable things, like "Hey Tallie, I'm your boyfriend and I haven't really seen you in several months, can you at least tell me when I might?" This was especially painful for Jakob as her apartment was just seven blocks from his dorm. One of his roommates even got laid there, in that very building, after which Jakob called Tallie in a fit of lust only to find that she either wasn't home at nine o'clock on a Tuesday or she was ignoring him.

Tallie had come to resent Jakob, resent his age, his lack of maturity, his hold on her as an attractive woman in a hip neighborhood of a big city. She punished him with meanness and cold shoulders and told her new friends she was single. Soon enough, in her mind she'd broken up with him. He was just a needy ex who couldn't take the hint and move on. Except she never actually sat Jakob down for the conversation. She put it off and put it off and soon enough she found herself getting riled up that he couldn't just get a clue and fuck someone his own age. And Jakob fought harder and harder for her, and like quicksand this made him sink deeper and deeper out of sight.

The first time they laid eyes on each other in Chicago was by accident on the street. Jakob and some friends from his dorm had been north in Evanston partying at Northwestern. Jakob hadn't yet activated his L pass through the school, so he and his friend, Colin, took off on the walk south when the cops arrived to bust the party. They intercepted Tallie a few blocks north of their dorm, coming out of the bar on the arm of a hunk in a cluster of spray-tanned, makeup plastered girls who seemed much more than five years older. Jakob couldn't believe his eyes and almost continued walking for fear of making a fool of himself in front of a girl who wasn't Tallie. But it was definitely her and a second, harder glance confirmed this.

"Tal... hey, Tallie. TALLIE."

Tallie stumbled around in a half circle and looked inquiringly at Jakob and Colin, about ten feet away. She was very drunk.

"Who the fuck are—ohmigod, Jakob. Jakob! Oh my god guys! Guys! This is Jakob... he's a friend from back home! Jakob come meet my friends!" Jakob approached slowly, a little drunk himself, and shook the flaccid hands of two girls. The guy offered his hand but Jakob was staring fixedly at Tallie.

"Ohmigod Jakob! Don't be rude! This is Cam! He lives on Michigan Avenue, Jakob! Isn't that crazy!" Jakob was desperate to flee the scene but saw an opportunity to corner Tallie.

"Hey, remember the plans we made? Brunch tomorrow, I forget what place, but you mentioned it on the phone?"

Cam closed in and put an arm around Tallie. "We're actually going on a day trip," he said. "My father's got a place on Lake Geneva, a couple of jet skis. We'll be back in the evening."

Jakob spoke in barely a whisper. He looked at Tallie. "That true, Tal?" and Tallie, hammered though she was, began to sense that she might be in trouble.

"Jakob, honey, let me call you tomorrow and we'll talk about it! Or maybe you can come over! That's it, you should co—" But it was too late. Jakob lunged forward and threw a rapid combo that connected with Cam's stomach, nose and jaw. Jakob threw him to the ground and pounded Cam's gym-toned stomach and finished him off with a savage kick in the ribs. He would have continued the beat-down but Colin had yelled "COPS!" the one word which he knew would penetrate Jakob's rage. There weren't actually cops but it did the trick. Jakob popped up, looked at Colin, looked down at Cam's bloody, crumpled figure on the ground, and took off down the street.

A day tailing Cam the following week confirmed Tallie's claim that he both lived and worked on Michigan Avenue. Jakob was tempted to ambush the rich prick for round two but held off when he saw Cam shaking hands with two police officers outside his building.

As summer turned on a dime to fall and the trees sported freshly naked limbs, Jakob's college life imploded. He refused to go to class, spending his days drinking and smoking pot in his dorm room. He acquired a taste for cocaine and Adderall. By Thanksgiving he was selling pot again, this time mostly to Loyola freshmen and anyone to whom they passed along his phone number. He was kicked out of his dorm, and a week after that he dropped out. He moved in with an old hockey friend, Jeremy, who coincidentally had also quit school to sell pot. Their house looked like it had been picked up high off the ground and then dropped; none of the right angles were right, the door had to be slammed shut because it scraped the floor, each wall had its own unique pitch and shade of beige or gray, the windows extra drafty in the winter months so you had to saran wrap the entire unit twice.

When Jakob went to prison three years later, Niklas imagined that, in retrospect, his brother's life before incarceration was probably a direct line to his incarceration, a downward spiral of chemicals and violence and destructive decision making. This was not the case. In fact, it was quite the opposite, though the source of his potential salvation turned out also to be the source of his destruction.

He met Ivan Medvedev at a party hosted by the Delta Upsilon fraternity at Northwestern. Jakob and his roommate had a former teammate in the frat and the plan was to go with a big bag of weed and take advantage of a cohort who paid enough tuition each semester to buy a Lexus, and also maybe bang some rich girls, but that was strictly secondary to business. Fortunately for them, Ivan ran into them on the second floor landing selling a gram to a tall, thoroughbred girl who looked like volleyball player. He watched her saunter away down the stairs and then turned to Jakob and Jeremy.

"How much have you got?" Traces of a Russian accent.

"How much you need?"

"You got an ounce?" That was, in fact, all they had. Jakob nodded.

"How much?"

Jeremy shot Jakob a glance and a shrug. "Two-fifty," he said experimentally.

Ivan laughed. "OK, you got me. Whatever."

He obviously knew the price was ridiculous even for Northwestern, but then he pulled a roll of twenties from his pocket and peeled off two hundred and sixty dollars. He handed the roll to Jakob, and Jeremy passed over their sandwich bag full of weed. Ivan studied it, then looked at the boys.

"You guys want a blunt of this in my room? I'll roll. Shit has been dry as hell recently and you two basically delivered to my doorstep. My name's Ivan. C'mon," and he headed up the stairs to the second floor and led them into the third room on the right.

The second Jakob was over the threshold he smelled money. It was everywhere—booming from the massive speakers in the corner, blaring from the fifty inch TV, dripping from silver silk sheets and the MacIntosh computer and the Louis Vuitton bag filled to the brim with (...really?) dirty laundry. It was a filthy display of wealth, and yet it was all very disheveled and clearly not cared for one bit. Pride of place went to a full eighty-eight key keyboard sprouting wires, and what looked like recording equipment connecting the keyboard to the Mac. Two big twin bean bags sat beside the bed, on which Ivan was bent over a rolling tray, emptying a thin brown Swisher of its guts.

"So I'd bet my bottom dollar you guys are UIC or something," he said, looking up at them while he twisted a large silver grinder full of weed. Jeremy looked at Jakob, indicating he should answer for the both of them.

"Uh, Yeah." On the other beanbag, Jeremy did his best to not act surprised. Ivan was sealing the blunt with his tongue, and retrieving a lighter from his pocket with which he roasted the licked side and sparked the thing up. After starting a nice, even burn he passed it to Jakob and expelled a cloud of pale, used up smoke. His voice pierced the smoky silence after a moment.

"That's cool, man, no shame whatsoever. You a fan of choral music?"

"Not particularly," Jakob said, though he knew that Hannu was, remembered how when he and Niklas couldn't sleep Hannu would put on a tape of a British boy choir singing the Psalms. He tried to remember the names of his father's favorite groups.

"My dad is, though. I can't remember what he liked, though, besides Sibelius."

"No flies on Sibelius," said Ivan. "You ever heard of Rachmaninoff?"

"Uh, maybe? Couldn't tell you."

"Well that's my great-great-uncle I think on my mother's side. He's long dead but somehow I am the sole living heir to his musical estate." Jakob took a moment to calibrate his reaction.

"Uh, wow, that's tight. Is that just a bunch of money, or...?"

"No, man, I'm telling you, it's even better than that," said Ivan with relish, taking a long drag from the blunt. "I own the rights to the music. Which means I collect royalties whenever people use it or download it or buy it or whatever."

"That's sweet," said Jakob, for want of anything else.

"But the thing that made me rich is I found a loophole in the copyright laws. As long as I change, like, one note in a piece every year, contractually it counts as 'New Music,' and everyone who listens to the piece is actually listening to technically a *new*, *different* Rachmaninoff piece, but now I get composition credit for whatever little tinkering I did." He sat back and waited for them to react.

Jakob, for one, was charmed by the romance of a get-rich scheme that involved high art. He should have hated Ivan, but he found himself liking him more by the minute.

"That's clever," he said, accepting the blunt.

76

"So, what, you just, like, change a note and cash checks? Like that's it?" Jeremy was skeptical.

"Basically, yeah, once I figured this out. I'd get royalties anyway, since I'm the sole heir, but the copyright fraud that I technically commit every year is the thing that really pays."

Jakob and Jeremy each asked a few more polite questions, on the same page that this guy was a customer to cling to, and then followed Ivan back to the party downstairs. Having rid themselves of all their weed, Jakob and Jeremy had no reason not to join the party, and join it they did.

The next morning Jakob peeled himself out of some freshman girl's criminally cramped dorm room bed and into the overcast winter morning. He wondered whether he should wait or look for Jeremy, then decided that Jeremy'd be fine. As he sat on the platform waiting for the train, thought about what an eccentric personality they'd found in Ivan and how it was too bad they'd probably never see each other again. He'd never liked a guy so much right away, especially a guy who on paper he would probably dismiss out of hand. And he was wrong. Later that week their phone rang and when he picked it up, Ivan's voice rang out from the receiver.

"Yo, man, it's me, why the fuck didn't you leave your number? I need weed, man, come take my money."

Twice Jakob dropped off engorged sandwich bags full of weed, and twice he collected more than anyone else in the city for that amount. The third time, Ivan invited him out for a drink and the two of them didn't return until the bars closed and everyone else had left. And thus began the friendship that Jakob hadn't known he'd been missing but now couldn't live without.

They tore up parties as each other's wingmen and breakfasted together the morning afterward. They called each other up with crackpot urban adventures and laughed breathlessly after escaping the cops or whomever. They started beefs in bars and rarely fought, but when they did they rarely lost. Jakob taught Ivan that if you hit with an open hand you won't break your knuckles. Ivan regularly paid for expensive dinners and bar tabs with his royalty-engorged bank account. Jakob was having far too much fun to realize that the party would have to end, someday. Eventually he'd have to call his parents and his brother and maybe let them come and visit. But not right now. He was intent on riding this current wave of good times until it crested. Unfortunately, it would continue to accelerate until its abrupt end.

They'd been friends for two years when it happened, coming out of McGee's after celebrating Ivan's twenty-fourth birthday. It was a month or so after Jussi died.

Jakob had just taken his arm from Ivan's shoulder when Ivan rolled his ankle on the curb and pitched into oncoming traffic. A merging SUV hit him square in the head and torso with a crunch. The car stopped and the driver fell out and then drunkenly got to his feet, staring in horror. Jakob lost his mind.

He charged and launched a brutal kick to the groin, followed by a series of hooks and uppercuts that sent the man tumbling into the gutter. He wound up and began to kick the man in the kidneys, stooping to land a punch every so often. He rested, and went to check on Ivan. Ivan's face was mangled and Jakob couldn't feel or hear any breath or pulse. Fresh rage and despair boiled up inside of him and he went back over to the drunken man who was groaning on the ground, and shut him up with a stomp to his jaw. Then Jakob blacked out and the first sirens began to approach, a crowd gathering around the awful scene.

He came out of his blackout in the back of a cop car. His head thumped and felt woozy. Afterward in the holding cell, staring at his bruised and bloodied knuckles, Jakob wondered why he hadn't taken his own advice and struck with an open hand. It was actually Uncle Jussi's advice, given to him and Niklas as little boys the year they started playing hockey. Jakob looked through the bars of the holding cell wishing he could puke, wondering to himself what the hell he was going to say to Niklas and Hannu.

⚡ **13** ⚡

After breakfast with his old coach, Niklas decided to walk back to the farm, knowing it would take several hours and hoping the pretty day would make it pleasant. After a mile he was tired. The slope of the canal road wore out his thighs and lungs. It was pretty but after an hour of walking his eyes barely strayed from the pavement beneath his feet.

By the time he got to the long hill of Liminga Road his hoodie was tied around his waist and he was sweating bullets. He took a long look back at the canal, its surface rumpled in the wind. He'd realized about half an hour ago that coming up with Peter had been his fatal mistake. How easily he'd been convinced that it could really be just a trip! Coach Klingberg had assured him that forty acres would probably get snapped up pretty quickly by some neighbor or other who'd be eager to sell the timber or merely to put more distance between them and the other neighbors. Niklas felt for a second that perhaps he actually was truly on the brink of losing the place to Peter's short-sighted greed, but a large piece of him still viewed that as impossible.

He reached the top of a gentle rise and put his hands behind his head and panted. He saw cleared fields and logged forest and fallen down outbuildings next to abandoned orchards and beyond, the hills of South Range. He felt he understood something about his place in the world here, and the world's relative significance, and his own insignificance. He felt safe. The midday sun burned hot overhead, the shadows of the trees were shallow, and creatures in the roadside brush made quiet while Niklas lumbered by and came to life again once he was safely distant.

Folded in the pocket of his jeans were the envelopes with Jakob's letters, nearly equal in their soiling from being read over and over again. It was a miracle he'd even gotten the first one. He'd been in Chicago prior to Jakob's imprisonment. One day after work, a month and a half after Uncle Jussi's funeral, walking home from the bus stop covered in sawdust, Hannu had called.

79

"Hello?" Niklas had been apprehensive, given the typical regularity of their Sunday evening calls.

"Hey, buddy," Hannu said. "Are you at work right now?"

"No, I'm on my way home. I just got off the bus."

"Ah. Well, um…" Niklas could hear the edges of his father's voice cracking.

"Dad? What's up? What happened?" In his heart, Niklas felt a malignant seed of an idea sprout and take root.

"Your, um… Your brother has gotten himself in some trouble." Hannu coughed. "He'll probably go to prison." The sprout having budded, Niklas wondered what to ask first.

"What did he do?"

Hannu explained how Jakob and a friend, Ivan, had been walking outside of a bar in Uptown and his friend had been hit and killed by a drunk driver. Jakob pulled the drunk driver from his car and beat him to death right there on the curb. When the cops showed up, Jakob had told the whole thing exactly how it had happened, as though that would somehow vindicate him. At this point, Niklas was already crying, and started to laugh at the same time. If you'd asked me or Peter, he thought, miserably pulling chunks of sawdust from his hair, or any of the neighbors, they'd say it was inevitable. Hannu and Pernilla were shocked to their core, of course. Everyone had their fingers crossed that he would be out in time for Thanksgiving four years hence.

Niklas cracked up, psychologically, emotionally, in the immediate aftermath and ended up back in Marquette with his mother and father. When he returned to Chicago that February, having long since lost his job in the scene shop of the Lyric Opera, there was a letter waiting for him from Jakob, untouched since its delivery several months prior. Niklas was surprised—they'd spoken a few times on the phone and Jakob had made no mention of a letter. Niklas wrote back to thank him and inform him that he was moving to Milwaukee, to address all future letters there. Two more letters had followed, separated by several months and, given their tone and content, more than hinted that Jakob was emotionally on the ropes. They read sometimes like letters to himself, or to someone other than Niklas. It was the first time in his whole life that Niklas saw his older brother utterly naked and disarmed in front of him.

He rounded the last bend and saw the fence posts that flanked their gravel driveway. Shuffling down the stretch, careful not to further tear or distress it, he pulled the first letter out of the overstuffed envelope. He knew every step from here to the cabin door in the bones of his feet. His pace slowed as he read, the words like molasses gathering around his body and mind in a mummy of apprehension and longing.

Dear Niklas,

Christ what I'd do for a warm, flat Miller Lite. I remember dad always going on about how self-denial and boredom can be liberating. It's been a blessing but mostly a curse having to figure that out on my own. I'm sorry if this is out of the blue—our phone calls have been great, but this is something different that I'm trying. I've been meaning to try and write someone, and obviously who else would I write to, but there's always some damn thing that comes up every time. What finally drove me to do it was some trouble I got into last week: I swung on a guard that called me a faggot and got two nights in solitary. Jesus F. Christ. Do you remember all those nights at Uncle Jussi's around the fire, before we started throwing our own parties? I'm sure you do even better than me. After about six hours alone in solitary they all sort of sprang up around me. I could see the flames dancing on the walls, could hear Dad singing "Angel From Montgomery," could see the stars coming out above the shadows of the trees against the night sky. How did we ever get too cool for that? I guess it was only ever me with the parties, though you came out, as I'm sure you don't remember (haha). I guess when Peter moved to New York that kinda served as a marker for a new era. I know Dad was upset about it, the partying, and when Uncle Jussi died I beat myself up about it for a while, but I'm not really sure what to do now. I wanted to party and they said it was cool to bring friends. I didn't know it would end up like that, like it was, a gulf which hurt Dad and Jussi, but even then I remember having a ton of fun at the time and only ever regretting things after Jussi died and Dad had given the place to us. And by then we'd lost something permanent. If I'd known things were going to evaporate so quickly, I wouldn't have been so careless with them.

Anyway, I was in solitary and all this stuff was swimming around in front of me and I felt like I was tripping in the woods. Remember how Pete always insisted on cooking even though he sucked at cooking over the fire? A couple weeks in here I started imagining that the food they serve us was actually made by Pete, and it's brought me some peace. They forgot to bring me dinner my second night in solitary and I just imagined that it was that time we all took acid and after romping around in the woods all day we tried to cook brats but Peter burned the shit out of them, for sure inedible, and by the time we sobered up our stomachs were echoing with screams let loose by their utter emptiness. Honestly, everything after my first few hours in solitary felt like a horrible acid trip, but I'm not sure if that's just my memory of time dilating and days lasting years in there. A buddy in my block lent me this book on Anishinaabe religion. I thought of you when he showed it to me, you'd love it. It's pretty cagey about their specific practices but I found an anecdote about a practice where a man would find a spot deep in the woods or unprotected on a mountainside and go for three days and three nights without food, water, or shelter. It was said to bring visions about the true nature of reality and to lower the barriers between the human world and the world of spirits. There's a Hindu guy who spots me on benchpress in the yard, sometimes and when I told him about this, he chuckled and said that it was very similar to the idea of the veil between the world of illusion and the world where all things are true.

Speaking of which, send me some books if you can. Your favorites, whatever, I don't care. You always took after Dad much more than me in that respect. I'm sure he'd be cool with sending me some stuff from the shelves at home. I miss Chicago but I'm glad in a weird way to spend a winter further south. They say that fall lasts forever in southern Illinois. Fuck frostbite through our heavy coats like up in Marquette. Though I'd give a hand to frostbite to be free. My hand is cramping up. How the hell did those guys back in the day write so much by hand? It's getting loud in here—it's all in Spanish, but they're getting louder and angrier. Everyone here seems to attract trouble like flies to honey. Their brains are constantly getting them into trouble, their minds the only refuge during punishment. Troubles notwithstanding, I've always felt the opposite to be true about you, Nik: your brains help you out of the trouble your mind gets you in. Does that make sense? I think so, but I just reread that sentence and my eyes hurt in addition to my wrist. I'll write again sometime, probably soon. I'm sure we'll talk by then. Stay out of trouble. Thank Dad for all of his letters. I promise I'll get back to them soon.

I feel like a coward for asking but could you pray for me? This is the kind of place that makes you wonder if anything was ever true.

Love,
Jakob

Niklas, having read the last several sentences sitting on the steps of the cabin, folded the letter and carefully returned it to the front of the envelope. Inside the cabin, he put the envelope and his balled-up jacket on his cot and returned to the porch. He looked out to the left toward the orchard and the vegetable patch beyond. Clumps of chokecherry had thrived in the boys' long absence. He realized he hadn't yet gotten a good look at the orchard in the daylight.

Niklas had to fight through a "mothership" chokecherry bush, as Hannu called them, on his way to the orchard. He unlatched the rusty chain and let it dangle as the gate swung open.

There had once been a patch of lingonberries down the hill on the south end of the first fenced section, about ten apple trees in the middle chunk, and twenty or so blueberry bushes up the gentle slope on the eastern end. Farther south, barely visible through the trees, you could see the vegetable patch and the white-painted tires that had held potatoes; to the left of this there was a third patch, though invisible, which was exclusively lingonberries. Fenced off individually along the overgrown path between them were five cherry trees.

Hannu had always fancied himself a farmer, though up until he acquired this very property, it would have been more accurate to call him a gardener. Jussi was a willing, excited participant—he was perfectly suited to the task of helping Hannu with whatever was next, mostly as an extra set of hands, and Hannu in turn, thanks to deep reading on the subject, broke down the necessary tasks of farm care into consumable bites for Jussi.

And so they had gone in first with the brush cutter, blitzing the invasive chokecherry clusters that came back so quickly you felt like you were playing Whac-A-Mole. Hannu stayed out on the property for several weeks that first summer, crumbling the soil between his fingers, buying drinks in Schmidt's Corner and the Range Lounge; after a beer and a quarter of football just about anyone would answer his questions about how to supplement the soil (compost, mostly, except for acidifying the blueberries which takes sulfur or whatever they tell you to buy at Erickson's), where to get the best mulch (don't purchase it; get yourself a wood chipper and take a hatchet to any dead pine. It's acidic enough and the machine will pay for itself after twenty loads of the wheelbarrow), where he could get a fifty gallon rain barrel to store fresh water on the property (call Calumet Electric—they got extra sometimes and all you gotta do is call and ask). And Hannu took this knowledge back to Jussi and the two of them got to work. They marked out which areas would get fencing; they turned the earth carefully to avoid stretches they agreed would eventually become paths, lanes from which they could tend to the berry bushes and fruit trees in their youth. They went to Tractor Supply and purchased rolls of fencing and bundles of posts, a post driver and two pairs of fencing pliers.

They swaggered into their clearing laden with tools and materials and Hannu marked out where each post was to be driven. Hannu held the posts steady as Jussi drove them in, using the post-driver's momentum to work the posts inch by inch into the ground. One day it rained and, suddenly, the posts sank easily into the ground, welcomed by the softened earth. And when Hannu was finally pleased with the layout, they started on the fencing. Jussi stretched the rolls of fencing, wedging his pliers in through the fence and against the next post, with Hannu following close behind, twisting bits of wire through the fence and around the post, finishing with a pinch, twisting the wire until it was taut.

Several pieces of connecting wire snapped before Hannu learned just how far he could twist before it was too much. They were halfway around the first plot of land when Hannu ripped his pants on a stray end sticking out at knee level, learning the lesson of turning your loose ends inward to avoid the barbs on bare skin or clothing as you walked by.

They repeated the process twice more to separate different kinds of fruit and vegetables. In the first and largest section: lingonberries and blueberries, the former at the southern end of the patch. In the second section: cherry trees and apple trees and one little oak tree down near the end, planted for sentimental value with an acorn Hannu had saved from their backyard oak tree in Marquette. And in the third section: peas, tomatoes, beets, turnips, peas, acorn squash, and potatoes. The potatoes grew in towers of two or three tires placed one on top of the other and filled in with dirt. For Jakob's first birthday the next year, Hannu dug up several fat ones and fried them next to the bacon, and the bacon made him wonder if Jussi could manage a couple of pigs. But it never got that far.

The lingonberries spread sprout by sprout and the apples grew plump and slightly sour in their sweetness. The cherries came quickly and in vast quantities, making up for the blueberries' refusal to cooperate. By the time Niklas and Jakob and Peter were old enough to comprehend it, the orchard was bursting with life. Hannu's final project before Uncle Jussi's death was rigging up an irrigation line from the rain barrels at the back of the shed to the lingonberry patch, which had become a point of pride and something to brag about in the Range Lounge or at Schmidt's Corner, where he'd quickly become a friend and a fascination among the rougher men who drank there. Hannu always brought a deck of cards and, with Jussi as his partner, played euchre with anyone who would sit down. After people started to recognize Hanu and Jussi, they joined in the euchre, and few came away victorious thanks to Hannu and Jussi's knack for nonverbal communication (which years down the road was passed along to Niklas and Jakob, who took great pleasure in thrashing Peter, who never quite got the knack for playing with his uncles). Hannu was an honest man who spoke always in earnest, with great wisdom and broad humor, and men couldn't help but warm to him and feel comforted by his willingness to adapt, his dogged persistence in stewardship of Jussi, his capacity for neighborliness, and his infectious desire for brotherhood. It must be his beard, they said. Hannu had an excellent beard.

* * *

Niklas broke through the chokecherries and looked at the remains of the three patches. The posts remained strong and upright though rusted, and the bottom of the fence no longer ran flush along the ground where rabbits had invaded. Tall grasses and wildflowers had leapt up among the neglected plants and a fresh phalanx of chokecherry was beginning to leaf among the weeds. Niklas remembered hours on his knees with Jakob and Hannu and Jussi, each with gloves, scouring the ground and pulling up any competition by the roots. The ribbed razor's edge of the choke-cherry leaf was their main target. Sometimes Niklas once he grew older would get a turn with the brush cutter to fight off the massive groves of chokecherry that were always looking to invade around the cabin or in clusters by the fruit trees. "We gotta take care of that mothership or she'll crowd out the blueberries by October," Hannu would say. "We gotta take care of that."

And now, standing at the edge of the first patch, looking out over the little farm that took twenty years to bring to life, Niklas' heart was torn over one certainty: the chokecherries had won. The little orchard had been swallowed by the plants he'd spent so many hours weeding. "We're in priest territory, not doctor territory," Hannu used to say. And within Niklas, deep in his breast, he felt the need to bring it back to life, to massage the land back into fertility, to pick the weeds in the dirt on his knees and pour his own sweat into fruit bearing plants; to be an agent of life, and of growth, for if he didn't something larger than any one man who'd helped bring the orchard to life in the first place would be lost. His father's dream of years ago would be forever fumbled by his sons. And then the wind rose and the flutes in the tops of the trees came to life—one single, wavering note, like the call of an airy loon, beckoning from beyond the veil. And Niklas knew he could not sell this land.

He turned to head back to the cabin and to shake off the tears. Once inside, he lay down and a tidal wave of fatigue crashed in his ears. A swirl of thoughts about the orchard and the land and Peter and Uncle Jussi carried him down, down past his fears and his affections and everything in between. At the edge of sleep, he heard

86

the crunch of gravel and killed engine that indicated Peter's return. Niklas sat up on his cot. Outside a car door slammed, followed by a "Fuck! Shit!" Peter had likely closed the door on his finger. Niklas went to the door to gloat. Through the screen door he saw Peter staring down at a finger cradled in his other hand, grimacing. He lurched forward, apparently not seeing the steps when he arrived at them because when he did he just kept on walking and tripped and fell on his face, legs sprawled out over the three steps up to the porch.

"Dude," said Niklas. "Are you good?"

Tina Kinnunen, née Watson, fretted about her husband Peter as she attacked her hair with a cheap plastic brush, wondering if her mother would consent to yet another last-minute babysitting gig. Tina suspected yes and also suspected that she would be expected to stay for a chat and maybe a cup of tea. It was less than an hour before her son, Olly, was appointed to see a specialist at Columbia St. Mary's, just ten minutes north of their apartment on Water Street. In light of her mother's probable desire to socialize, she'd decided to get ready early.

She tossed the brush into the cabinet behind the mirror, calling out for Olly and his cousin, Josh, as she did so. "Olly, Josh, are you dressed and ready? Shoes on?" She left the bathroom and found the boys waiting timidly in the kitchen, Josh bent over on the floor, trying in vain to tie his right shoe.

"No, here," said Olly, bending down to assist his little cousin. "You need to twist the bunny *together*, Josh. Here."

Olly untangled the knot to its original loose twist, made bunny ears out of the ends and demonstrated slowly how to finish tying a bow. Then he undid the bow, redid the initial twist and handed the loose ends to Josh. "Here, see? Now you gotta."

Josh picked up the two loose ends in wonderment, then looked up as if to notice Tina for the first time.

"Aunt Tina! Olly taught me how to tie my shoes! Watch! Are you watching?"

"Yes, sweetheart," said Tina. "I'm watching but we're in a hurry, OK? Let's see that bow real quick." Josh doubled down and stared hard at the shoelaces in his little hands. His eyes had drained all the confidence of a moment before. He looked up at Tina again.

"He taught me, Aunt Tina. I forgot but I knowed how!"

Tina bent down to help him but Olly beat her to it. "Here," he said. "Just twist, over and under, then you make your bunny ears, twist 'em again, and there's your bow!" He looked proudly up at his mother.

"That's kind of you to teach him, Olly," she said. She reached out and grabbed Josh's hand. "Come on, sweetie, we gotta get going! Olly's got a very important appointment so you're going to hang out with grandma for a bit, all right?" She herded the boys toward the door. "Olly, could you get the door... thank you, sweetie," she said as he held it open for them.

Tina hooked her purse down to the crook of her elbow and fairly pulled Josh out the door with her. Olly rushed ahead down the hallway to push the down button on the panel between the elevators. Tina walked down the hallway clutching Josh's hand, eyes roving, dancing from the ghastly carpet over to the paintings on the walls, catching the gleam of chrome from the table near the elevators that held a fresh vase of fake lilacs. She drank it all in, knowing her days there were likely numbered, and feeling guilty that, given the circumstances of today's errand, the condo was what she was worrying about. She took a deep breath while waiting for the elevator, picking up the smaller boy, bracing him against her hip, ruffling the messy mop of her son's hair with the other hand. The elevator dinged and she hustled them inside, letting Olly push the button for the ground floor.

Outside the air was unseasonably crisp though the leaves had yet to begin changing this far south. The sun sparkled off the pavement and glared off the windows of the buildings opposite. A light breeze over her exposed arms made her shiver. She worried for a second that the boys would need the jackets that were still hung up in the closet upstairs, but once they'd passed from the edge of shadow cast by their building and into the direct sun, she realized they'd be fine, that it was sixty degrees, the boys didn't care, they'd be fine. The car was parked on the corner, just before the hill up to Brady Street.

She fastened Olly in the backseat, then made sure Josh was securely buckled in his booster seat on the other side. She took a breath when she settled in the driver seat. At a break in the traffic she gingerly pulled out and headed north toward her mother's place by the hospital in Murray Hill.

She rehearsed the conversation that was waiting for her at her mother's. No matter how much she tried to anticipate the things her mother would say, she'd never once felt sufficiently prepared in her mother's company. *Bring Josh to the door, summarize the situation early, protest at least once before accepting a cup of tea;*

don't take the bait about my marriage, don't let her sensationalize the mess the world is in; maybe, because he'd been a prick this morning, let her gossip about Rick—Rick was Josh's father, in the middle of a nasty divorce Tina's Catholic mother resented, in part because it meant the rest of the family had to raise his son on short notice. Tina turned on to Farwell and made for Oakland Ave., the streets too full before midday with college students Tina suspected were skipping class. She took a right on Bradford Street and then a left on Murray. She nestled the little Toyota sedan neatly against someone's driveway, then turned off the car and went to help Josh out of his seat. She picked him up and told Olly to wait in the car, locking it anxiously.

"Mom! Why can't I see Grandma?"

"We can visit her when we pick your cousin up," said Tina, bracing to close the door. "I'll be back in a moment, it's always good to show up early." And she marched across the street toward the maroon front door of her mother's duplex. She rang the doorbell with a lingering thumb and waited. Several moments later the floorboards inside creaked announcing her mother's presence.

"Oh, my, Christina darling!" she said with shining eyes. "Your timing is wonderful. I've just made some—"

"That's good, Mom, thank you. I was actually going to ask if you could—"

"Christina! Come on in out of the cold first."

"It's sixty degrees, Mom."

"Well, maybe for you, but that young man is probably freezing? And how are you, Joshua dear? Are you hungry?"

"Hi, Grandma," Josh said shyly, looking to his aunt for help.

Tina walked through the front door and set Josh down on the arm of a puffy red chair. She turned to the window to avoid her mother's gaze.

"Mom, Olly's got his appointment today, the one I mentioned on the phone with Dr. Billings in oncology, and I was hoping you'd...." Tina looked around, surprised at having made it this far without interruption, to see that her mother had left the room. She appeared again from the hallway to the kitchen with a tray heavily laden with cookies and tea. She looked up in surprise at Tina's face.

"I was just getting the tea. What were you saying?"

"Olly's got his appointment today, and I—"

"Oh, that's right, he does! I remember you telling me on the phone. I'm so glad you two are getting him a second opinion. You said Dale Dribblet got you in with this man, correct?"

"Yes, Mother, and if you'd let me finish you'd hear what I'm asking—"

"Well, what do you expect me to know? This doctor should be able to answer your questions better than me."

"Can you watch Josh while I take Olly to his appointment? We'll be finished by one, one-thirty latest. I'd really apprecia—"

"Aren't you at least going to have a cup of tea?"

Tina took a deep breath, exhaling through her nose. "Sure, Mom. But it needs to be quick." She turned to Josh who was playing with his zipper, letting his legs dangle over the edge of a chair, which was much too large for him. "Josh, sweetie. Run on upstairs, OK? Auntie'll be back in a few hours, OK?"

"OK!" And he ran toward the stairs, looking back to see if they'd been watching him. He saw that they were and slowed, climbing each stair around the corner with only his right foot. Three stairs up and out of sight of the adults, he leaned forward and helped himself up with his hands, climbing the stairs on all fours. Back in the living room, Tina scalded her lips and tongue on a boiling cup of tea. Her mother watched her wince in pain, gave her a moment, and began the obvious line of questioning.

"Honey, where is Peter?"

Tina bit into a cookie to buy herself some time. "He's away on business."

"What business?"

"He's doing some family business with Niklas. It's OK, Mom," she said, reacting to the harsh look of disapproval in her mother's eyes, "It's going to bring in some money. I think we're gonna have to move."

"Well, I could have told you that. That swanky apartment on Water Street. I told you it was a bad idea."

"Yes, you did. It's going to be fine, Peter says he'll be promoted pretty soon, and the money from this land sale will definitely get us through."

Her mother looked perplexed. "But, so are you going to get a job?"

"That's not the plan, no."

"How's your insurance?"

Tina took another gulp of hot tea. "Our what?"

"Your health insurance? You know, for..." and here she mouthed *Olly*.

"Well, and that's part of why he's up with Niklas selling family land. We need some cushion in case treatments are out of pocket."

"Selling family land? Is that really the best idea? Does the rest of his family know he's pawning off their land to pay for a swanky apartment?"

"Mom, what? A second ago you were asking about insurance, then—"

"Well," said her mom, raising her hands in surrender. "It's really not my business."

"That's right. We'll be fine. Seriously."

"I'd offer you some money, but you know your father wiped me out in court and—"

"No, it's fine. Seriously." Tina got to her feet, setting her empty mug on the tray and stuffing another cookie in her mouth. "Ok, Mom. I'm going to go now. Thanks for—"

"Christina, I told you this so many times. Those boys, Peter and Niklas and Jakob... that's the thing, they're still boys. How do you know this isn't just an excuse to go party together in the woods and leave you out to dry?"

This had occurred to Tina. Her words came through with a sharp edge.

"Mom, he's going to be back soon with a big bunch of cash for Olly's treatments and rent and whatever else. He knows," she said, almost to herself, "he knows this can't be just another one of their adventures. He knows it."

"All right, sweetie. Don't rush, you'll get in an accident. Hold on, I'm getting slower." Tina suspected foot dragging was mostly a performance. Once out the door, she turned back. "I'll be back soon, Mom. Don't ruin his appetite. I'll be back in a little while."

Her mother put a hand on the door as she turned to leave. She called after her daughter, "Don't let them push you around! Ask questions! Say hello to Olly for me!" And Tina assured her she would, and turned back across the street toward the waiting Olly, who was staring out the window watching a plastic bag furling in the wind, falling gently toward the curb.

92

⚡ 15 ⚡

"Unhhh."

Peter groaned as Niklas attempted to roll him over off the steps and into a sitting position. His head bobbled back and forth a few times before settling upright; his eyes were half closed.

"Dude, are you hammered or what?" Niklas laughed. He'd known Peter was headed for trouble ever since he'd made himself known for passing out after beers and shots in quick succession at Jakob's parties in high school. They usually put him to sleep in a corner with a balled-up coat beneath his head, near the fire but also under a tree. Seeing him now, laid out across the front steps in broad daylight, Niklas was not surprised. It was a very small dose of what he felt when Jakob had gone to prison—these things, if they indeed had telegraphed themselves in early and subtle ways, implicated everyone who was present in their aftermath. Niklas sniffed around Peter's collar for vomit and detected none, thankfully. Peter was mumbling something now, one eye slightly more open than the other.

"What was that?"

Peter garbled something indistinguishable. Niklas caught the words "Olly" and "pissed" before Peter began to tip over again. Niklas caught him and leaned him up against one of the thick posts that held the porch roof up. He stuck the hoodie that was tied around his waist between Peter's head and the post.

Inside, Niklas retrieved his pot and pipe, grinding himself a bowl's worth. He sat down next to Peter on the porch. The sun was starting to sink again, though still several hours from the tops of the trees beyond the cherry orchard. He fired up.

The first hits spread peace throughout his limbs. Peter groaned, making him laugh. Peter mumbled some more, slouched his head to the other side, and fell back asleep.

An hour later, Peter's snoring became irregular. Niklas, waiting for him to awaken, had packed another bowl. Peter began to stir, twisting his trunk around and trying to push himself upright. His hand slipped, forcing his eyes to open wider. When they were open enough to take in the world, he looked around, bewildered. Niklas watched in amusement. This was a moment he'd been present for numerous times before, one that Jakob had identified years ago. Peter looked around; Niklas passed him the lit pipe. He waved it away with a grimace, then thought for a second and beckoned it back. Niklas cracked up, took another rip for himself, then passed it on. Peter coughed quite a bit at first but still went in for a couple of hits.

"Don't fall back asleep on me now."

Peter exhaled pale, used up smoke and passed it back with a look of concern. "How long was I out?"

"A while. Were you at Schmidt's?"

A cloud passed over his expression. "Yeah. I got talking with these two guys. I didn't even have that much to drink," he said, incredulously.

"You looked blacked when you stumbled up and fell over."

"Yeah."

"Were you?"

Peter looked off into the trees. "I guess. I remember getting in my car, but I don't remember much besides getting into it at Schmidt's and coming out of it here."

"Geez."

Peter said nothing. He stared hard out beyond the yard into the woods. There was too much afternoon left. The pot had taken the energy out of Niklas' feet. He wanted to sit by the fire and listen to the quiet but he felt he didn't have the strength. What he really needed was an audience with "Mother Superior," as Hannu sometimes called the greatest lake. The roiling waves and stiff wind always awakened a sense of the massive scale of the cosmos, setting off his own insignificance. A thought occurred to Niklas— the smokestack. They could have a fire and the lake all at once. His mind was made up in a second. It was a remarkable place and he wondered what memories would float to the surface as they walked across the concrete rubble next to the crashing dark blue lake beyond.

"Let's go to the smokestack."

Peter looked confused. "Right now?"

"Sure. Yeah."

"Why?"

"I want to go see the lake. Also, it's a cool spot. I can't believe you don't remember smokestack fires. I'm sure you came to the first few."

"I don't know. I'm pretty beat."

"Bring the blow."

"It's nearly gone."

"Jesus, dude. Already?"

Peter nodded.

"You don't have to do anything. I'll drive and build the fire. Just come."

* * *

Every atom in Peter's body wanted to just stay right there and fall back asleep. He remembered the smokestack, but just didn't care for it like Niklas did. He'd seen the lake before. You could get just as warm in a heavy coat as you could by a fire. Or, better yet, inside an actual building, rather than holed up in the ruins of a factory whose detritus probably poisoned the very smoke that rose from the fires you made in the smokestack. But he looked across at Niklas' beseeching expression and couldn't say no. At least one of them could still drum up enough vulnerability to get attached to things. Yet as Peter looked around and thought of his son at the specialist's office, he knew that even in his emotionally impoverished state, he was still attached, however fretfully and resentfully. He still loved the places and people of his boyhood, and he wished he could be earnest about it all the way Niklas was. But he truly just wanted to sleep, to not feel these things. Because he knew he would eventually have to let it go. And that eventually might as well be now if it meant more agony like this. He wasn't strong like Niklas. He couldn't bear the agony for the sake of milking every last moment.

But the time had not come quite yet, and while he could, Peter figured he'd better go along with Niklas to the lake. So he kept his mouth shut and dragged himself to his feet, accepting and draining Niklas' half full water bottle on the way to the car. Out of habit he went to open the driver's side door.

"Uh, I'm driving, man," said Niklas as they bumped into each other.

"Right," said Peter, once again feeling pathetic, once again keeping his mouth shut.

They parked way out at the top of the outcropping. The only things obstructing the view of Lake Superior were the board listing residents of Freda who'd died in foreign wars and a couple of scrubby cottonwood trees. The wind off the lake blew stiff in their faces as Peter followed Niklas along the trail through the trees down the hill to the ruins, which spread out like a football field of concrete dotted with head-high protrusions of metal and more concrete arranged in lines to the perimeter where the old outbuildings sat, more whole but still crumbling. A black circle, twenty feet in diameter, filled with weeds and dark puddles and rubble, was all that remained of the crusher that Jim's father Jim Sr., and their grandpa, Teemu, had managed. A Finnish flag was spray-painted way up on a crumbling wall; overtop, in black letters were the words, INDIGENOUS SUPREMACY. There was more graffiti, but it wasn't political or nationalistic, only vulgar. One bit, on the side of a sandstone outbuilding's crumbling wall, merely read CUNTS. In the far-right corner as you looked, just twenty yards from the lake on the far side of the ruins, was the smokestack: two-hundred-and-fifty-feet tall, slate brown, ungraffitied, it towered over the area.

The boys scrambled down the rocky, rooty hill and walked toward the stack, skirting the fossil of the crusher. Niklas strayed out to the lakeside edge of the concrete. Peter didn't notice because he was looking at the ground, afraid he might trip. He said, "Do you ever," looking up and noticing that Niklas now stood at the edge of the concrete gazing out at the lake. Peter went to join him. They stood for a long time without speaking. It was partly cloudy now, with the dark gray-blue lake lit up in patches by beams of sunlight through the clouds. There was a tiny bit of visible blue sky to the north, which spread from the lake over the land. The lake itself stretched out to the horizon, and the land bent convex on either side of them. The shifting, rumpled, roaring water mesmerized them, and the patchy bits of sunlight were ethereal. Everything slowed into one continuous moment until the clouds stitched themselves up and the patches of sunlight were gone. Peter repeated his question:

"Do you ever wonder how they stood it?"

"All the time," said Niklas. "What do you mean, though, like, specifically?"

"Well, I was thinking of the guys who worked in this factory, but the Indians that lived here had to be tough as hell, too."

Niklas nodded. "It puts things in perspective." He paused. "We have different things, though, new things that we have to deal with."

"I know. Still, there's a lot of advantages."

"Yeah," Niklas said with a sigh, still looking straight northwest, into the lake. "But here we are, standing on the ruins of a factory, talking about how beautiful the surrounding nature is. But it's not even nature."

"It's still remote."

"Remote. The best you can say about anywhere anyone can live." Peter was surprised at his bitterness.

"Don't you like Milwaukee?"

"I do. But if I could trade my life and its comforts for a time when people really lived out in the wilderness, like that's just how it went, I would do it in a heartbeat."

"Huh. I'm just not nearly tough enough."

"You'd figure it out."

"But I don't want to."

Niklas looked over at him with a sad smile. "That's the thing," he said. "Part of the deal back then was less individuality. You relied on people, they relied on you, and kinda to that extent you were one organism. We used to be that way—you, me, and Jakob. It worked great out in the woods, playing hockey together, all like that. But the world we live in isn't meant for that kind of operation. And when we all split up, things all went to shit. Jussi dead, Jakob in prison, Dad depressed, Jim lonely, me psychotic or stoned, you—" He pulled up short, not wanting to pick a fight. Peter just laughed dryly.

"No, you're right, Nik. So, do you think we shouldn't have done things the way we did? Should we have stayed in our rooms and played video games?"

"Of course not. We're just on the other end of that bargain now. First comes the laughter, now come the tears. Seems to be the way it works for guys like us."

"I still suck at video games," Peter said ruefully. "And they're such social currency that it actually kind of sucks."

"You sucked at building fires, too. Honestly, all is not lost, we just got out of practice. Once Jakob is out we'll all find some

97

routine. We've got the farm. He won't be able to cross the Illinois state line for a year or two. I mean, he'll probably live with me at some point after he's off parole."

Peter fell silent at this, not wanting to kill the camaraderie yet knowing that a future that at all resembled the past was a fantasy. Niklas clearly still thought that things were undecided.

"Speaking of fires," Peter said, "I'm a little chilly. Let's go make one in the stack."

Niklas turned and followed him across the rubble toward the smokestack. You had to walk to the edge of the concrete and then down a hill through some brush into the woods, then over a creek, placing your crossing feet on island rocks. The structure was just beyond the creek. You had to climb or hoist yourself up onto the head-high ledge that led inside. Once up, the place felt small, the remains of old fires sitting in the center swirling black and gray in the occasional draft. It was circular and felt more than a little post-apocalyptic, a coin of sky visible far overhead where the smoke had once billowed out. The inside was graffitied, though not legibly, and in places rusted bits of rebar stuck out from the walls, waiting to catch and tear an errant pant leg. Before they ascended into the stack, though, they needed to collect firewood.

They spread out in the woods in a practiced fashion, each looking for little stuff to get the thing going and thicker sections for warmth and longevity. It had rained recently and lots of it was still damp. The ground was soft beneath their booted tread, sticks snapping only occasionally. Niklas struck gold with a dry maple branch, broken and lying on the ground, its central bit three inches thick with brittle twigs sticking out in every direction. He hauled the thing back to the stack and loaded up all he'd collected onto the ledge, scrambling up the crumbling brick behind it and into the central chamber.

It was about ten feet in diameter, with the fire ring in the exact center. Light came in barely from above and strongly from the entryway, more a doorway than a corridor but still enough to keep out the worst of the wind, though not the snow, which in winter came through the top of the stack and, because of its angle, fell in a small circle right about where the remains of the fires were. If it was snowing while you were in there, you could watch the circular beam of flakes fall and melt at eye height just before they made landfall and dripped into the fire. Peter scrambled in with few thicker branches which required Niklas to place them at an angle against the wall and stomp violently until they snapped. Niklas had a moment of panic when he couldn't find the lighter; it turned out to be in the opposite pocket, buried deep. It took about ten minutes to really get going, but then the blaze reached the bits that had had to be stomped on, and the flames needed no more deep breaths or coaxing or fuel rearranging to maintain their momentum. The chamber grew warm quite quickly. The boys stood back and stared into the glowing embers.

"You know, I thought I was going in for a while too," said Peter.

"Huh?" grunted Niklas. He was deeply focused on the fire.

"Back last spring when things went to shit and I lost my job. There was a rumor we were all going to have to take the fall for the bosses and do time."

Niklas turned, his attention now fully on Peter. "Seriously? Like, at Wells Fargo you're saying?"

"Yeah. I even had a note written to you and Jakob. Of course, in the end it was all just people sensationalizing. No one individual with the banks really got punished during the whole crash I don't think. But I was worried there for a while."

"Geez," said Niklas, looking at him in a new light. "What happened? I never really knew what you did there."

"I sold mortgage-backed securities, dude. Like, the thing that brought the economy down. I was on a team of underlings, not like, calling the shots, but you know that's who gets punished in situations like that."

"Holy shit, dude." Niklas laughed. "Of course you were at the center of our country's economic collapse."

"Not the center at all. You know who was, though?"

"Who?"

"Tina's father. He was the one who got me the job in the first place. When she got pregnant in college and decided to keep it, her family flew out and had a talk with us. Part of the deal was marriage, another part was the move to Milwaukee so I could work a job her dad had lined up for me. At Wells Fargo. That's the type of family they are. Won't spare a penny of their own for us, but will bring me in on all the illicit shit so I could make my own share. Or so I thought. It was OK for a while. But toward the end we knew we were up to some sketchy shit."

"Damn. But, so didn't her dad get you the job with the city afterward?"

"Yeah. When everyone was getting fired and we thought some of us would do time, he called me up one day and told me I didn't have to worry, that as long as I stayed under the radar I'd just get laid off. And of course I was like, 'Well, OK, big whup.' But he told me he had friends in the mayor's office, that he would pull some strings if I found myself out of a job. It just took so long once I was finally laid off. That's what really got me. I was unemployed for eight months, we had Olly and the place on Water Street. Too damn much, man, and I just kept waiting, paralyzed. But with Olly and the job and everything, it just all happened so naturally. I don't know. The sum of everything now feels fucking idiotic, and wrong, Nik, and I know you think it is too. I know. But each step was so reasonable, you know? Only now do I see it as one long backslide into a life adorned with bullshit. Or at least adorned with so much bullshit it's hard to tell the difference in situations. And then..." He trailed off, looking around slowly, then back at the fire.

"Then what?" Niklas asked, kind of awed by this raw honesty. Peter was usually defensive beyond a fault.

"Nothing. Shit is just... wack. Just brutal."

"Yeah, well. This place isn't."

"No, you're right. It's not."

The silence that followed felt delicate to each of them, Niklas for having seen a side of Peter that he'd suspected was there somewhere but long dormant, Peter for having confessed things he might later have to refute or at least contradict. He was, at the end of the day, protective of his family and loyal to their patch of wealth in Milwaukee, and despite his desire to prioritize his better instincts under the influence of the woods and his cousin, he knew the rest of him would rationalize anything for the sake of his own desires vis a vis wealth and material scorekeeping. And on top of that there was Olly and whatever the doctors found with him.

The fire burned low once they ran out of things to feed it. Niklas tended it, pushing the unburned ends around into the hot coals where they would begin to smoke and finally come alight. Toward the end he had to blow like a bellows to keep the flame alive. Soon it was all the way done. The boys stood up.

"Piss it out?"

"Of course." They sent their eyes to the sky out the top of the smokestack, unzipped their flies, and extinguished the fire.

Peter went first, Niklas scrambling down after him and across the creek back to the ruins of the crushing plant. They walked silently back to the car, heads turned to the left to watch the lake until they arrived at the hill where their car was parked. They wrenched their heads away from the heaving lake and began to climb. At the top of the hill they examined the lake again, churning, the sky still overcast, the air still slightly crisp and then, in unison, they turned and got in the car to head home.

* * *

On the way back, the boys decided to get groceries in town and cook out at the farm. The shop was routine—onions and garlic and a green pepper from the produce section, a small sack of potatoes, a quick stop at the beer aisle, then on to the back for the cheap pork ribs that do so well over the fire. Niklas paid for the meat, onions and potatoes; Peter for the garlic and the pepper and the beer. In the parking lot, they realized they forgot ice for the beer, so Peter turned back and went in for some, though Niklas protested, saying it would be cold enough at night to keep things cold. On the canal road headed back to the farm, the clouds finally broke in the southwest and the late afternoon sun broke through at a shallow angle, casting a spooky pale yellow light that clashed with the dark green of the trees that flanked the canal and with the dark gray underbellies of the clouds to the north. Niklas, staring for long periods at the western sky and the hills beyond the water, had to jerk the wheel to stay in his lane a couple of times. Once inland he sped home, shooting bits of gravel behind the tires.

Back at the farm, Niklas gathered the groceries and went to the old fire ring between the cabin and the trees. It was an old piece of metal sheeting curled into a circle and stuck halfway into the ground, so that eight inches protruded above the bed of dead pine needles. Around the ring were large stumps to sit on or use as a table surface. Niklas deposited the groceries on one of the wider stumps. The old woodpile still had a couple of dozen chokecherry logs, plus the pile of twiggy kindling that lay on the ground beside it. He wished for a good split pine log but couldn't find one. He placed a fistful of dry pine needles in the center and soon began to add larger and larger sticks around it. The fire would have to burn for at least another half an hour before it was ready to cook on, and they could see it from the window of the cabin. Inside, Peter was sitting at the table holding his head. He didn't look up when Niklas approached the table.

"You good?" Niklas asked gently.

"Yeah. Just hungover as hell. It started to hit me in the grocery store. My head and stomach are rotting."

"Go get some water, then. We'll need some anyway."

"I don't think I can move."

"Well, the cooking fire is going. We can probably eat an hour from now if you let me cook."

"Sounds great. Hey."

"Yeah?"

"Can you pack a bowl?"

Niklas laughed. "Sure, if you go get us some water."

"Fine."

"The jugs are in the shed, the rain barrels are side by side behind it. Should be full, I'm not sure when anyone drew water from them last."

Peter looked up for the first time from his hands. "Is that stuff safe to drink?"

"It's rainwater."

"Right, it's been sitting there God knows how long. Standing water is a no-no, I thought."

"Dump the first inch if it makes you feel better."

"Are you sure, dude? I really don't want to get sick for the sake of toughness or whatever."

Niklas looked at him hard. "Pete. It's rainwater. You're welcome to boil yours if you still aren't sure."

"I'm just saying. How long has it been sitting out there?"

"Well, judging from the shit I just used to start the fire, it rained not too long ago. So at the very least it got refreshed recently."

"But doesn't it run through those gutters on the shed? There's no way those stay clean."

Niklas snapped. "You are an insufferable pussy, you know that, right?"

Peter got up and headed out to the shed. "If I get sick, you're paying every related bill."

"Deal."

Peter paused on the porch, flipping up the hood of his sweatshirt against the bite of the early evening breeze. The sun hadn't set yet, but it would soon. It was far below the tops of the trees, barely visible in glimmers through the western flank of the forest. What sounded like a logging truck roared past, and the silence in its wake left Peter staring out after it. He stepped gingerly down the stairs, careful not to rattle his pounding brain or jostle his roiling stomach. Slowly he walked toward the setting sun and the green shed that sat in the woods beside the driveway. The ground was soft beneath his feet, the long grass dancing in the breeze; the snap of twigs beneath his shoes and the slight incline up toward the road was all he could manage to focus on. After about thirty yards, he got to the trees by the shed. He could see an upturned wheelbarrow, one that Hannu and Niklas must have left when they cleared the place out. Peter pulled open the plywood door and found the two blue plastic water jugs right in the corner, next to a rusty pickaxe and an ancient crosscut saw leaned up alongside some scrap two by four. Evidently, Hannu had left just enough of himself here so that he could return in a pinch. A thought occurred to him: Would it be a violation of some extralegal law to sell the place without consulting Hannu? He'd drummed up a fairly weak rationale for strong-arming Niklas and bypassing Jakob, but Hannu was a whole 'nother thing to consider. Peter realized he didn't actually know where or how the land had been acquired in the first place.

He took one of the two-gallon jugs out behind the shed to the rain barrels, full to the sixty-gallon brim of rainwater. He listened to the twangy gush as the brass spigot spat cold, clear water against the side of the plastic jug. It was full after an eternal twenty seconds, while Peter stared at the shed's cinder block foundation in the sand and marveled at its durability. He'd never really thought of his uncle Hannu as a tough, handy woodsman, but it appeared now that, intentionally or otherwise, much of the place had been built to last.

He lugged the full jug back down the slope to Niklas, who waited out back at the fire ring, feeding bits of birch and maple branches to help the fussy cherry logs get properly alight. Peter set the jug on the porch and got down on his knees to tip some into his mouth. The water tasted unbelievably refreshing. Gasping, he took several deep breaths and went back for a second draw. He sat down on a log and watched Niklas tend the fire.

"We should get to chopping," Niklas said, setting one last cherry log on the blazing fire. He pulled up his stump to the wider faced one that held their dinner. He broke a clove of garlic in half and handed half to Peter, who looked like he didn't know what to do with it. Niklas pulled his multitool from his jeans pocket and, after wiping both sides of the blade on his thigh, began chopping the garlic nice and fine on a relatively clean-looking foot-long hunk of two by six. He looked up after mincing a clove to see Peter standing in the same confused position.

"Just peel it and give it to me. Same with the rest of this." He handed Peter the rest of his unpeeled cloves. "And an onion, too. I'll do all the chopping if you peel."

"Sure," said Peter, and they spent the next twenty minutes chopping meditatively, smelling garlic and onion on their hands and feeling bits of dirty bark as they grasped more logs with their sticky fingers to feed the fire as it died. Evening deepened, and the sky above the tops of the trees was mostly pale blue now. The song of the birds had died down. No car had passed in a very long time. The only noise was the occasional nonverbal complaint from Peter at an especially troublesome onion. When the garlic was minced and the onion and pepper and potatoes chopped, all that was left was rubbing down the meat and frying the whole lot over the embers. Niklas went to retrieve the frying pan from the basin inside the cabin. When he returned, he took out the pork ribs and tore into the plastic wrap with his fingers. He made a rub of minced garlic and salt and red pepper. Soon three strips were sizzling side by side in the pan with onions and peppers and garlic popping in between them. The boys sat back on their stumps and looked on with lighter hearts. Now *this* really felt like the old days: the same food, the same dynamics alive during its prep and cooking, the same kind of wood in the fire as always—always, since Hannu had acquired the place. Which reminded Peter to ask.

"Say, Nik," he ventured forth inquisitively, "how did uncle Hannu get this land in the first place? Was it Grandpa Teemu's?"

Niklas stared into the fire. "No, it wasn't Grandpa Teemu's. Their place was over in Hancock, since Grandpa Teemu's dad, Olli, moved there from Calumet after the strike and Italian Hall and all that. Dad got this place from the father of one of his students, as a favor."

"A favor? How loaded was the guy?"

"Pretty loaded, judging from what Dad told me about it. It was mostly inheritance, though. His own dad had owned a lumber mill for a long time, left it to him and he sold it. I think this place, I think I remember Dad saying this, I think they used to log certain bits of this land."

"Really? I thought it used to be farmland. What about that head-high pile of field stones down the creek a little ways? I thought we figured that was a farmer clearing a field."

"Sure, but this would be after that. If this man, Bruce Gregson was his name, if his own father owned the mill since the fifties, it's totally plausible that the lumber company bought out the farmer to log the place around then."

Peter nodded. "But, so what did your dad do to make this dude just give the place to him?" Peter smiled. "It wasn't shady, was it?" he asked hopefully.

Niklas smiled faintly. "No. Well, a little bit, I guess, if you squint from the right angle. All he did was come to a troubled kid's aid, and the troubled kid happened to have a rich dad."

"All right, but, so, what happened?"

Niklas took out his knife and flipped each strip of pork, then stirred around the peppers and potatoes and onions. He pulled his hand away from the fire quickly, adjusting the pan with a cherry log.

"My mom was pregnant with Jakob," Niklas began, looking up at Peter from the fire. "My parents were real young, just starting out in Marquette. My dad had finished college and grad school and was teaching middle school at the time. There was this kid he kept having trouble with, this sixth-grader, Tommy Gregson. The usual stuff—not raising his hand and blurting things out in class, rambunctious, can't pay attention to one thing. It made sense, because his parents were divorcing and his dad had shacked up with this lady, and everyone in town knew about it. Tommy's dad, Bruce, was wealthy from the mill his father had owned and sold. Bruce's own father spent his fortune from the mill sale getting even richer, buying up quarter sections and logging them, then chopping the logged land into smaller lots and selling it off. Then he died, leaving Bruce with a pile of money and hundreds of acres in the Keweenaw and no ambitions to do anything but sit on it and spend the money. So Tommy's already a bit under the microscope, being a rich kid, and he's a big kid, too, and not very athletic, so he got picked on all the time.

So one day at recess, the sixth grade is out there with the eighth grade, and Tommy's so big sometimes it's hard to pick him out from the corner where my dad is standing. But so anyway some of the eighth grade guys had caught wind of things and started to give Tommy shit. Apparently the woman Bruce Gregson had shacked up with had been around long enough for some of the boys' older brothers to have seen her out around town and taken a swing at bedding her. Allegedly a bit of a cougar. That doesn't really matter. This group of eighth graders started in on Tommy bullshitting about how his dad's gone off with a whore and all that. Apparently, when they asked the group afterward in the principal's office, none of the kids actually knew anything, they'd just heard rumors. But unbeknownst to them, little Tommy had walked in on his dad and this woman the previous week. He hadn't told anyone."

"Jesus."

Niklas paused to push the frying pan off to the side to cool. Peter silently stared at the fire which hissed and popped every now and again.

"Anyway, so Tommy snapped, and started whaling on the ringleader, this kid named David Wexler. The teachers watching let him go for a bit because David Wexler was a bully and they knew he'd probably asked for it. But Tommy kept whaling on this kid, busts his nose, kidney shots, everything. It took a cop and a football coach to pull him off the kid. Wexler went to the hospital overnight, had to get a shit ton of stitches. It was a mess. The parents all got called down. The Wexlers were talking about pressing charges. Bruce Gregson was pissed because Tommy had mentioned the bullying before and nobody had done anything about it. So the school sends everyone home and says they'll have a conference and decide what's going to happen the next day. Dad goes home, talks to Mom about things.

"You know my mom—fierce, opinionated, unafraid. She gives him a piece of her mind about how the blood is totally on the school's hands, that it really shouldn't be treated as all Tommy's fault. And my dad says he's afraid they're gonna kick him out.

"So my mom tells him a story, and this really affected him because he told me this part like it was the point of the story when he told me, about how her own father was working as a farmhand in Minnesota in the fifties. He spoke no English and was the butt of many of the other hands' jokes. One day, for a joke, a big group all rode up on him screaming about redskins and an attack and he took off and hid in the hayloft all the rest of the day. He heard the cowboys laughing about it the next day. He was so pissed off he decided to leave once he'd fought them. After the next day's work he packed his bags and found one of the cowboys out front and beat him to within an inch of his life, right by the clump of lilacs next to the ranch house. Somehow that detail about the lilacs was important to my dad. Anyway, the owner of the farm came out and saw Grandpa's bags zipped up next to him. Took him inside and found out all about what happened. He was furious at the cowboys; fired two of them (he was looking for an excuse with these guys) and let the third stay with an apology. The owner then apologized too, saying he was sorry they'd treated him lesser. Now, as my mom told it, they could have easily fired Grandpa for being violent, but they saw the toll that everyday ribbing and pranks had taken. Anyway, a few weeks later, according to Mom, a Dakota girl showed up to work in the kitchen after her dad had been allowed to stay. A year later they were married. I've never heard Mom tell the story, but when Dad told me that part he emphasized how much the whole thing meant to her. Had her father been fired and banished, he would have never met her mother."

Peter shook his head. "So what happened to the kid?" He tested the pan's handle, then picked it up and set it on one of the stumps. He popped a green pepper in his mouth and winced at the heat.

"Yes, anyway, so Dad goes home and mom tells him that whole story of her father and the cowboys and the benevolent boss, and he goes to sleep trying to figure out if there is any recourse with the kid or if the degree of his violence on the playground had sealed his fate. So the next day, they have this big meeting with all the kids involved and their parents to try and figure out what to do. And Dad, my dad, totally goes in on behalf of Tommy Gregson, blames the faculty for not spotting the bullying sooner, gives a hard chat to the eighth graders about leaving people's families alone when talking shit. They decided to give him a week of in-school suspension. The Wexlers were pissed, but my dad totally had the principal's ear. Afterward, he was talking to Bruce Gregson in the parking lot, and he gave him a bit of a sermon about ignoring Tommy and chasing floozies. He said that when Tommy lashed out at those kids for talking shit about his dad, he was fighting for his dad's honor, but also maybe a piece of him suspected the things they said were true, or in this case knew it, since the walking-in-on had already happened, and that maybe the punches were not just thrown in anger for his father, but thrown in anger *at* his father.

Standing there out in the parking lot on a cold spring day, Dad said he never saw a guiltier face than that of Bruce Gregson being told he was coming up short as a father. It had never even occurred to him. They stood out by his car for hours. They got to talking, and when Dad's eyes lit up at the mention of all that land lying fallow in the Keweenaw, Bruce asked how much of it he wanted. Dad balked, but Bruce was serious. Forty acres wouldn't even be a tenth of Bruce's total holding out there, which he didn't really care for anyway other than as numbers to brag about with women and his buddies. So they made plans to drive out there once the summer came, and they marked out with fence posts this forty acres that were standing on right now. Dad made sure we got the creek, and Bruce suggested he take the portion with the clearing and the largish hunting cabin, since he couldn't log it anyway, if he ever wanted to. Dad and Bruce still keep in loose touch."

"Holy shit. That's wild."

"I know. It was perfect, too, because they needed a place for Uncle Jussi. He was living in a group home in Marquette that was absolutely miserable. Dad said he called Jussi the second he got home and told him about the place before they even had any kind of plan. By that fall Jussi was out there full time in the cabin, and Dad had met Jim, and they'd started clearing the brush and prepping the ground to plant the following season." Niklas looked like he was about to continue, but all he said was, "Well let's have some dinner, why don't we."

They each took a strip of pork and about half the vegetables and potatoes. Niklas took the much larger half of veggies because Peter didn't like too many onions. Niklas went to grab a beer, asking as he went, "You want one?"

"I think I'd throw up," said Peter, "but yes, and thanks." They ate in silence, staring at the fire, vaguely aware of the dying light. The meat was juicy and not too tough, the vegetables sharp with flavor, the taste of too much garlic tugging on their heartstrings.

Niklas all of a sudden was buoyant with joyous energy. After a trip to the lake and the smokestack, a garlic-heavy meal cooked over an open fire, the relative solemnity of the woods compared with his regular city life, he felt like things were almost back to normal. In a few months, they'd be in heavy coats on snowshoes and Jakob would be with them and they'd probably be quite drunk. For now, though, the breeze was gentle with just a little bite. It felt like all those other summer afternoons with the boys around the fire bone tired after a day of work or play. Niklas silently devoured his pork and potatoes and peppers and onions. After a while, Peter spoke what Niklas was thinking.

"All this garlic makes me think of Jussi."

Nik smiled. "Yeah."

They thought about Jussi then, who used to insist on a whole clove for himself for every meal.

"It's 'cause Jakob came home one day about the mosquito thing," said Niklas.

"What mosquito thing?"

"How the odor of garlic keeps 'em away."

"I don't remember that."

"How do you not remember? Jussi always walking around with half a bulb in his lip like a plug of tobacco. You thought it was so gross."

"Oh, yeah, I do remember that. I just don't remember where it came from."

"Ah, yeah, one summer Jakob went fishing 'cause one of the dads on his team took a bunch of the boys out. He came back with that garlic thing. Jussi was delighted. It was just another excuse for garlic."

Peter nodded. "I haven't fished in years."

"We'll go sometime back in Milwaukee. I've seen dudes fishing under the Locust Street Bridge. We could go by your apartment."

"Do you have rods?"

"I've got mine. I think my parents have a few extra in Marquette."

"Cool, yeah, for sure."

Niklas had scraped his plate clean. "How much of this last bit of rib do you want?"

"That's all you." Peter's first rib was barely half finished. Niklas took the third strip of pork and munched on it standing up, like a candy bar. The wind moved through the branches, swaying, trunks heaving, and both of them shivered a little. Peter tried to kick the fire back together. Eventually he just gave up and let Niklas coax flame back into the ring. He pushed all the coals into a pile and put a handful of pine needles on top, then pushed the remaining bits of cherry around and on top of it.

"You gonna finish that?"

Peter shook his head and offered the plate.

"You sure?"

Peter nodded yes.

He was getting fidgety on the stump. He wondered if he should call Tina or not. He knew he wouldn't, but he also knew he would worry about it. But they'd already spoken today, albeit briefly and before the appointment. Should he call? It was getting on toward seven-thirty he guessed, and she'd be putting Olly to bed soon. Suddenly Peter realized his whole rationale for being here in the first place and trying to sell this land hung on the prognosis that had been delivered to his wife earlier that day. Niklas knew nothing of it, and perhaps the knowledge would make things easier, or at least less difficult. All at once, Peter made a decision, which didn't necessarily have any bearing on whether or not he would call his wife, but in reality meant he definitely wouldn't.

"I'll be right back." Peter disappeared into the cabin for a second, returning moments later with his zip lock baggie. He sat down again by the fire and took out his keys and scooped out a bump, which he promptly hoovered. Then he passed the baggie to Niklas with his keys.

"You sure, man?"

"Well, we're going out tonight, right?"

"I guess."

"No way I'm going out without some."

Niklas nodded, seeing the logic to this, and gingerly scooped himself a modest bump and passed back the baggie when he was finished.

"Thanks for sharing, dude. You're looking pretty light there."

"I know. I'm hoping someone at Schmidt's will be holding."

Niklas looked at him askance. "I don't know about that, man. That might get weird if you hit up the wrong people."

"Not my first rodeo, Nik."

"I'm just saying. You know how it can be up here."

"I'll be careful."

"All right." Peter scooped himself another bump. The fire was dying around the last two cindered logs. "Piss it out?"

"Not just yet. The sun isn't even all the way down."

"We're out of wood."

"I'll do a run to the woodpile."

* * *

The woodpile was much smaller than it used to be. The light that fell was a fading blue; panic rose in Nik's throat at the pace at which time passed. He loaded his arms and went back and fed the fire and stoked it up with pine needles.

Peter looked over at him. "Remember when we hucked it out here for my sixteenth birthday, and it got down to twenty-five and we almost froze to death?"

"I was fine. You just didn't bring enough clothes. Also, did it really get down that low? I thought we made that up for people at school."

"No, it was twenty-five. I looked in Uncle Hannu's paper the next day."

"Huh," said Niklas contemplatively. "Wasn't that the summer we all tripped and we made you cook because you wouldn't take a full tab?"

Peter shook his head. "I think that was a year or two later. I was already at Beloit. Tina was pregnant."

Niklas laughed. "I didn't even take a bite, man. My stomach knew those brats were not done. I remember watching Jakob tear into his; his eyes just rolled back into his head and he bent over in the bushes to yak."

"It was a dick move making me cook. I was still tripping and I hadn't eaten breakfast like you guys had."

"Yeah, I know. I mean it was my first time, so Jakob wanted to show me around, kinda."

"I know."

"Jakob took me out to our old spot past the rockpile by the creek in the woods. I felt like we hadn't been there in forever. Once we started making fires and food we stopped playing at that spot by the creek. That day, being back there, I felt just like a kid again. We sat still for a long time and saw a bunch of rabbits and deer wander by. Jakob caught a toad but I got overwhelmed. Then he climbed a tree and I really freaked out because it was swaying back and forth in the wind."

"The trees always did that, though. Jakob would climb them intentionally for the sway."

"I know, but I wasn't very level-headed about it." Nik looked at his feet.

Peter shook his head. "That shit was strong. I only took a third of a tab and it totally got me there."

"I didn't realize that 'til later. When I was tripping it felt like I was discovering the whole universe for the first time." Niklas played with the twin strings that dangled from his hoodie. "He talked about that day in one of the letters he wrote me."

"You still have those letters, right?"

"Yeah. You can read them if you want."

"No, it's OK. They're your letters. Only if something, like, happened." Peter paused. "Nik, did he ever mention me?"

Niklas nodded. "Yeah, definitely. In the first one, he talked about that time we were out here tripping. He asked after you in the last one, but he was basically just signing off and wishing us well collectively. Said he wanted to have a big Thanksgiving dinner in Milwaukee if he gets out in time. Maybe come up here the weekend after. He wants to ski."

Peter looked long into the fire. "That's good. You've talked to him on the phone, too, right?"

Niklas' face darkened. "Yeah. Well, not since the Fourth of July, that was the last time. I don't know. He sounded OK but really didn't want to talk long. Said he'd gotten in a groove with reading and exercise. Super stoked to be out soon. Probably half the conversation was about Thanksgiving. He hung up after a few minutes."

"Huh. Well you guys are welcome at my place for Thanksgiving."

Niklas smiled. "Thanks, dude." They both stared at the fire for a while. "It's really hard to say, you know? It's been two months since we've talked, which is the longest since he went in."

"You ever write back to him?"

"Once. I don't know. It was weird. His letters to me weren't really the type you respond to, you know?"

Peter didn't know, but he nodded anyway. There was a long silence. It was dusk, now, and the creatures of the night could be heard stirring in the woods just beyond the shadow of the fire.

* * *

An hour later, when they'd pissed out the fire and gathered all the remains of dinner to be brought inside, when they'd each had two beers and were thirsting for more, Peter remembered something funny that had happened that day.

"I ran into Hayley today."

"Holy shit—like Jakob's Hayley, from Schmidt's?"

"Yeah."

Niklas cracked a smile. "In what capacity?"

"I saw her today coming out of the library. She's pregnant."

"Huh. That's wild."

"Yeah. I talked to these guys when I was there this afternoon and they had a whole lot to say. Apparently she's marrying Cory Eskola in the spring."

"Wait, really?"

"Yeah, why?"

"Is it his kid?"

"I assume."

Niklas cracked up. "That is so funny, dude."

Peter frowned. "I don't get it."

"You remember our connection to Cory Eskola, right?"

"You mean besides boozing with him at Schmidt's?"

"Yes, besides that. He's, like, Jim's second nephew or something. I'm not sure if he remembers but he came and redid the roof on this place so Jussi could stay here over the winters. He was a kid back then. So, but later he came to check it out, I think I was ten and Jakob fourteen or fifteen."

"I still don't get it."

"Well, shit, he's gotta be in his early thirties. Getting married to someone in her late twenties, whom Jakob banged when he was nineteen."

"Oh, I guess, yeah. Jakob should hit her up when he gets out."

"Fuck that. I don't want half that bar trying to fight us the next time we show up."

"That's true." They had been standing outside on the porch, arms laden with the dinner things, and now they went inside through the screen door whose bottom scraped the porch boards and they set things down on the table in the dark. It was fully dusk now. Niklas lit a candle.

"Is she still hot?"

"It was hard to tell from the car. I mean, she's pregnant."

Niklas laughed. "I guess." He rose and set the dirty plates and utensils in the ceramic basin and sat back down at the table.

"We going out?"

"In a little," Peter said. "How was coach?"

"Huh?"

"You saw Coach Klingberg this morning, right?"

"Oh, yeah."

"How's he doing?"

"Fine, I think. Lonely. Since he moved out here from Marquette, things have been pretty lonely. I think he was counting on Dad and Jussi being around for a while. He doesn't have many other friends, and talking to Dad on the phone is a tough replacement for being together."

"Really? I didn't think Uncle Hannu and Jussi spent much time with anyone but themselves when they were up here. Besides us, I mean. And Jim I guess." And even as he said this, Peter reflected on his chat with the men at Schmidt's who'd known Hannu by reputation and had asked about Jussi by name. Peter wondered how much he'd missed during all his years away. So much had happened, yet all of it was gone so quickly with Jussi's death and Hannu's departure. He'd only really made it back for Jussi's funeral.

"Yeah," Niklas said, "Thanks to Jim, they got around quite a bit. They went to church every Sunday they were up here together at Trinity Episcopal in town. My dad even gave a sermon or two toward the end, in the middle of winter when whoever was slated to preach was sick or whatever. When he first got the land, he drove around to bars and diners in various towns and asked about berry farming and bought people beers and stuff. He was a good neighbor. And everyone was charmed by Jussi. They loved my dad, and they grew to love Jussi that much more. Very protective. Dad said toward the end he didn't even need to visit Jussi, because people were always calling with updates anyway. Of course, he still did." Niklas paused, looking over his shoulder at the dying light in the western window. "You know, maybe Coach didn't see them all that often, in the grand scheme of things, but at least having visits to look forward to helped... you know? Could go years without seeing someone but the second you hear they're dead or gone, something changes. I don't know. He'll be fine. I mean, what don't we know about it?" Niklas concluded, leaning his chair back on its two rear legs.

"And he gave you a ride back, I guess?"

"No, I walked."

"You *walked?*"

"Yeah. It wasn't that bad. The weather was nice, and most of the walk was along the canal."

"Huh. I thought about coming to get you after I finished at the library."

"It's all good."

Peter thought for a moment, casting a quick glance at Niklas out of the corner of his eye. "I realized at the library I don't know shit about listing a property. I put a few ads out online, but I wasn't sure if I should print out flyers, or something."

Niklas looked up and started to speak, but stopped.

"I think I'm going to ask Jim about it. I'm sure he sees land get bought and sold all the time."

"Peter, man," Niklas said quietly, "I can't get on board with it. I've thought about it all day. We just need to find some other way out of this."

"What do you mean?"

"I mean I didn't... I guess... I don't know. I got in the car thinking you weren't really serious, or, I don't know, that once we got up here you'd see that we couldn't or... I don't know. But you're talking about this place like it's decided. And I guess I'm just saying, I'm not on board. I just," stumbled Niklas, casting about for the words which would not come. "I just think we'd be making a mistake. These are our people up here. You know neither of us is going back to Marquette any time soon. And that's the city, anyway. We're older and all spread out, but this land, Pete. This is all we got."

"Nik," said Peter with enforced patience, "come on. We talked this through weeks ago."

"Yeah, I know, but we talked it through in Milwaukee, man. That's no way to do it. And now we're here, and I got the smell of pine in my nose and air in my lungs and now I just don't think it's right. Uncle Jussi left us this land, his land, my dad's land. This is

115

the last piece of our childhood that isn't in pieces. I'm sorry, Peter, I'm out. And you can't sell without two signatures."

Peter, seething mostly with apprehension about his next phone call with Tina, got to his feet. Niklas did as well.

"Come on, Nik, let's just head out."

"Um, so but don't you want to talk about this?"

"Nik, we're selling the land. We agreed. We both got bills to pay, especially me. I know this is painful, feels wrong, but it's not a choice."

"What do you mean it's not a choice?! I haven't even told my dad yet, he's gonna be beside himself. I put that all aside 'cause you convinced me back in Milwaukee but we're not in Milwaukee right now. We're here. I went out to the lingonberry patch earlier. Uncle Jussi must be rolling in his grave. Even if my dad saw how we've just ignored the place he'd be livid. Forget about selling it, we need to get this place back to something dignified. Feels like we're pissing on Uncle Jussi's grave. Look around you, Peter. Have breakfast with me at the Suomi tomorrow and then tell me again how you want to sell this place. A piece of our soul, that's what it is. It'd be like killing the kid you used to be. These neighbors are all we have left of Uncle Jussi."

Peter looked out the window for quite awhile, at the deepening blues through which stars would soon begin to sparkle. He put his head in his hands. "Nik, I gotta ask. Is this one of your jags that'll be gone by morning or are you serious?"

"I know what you mean. And I'm serious."

"All right, Nik. I really hadn't planned on playing this card but you know we're both broke. I gotta worry about Olly. And Olly's sick and with my job gone, you know, dude. Hospital bills are expensive as hell. You know."

"What do you mean?" Nik swallowed hard, sensing something massive.

"My child is sick."

"How sick?"

"I don't want to do this."

"Dude, I don't think you understand me. Take out a loan or something." Niklas' eyes were wild and red around the edges in the candlelight.

Peter winced. "Come on, Nik. You can't lecture me about the recession on the way up and then tell me to take a loan. Please listen to yourself. Medical bills, man."

"How sick?"

"Leukemia. Probably."

The percussive blast of this news rendered Niklas deaf and mute for half a minute. He sipped his beer and thought about the little boy he tossed a football with at family gatherings. "My God, Pete, man, I'm sorry."

"Not your fault. We've known for a little while. We're getting a second opinion. Actually, Tina got it today. Supposed to at least. I still haven't heard from her. I guess I should call her."

Niklas pondered this, panic rising in his chest. "I think I need to go. No, look..." he said in response to outrage brewing in Peter's face, "I hear you. I... I get it. I just need to think it over on my own. I'm not bailing, I just need to go."

"All right," said Peter. After a long second, he added, "Call me if you need a ride."

"Sure," said Niklas, and he forced his feet into his boots, stumbling over his backpack and out the screen door into the deepening evening where the wind bit his ears and his cheeks reddened as the world disappeared into the tall black trees.

⚡ 16 ⚡

Winter 1935, Hancock

Teemu was an all-star bachelor and saw no reason to hurry toward matrimony as his peers were beginning to. He drank with his buddies from the crusher and played pond hockey on his days off. For a couple of glorious years, life settled into a familiar rhythm that was not unlike his skated feet carving up the ice on the canal, the freedom of a decent job and good friends stretching out before him like the canal in early February, eventually spilling its outstretched fingertips into Lake Superior. He could skate for hours, hours that felt like little sections of forever. And on top of all that, the whole region was experiencing something of a boom. Train lines ran like capillaries all over the U.P. and even the Keweenaw. Architects and engineers came north from Chicago and Detroit and Boston to work on the cities-to-be. Almost a hundred years later the population would be less than half of what it was as Teemu went to work every day with Jim Markham Sr., now a dear friend, at the stamp mill in Freda. Teemu fished, hunted, drank, worked, danced, and generally consumed as much of the world as he could. But when forever finally draws to a close, it feels as short as everything else that's ever ended. Teemu hadn't given much thought to the question of the future beyond the fact that he liked his job and his home and was content to continue as was. And then, in early 1942, he was drafted into World War II and his decade of roving bachelorhood seemed infinitesimal, unfairly, in comparison to getting shipped alongside his buddy, Jim, to Italy to fight for a country he didn't really understand.

For two years, Ana and Olli waited stateside, fingers crossed and heads down, not wanting to invite the attention of karma onto their family. The summers were tense and the town keenly felt its lack of boisterous young men. Many young families struggled with money, and mothers had to go to work.

It was a strange time indeed; and then, all of a sudden, it was over and Teemu returned in triumph with a beautiful black-haired Italian girl named Violetta all over his arm. To Ana, who'd fretted many a late night to Olli about whether Teemu would ever mature, it felt as though her boy had become a man overnight. The war had left a faraway look in his eye. She wondered briefly if his old ways would return once he was back to work and drinking in the same bars, but she needn't have worried. He graduated from the floor of the stamp mill and became a foreman. Less than a year home from Italy and the war, Teemu was a fairly well-off man with a gorgeous young wife and a child on the way. Beers were poured out by friends in his honor at social occasions, which he was now too busy with business and domesticity to attend. He grew a mustache and privately laughed at how silly it looked but wore it anyway, and was taken more seriously because he did. Once, in a restaurant with the five months plump Violetta, an old rival had come up and challenged him, only to shrink away at the sight of the changed man. It was a relief to be free of the burden of a pugnacious youth, and perhaps a little melancholy, too.

Violetta, meanwhile, was an incandescent source of levity and revelry. She was the youngest of five, seventeen when she arrived in America with Teemu, yet already possessed of the social maturity characteristic of youngest siblings whose elders are kind enough to include them. She laughed often and loudly, with her whole body, so that heads turned in restaurants and movie theatres, which Teemu was now rich enough to afford. She took up smoking the second they got off the boat in New York and smoked every day for the rest of her life. She developed a lifelong habit of hosting lavish dinner parties for their circle of friends in Hancock, which she relished beyond all other of life's pleasures. And her Teemu came to enjoy these parties despite their buttoned-up good manners that inevitably fell to pieces once Violetta had gotten enough wine in everyone. It was mostly a matter of getting into the right mood, which was easy when you loved someone as much as Teemu loved Violetta.

They had a child the year they were married, and another the year after. When it was time to name and baptize the kids, Violetta and Teemu cut a deal; Teemu was permitted to name them Finnish names so long as they were raised (Violetta was adamant) strictly Catholic. Their eldest son would be Olli, Peter's father. Their middle child would be Hannu, Niklas and Jakob's father. Violetta was pregnant with a third when tragedy struck.

Ana called in tears to say that Olli Sr. had fallen severely ill, that it was probably late stage cancer, that it was way too late to do anything about it, and that Teemu should hurry over to the facility in Iron Mountain to say his goodbyes. It was all very sudden thanks to Olli Sr.'s aversion to doctors, but the man was in his late seventies and had by all accounts led a full and wonderful life.

Early the next morning, Teemu kissed his wife and little boys goodbye, hopped in their trusted red Ford, and sped south to Iron Mountain in the hopes of catching his father before he left the earth for good. Only as he neared the end of his journey southward did he shed some tears for his father, who would never get to meet his third grandson. He pulled into the parking lot and hurried to their door, where a tear-streaked, haggard Ana pulled him inside. She hugged him quickly and took him into the bedroom where Olli Sr. was propped up on pillows looking gaunt and frail. He smiled at the sight of his only son.

"Sit," he croaked, gesturing to the chair that Ana had surely occupied for the last week or so. Teemu sat and leaned over to kiss his father's forehead. Olli's breathing was ragged but his eyes were bright.

"It looks like my time's nearly up," he offered as explanation for the state of things.

Teemu nodded. "How are you feeling?" he asked.

"Oh, I don't know. I'm just tired." He stroked his beard, looking down like he wanted to make sure it was still there. Suddenly he smiled.

"It's the strangest things you remember," he said, looking earnestly up into Teemu's eyes. "Like life flashing before your eyes but only the absurd parts." He paused. "It was right after your mother and I were married. I was in Houghton looking for a new pair of gloves with Jussi. We walked out of the shop and some ancient guy with a white beard walked right up to us. He pointed at me and said, 'Look at that beard. I bet they think you're Santa Claus, too, right? But we're not! We're just guys with beards!' And then he just walked away. Jussi wanted to buy him a beer but I had to get back home, so we never saw him again." Olli was breathing hard from the effort of so many words. He struggled to raise a shaking hand and gripped Teemu's wrist with surprising strength.

"Tell me how you are," he said. "And for God's sake make it pleasant. It's hard to maintain a good mood when you're dying." He glanced around after taking the Lord's name in vain, making sure Ana hadn't heard.

"I'm... we're doing well, Dad," he said. "Violetta had a party last Saturday and one of her friends got so drunk that he broke this chair to pieces somehow. I spent all day Sunday mending it. I told Violetta she probably shouldn't keep throwing parties because it'll be so hard for her to stay off the drink in the midst of a party—she's pregnant again, we found out a few weeks ago." He paused, realizing that was bigger news that deserved to be dropped casually in the middle of a complaint. "Yeah, we're having another. She says she's confident it'll be a third boy."

Olli Sr.'s face lit up. "Oh. Oh, that's wonderful. Have you chosen a name?"

"No. Well maybe Vi has, but she hasn't told me anything."

Olli opened his mouth to speak but the words caught on their way out. He swallowed as his eyes filled up and tears fell to his cheeks. Teemu put his hand on his father's shoulder. "It's OK, Dad. It's OK."

Olli found his son's gaze again. "It occurred to me. I will get to see Jussi again soon. It's a good name. He would be pleased to know it got passed down." And he waited expectantly for his son to answer.

Teemu vividly remembered his father's shining eyes as he told and retold his many stories of his dear friend Jussi and the adventures they had together when he was a young man. That his father had never grown tired of telling the tales of their friendship had made Teemu imagine that Jussi was something of a god among men, a mortal being inhabited by an immortal force who wished to visit the earth but only for a lifetime. Jussi was a good Finnish name and the nickname would surely stick from an early age.

"Sure, Dad. If it's a boy we'll call him Jussi."

"Call your mother for me."

Teemu did, and Ana appeared after a moment. They exchanged a few words in Finnish and then she left.

They went on to speak of the Lions and the Red Wings and had a snort of whiskey before Teemu left to return to the Keweenaw. By the end of their visit his father was clearly struggling to stay awake. After the whiskey he kissed his father again, tucked him into bed, and spoke briefly with Ana about making arrangements for his passing. He felt a strange lightness on the drive home, a relief where he thought there would merely be a void. He'd been struck and comforted by something Olli Sr. had said: "I'll get to see Jussi again soon." Surely Olli, too, would be waiting for Teemu when the time came. There was no hard evidence for this, but when every single culture across history and the globe believes in something, only children and the slaves of modernity believe otherwise. Teemu hugged his children and his wife with extra warmth and fervor upon returning home. When the children had been put to bed, he found Violetta washing up in the bathroom. It was agreed that their third child would be named Juhani, and everyone would call him Jussi.

When his father's estate was arranged, Teemu was surprised to find among his inheritance a silver-copper half breed in a small wooden box. He knew what it was, had heard his father's story of the precious gift, but he'd never actually laid eyes on it. A short note in Olli's messy hand said, in Finnish, "From my Jussi to yours. God be with you. Dad."

⚡ 17 ⚡

The following day, an hour after noon, Jim Markham called it quits after putting in another section of rafters for his extension and securing the plywood ceiling with screws. He put his drill battery on the charger inside the door of the extension, then went to his truck, which was parked close by with the doors open and the radio nearly blasting old country. He drove back around to the front of his house and parked. Inside Cynthia was waiting with a fresh pot of coffee. Jim sat down heavily and put on his reading glasses to look at the paper which sat on the kitchen table in front of him.

Cynthia put a steaming mug on the table. "What's going on there?" she said, with a nod at the paper.

"Oh, nothing," said Jim. "Dey're talking at da city council about da bridge traffic in the summers. Don't know how long dat bridge'll last."

"Just build another one."

"Dat takes a whole lot, darlin'. They might tear down da bridge and build a bigger one."

"Why dey gotta tear it down?"

"'Cause da roads on either side are only good for dat spot. Dey'd have to build new roads otherwise."

Cynthia huffed, unsatisfied, and went back to the sink. "When are da Kinnunen boys coming?"

"Wouldn't you like to know," Jim chuckled. "Nik said dey'd be here dis afternoon round one or two. Could be any minute now." He looked up and watched the old western on TV for a few seconds. Cynthia had finished with the dishes and turned around. Her eyes flickered past Jim to the protruding bay window facing the front yard and that, judging from the sloppy yet totally competent handiwork, Jim himself had installed, likely without help.

"And here dey come," she said. Out the window she saw Peter's blue sedan followed by the typical cloud of dust. Jim set the paper down and turned around to look. Niklas got out quickly and stood

123

beside the car, looking at the driver's seat and barking at Peter to hurry up. Peter finally got out and they walked up the gravel path to the front door.

Niklas opened it slightly and called, "Hey Jim! It's us."

"Hey, come on in," said Jim as they rounded the corner into the kitchen. Cynthia smiled her grimace of a smile as they took their places at the kitchen table.

"Coffee?"

"Sure, yes, please."

Once they had their own hot mugs and had tasted the strong, black coffee (cream, milk, and sugar were never offered), too hot yet to gulp, they looked at Jim.

"So," Niklas began, "extending back again? Looks pretty far along?"

"Oh ya, going well. I want to have it insulated by the first snow dis winter."

"Really? Last year though I thought it snowed around Halloween up here."

"Nothing dat stuck. We always get a little early here and there. But da snow didn't stick 'til Christmas."

Niklas shook his head. "Damn. Well at least that's plenty of time to finish up the extension." Peter was amused to hear a trace of the thick Northwoods accent slip into Niklas' speech.

"Should be. This guy, well, I also gotta sell this boat. He wants me to sell it for him."

"What kinda boat?"

"Sailboat."

"What kinda sailboat?" Niklas pressed, looking over at Peter. "Pete, remember the 420 my dad took us out on a couple of times?"

Cynthia, meanwhile, was amused. "What kinda boat?! Da kind ya put in da crik, and up it goes!"

Peter laughed at this, but Niklas was looking to Jim for an answer.

"Oh, nothing much," Jim said. "I'll show you boys. About twenty feet or so I think. Sail and jib."

"Cabin or no?"

"Little one."

"Could ya sleep?"

"Not me! Ha! Even for you boys it'd be tight. We'll go look at her in a bit."

"Sounds good."

"How'd you get stuck with it?" Peter asked.

"Dis guy, he's a buddy of my son Greg's. Greg's a police officer, you know, you met Greg? Yeah. Anyway, buddy of his, he's got this boat, guy wants to sell it but he moved out to Montana a few months ago before it sold. So he talks to Greg and calls me up, he calls me, he says, "Jim I need you to get rid of dis boat for me—"

"He's too nice," Cynthia broke in, gesturing at her husband. "I told him, I says, 'Dat boat is gonna rot in da weeds out back like da old planer and dat tractor we never done nothing with."

Jim was shaking his head in disagreement.

"What do ya mean, no?" Cynthia said with mild indignance.

"It's a boat, hun. Boat'll sell. Everyone's got a rusty old tractor won't start."

"It'll get ruined sitting out dere all winter."

"It's August. I'll be rid of it by Thanksgiving." To the boys, in a comically aggrieved voice, he said, "She's always trying to control people. I tell her, I say, hun, it's OK. It's fine."

"No I don't! I don't want to control people. Only you."

"Ain't I a people?"

A moment hung in the air and then they smiled at each other, leaving it be, like they surely had been doing for years and years.

"You were saying, Jim, about the boat."

"Oh ya! So dis guy, Greg's buddy, he calls me up in June, he says 'Jim! I need you to sell this boat. Try to get two grand but if you can't dats all right.' And I says 'OK, sure'. Den da guy calls me up a month later, telling me he's got a new girlfriend who likes sailing. 'Don't sell her just yet,' he tells me. 'Hold on to her'. So I says OK, stop asking around, until he calls me up after another few weeks, the guy, he tells me, he says 'Romance is off. Sell da boat.' Ha!"

Niklas and Peter laughed, Peter appreciatively, Niklas with his full gut because he actually thought the anecdote was hilarious. "That's excellent, Jim," said Niklas. "If I had a spare two Gs lying around I'd take it back to Milwaukee dis week."

"Yours if you want it! Tell your buddies back dere, see if any of 'em need a boat."

"I surely will. Say, Pete, your buddies might be more the type… or is two thousand too cheap?"

Peter rolled with the punch. "I'll see. I'll let you know, Jim."

"All right. Good. So, you boys. How's your father?" He asked Niklas.

"He's doing all right. Wants to retire soon but I know he plans on teaching another year after this one. Him and my mom went out to Isle Royale this summer."

"Oh ya? I heard it's beautiful out dere."

"They loved it. Afterward he said it made him want to retire somewhere quiet, away from Marquette. I tried a few times to get him to move back out here but, you know, he's, uh. He's still moving on after Uncle Jussi, you know."

Jim nodded. "Did he grow anything this year?"

"Just a salad garden in the backyard. Radishes and snow peas and kale and, uh, I'm pretty sure there was one more. I forget."

"Dey're selling a big buncha land, the logging company, you probably drove by on da way in. Hundred acres. He could have more lingonberries than Sweden!"

Niklas smiled wistfully. "I wish, Jim. I'll put a bug in his ear, we'll see."

Jim turned to Peter. "How's things with you bud?"

Peter, who'd been gulping his scalding coffee, set down his mug. "Oh, I'm doing OK, Jim. It's good to be up here." Niklas glared at him.

"How's your boy?"

Peter coughed. "He's, uh, he's good. Second grade this year. It's crazy, time is flying."

"He play any sports?" Jim asked.

"Yeah, he played baseball and soccer this past year. He's, uh, taking the year off, though."

"He sick or something?"

"Um, well, we're not sure." Peter looked guiltily at the tablecloth. "He'll be all right."

Jim looked worried that he'd touched a nerve. "Well. That's good." Both boys nodded. "Hey," said Jim, "I still gotta start da fire for da sauna. You boys want to come with me and den we'll go have a look at da boat?"

"Sure," said Niklas, draining his mug. They smiled at Cynthia as they filed out of the kitchen, following Jim out back to the woodshed to grab an armload for the sauna.

Once the sauna fire had been started, the three men walked downhill past the rusting tractor and planer and other assorted equipment, past a stand of birch trees, through the long grass and nettles, through a clump of spruce trees brushing the boughs aside with their hands, and into a clearing where a small sailboat sat on a trailer. Its sails were white and furled with crumples, the main tied loosely to the boom and the jib wrapped around the forestay.

Niklas went up and looked in the horizontal cabin windows. He walked around, looking for an intact rudder and tiller, checking for scratches in the hull, imagining himself piloting it by himself out on the big lake. He turned to Jim.

"You know where he sailed it, mostly? The guy you're selling this for?"

"Oh, I don't know. Portage Lake. Maybe da bay."

"Huh. I want to go sail up around Copper Harbor."

"Oh ya, its real rough there around da point."

"That's what my dad said."

"Is he still trying to sail around da peninsula?"

Niklas looked confused, then cracked up. "I haven't talked to him about that in ages. I don't know. It's an awful long way, and his boat is so small. Maybe. He hasn't said anything about it in a while though."

Peter looked confused. "What was your dad trying to do?"

"Sail around da peninsula, right?" Jim said, looking at Niklas.

"Well, I think the problem is that it'll probably be a lot of rowing," Nik said. "He's got this boat, called an Adirondack guide boat, it's like this little fishing dory that rows but also you can rig a little sail. It's fun. I've taken it out a few times."

Jim smiled. "You gotta be careful, or he's gonna do it. Your dad don't like people telling him not to do something."

"I know. We don't badger him too much. He's mostly dropped it."

Jim nodded. Peter said to Niklas, "I just remembered. It's like that lady at Schmidt's the night we got here. You remember that?"

Niklas' eyes lit up and he nodded. "That was crazy. Jim, we... Pete, you want to tell it."

Peter shook his head. "I was, uh... The details are fuzzy."

"Well, anyway, Jim, the first night we got here we were at Schmidt's Corner, and we got talking with this older lady about people doing crazy shit on the Great Lakes and she told us that she, like, when her husband died, she'd always been into hardcore camping, wilderness type stuff, so when her husband died, she had this boat, I think she called it a surf-ski, like apparently a rowing shell type thing with a hydrofoil, I'm not quite sure, anyway, she set out to circumnavigate Lake Superior on that thing. Think a tiny, like, sixty-year-old woman, you know, in good shape, but still. So she starts around St. Ignace as early as possible, like, still in June. She gets through the first couple of months all right, turns the corner at Duluth and gets into the Canada section. About fifty miles into Canada, she told me, the first crazy cold snap hit and a storm kicked up. Coast Guard came and rescued her at the last minute. But, so she gets warm, they let her go, she chills for a few days at her campsite. And then she starts again. Gets another ten days. Then, just as she's really getting comfortable, she got caught too far from shore on a really choppy day, and the coasties had to come and get her again. They told her that if they had to rescue her a third time, they'd take her boat. So she packed up and went home."

"Holy shit," said Peter.

"So you don't want your dad doing none of dat? Ha!" Jim cackled. "Yeah, it gets real dicey dere. I barely think it'd be up to a choppy day too far out." He gestured at the boat on the trailer in the long grass in front of them.

"How much he want for it?"

"Two grand."

"Huh."

Peter shuffled nervously. They all stood there admiring the boat for a long minute. Jim then grunted and they followed him back up the hill toward the house. As they passed the ancient, rusted planer in the grass, Niklas lingered.

"Jim, you ever used this planer? I always just seen it in the grass."

"Oh ya. Just gotta oil her up and scrape off some rust. Got a motor all ready for her. Your dad ever tell you about dis planer? It was my father's, but he got it from your grandpa Teemu."

Peter looked up with interest while Niklas stopped in his tracks. "Hold up, Jim. Really?"

"Oh, ya," Jim said.

"Is there a story?"

"My dad had to sell his one year before I was born when he was broke and selling off big tools. Dat was before he got da job at the Freda stamp mill with your grandfather. You knew dey were buddies, right?"

"Yeah, we did," Niklas said. "We went down yesterday to the old stamp mill. Or the ruins of it. It's by the lake and it's kind of desolate in a pretty way."

"I was on da crew that demo'd it in sixty-seven."

"Damn, really? How old were you?"

"Nineteen. I was still drinking like a fish then. Ha! Come on. Da sauna's probably hot."

* * *

"Do you think he knows?" Niklas asked.

They were sitting side by side in the sauna, sweat sprouting on their foreheads in the hundred-and-ninety-degree heat, staring at the rocks and the crookedly laid boards in the floor and walls, Peter feeling more than a little claustrophobic. Two buckets of water sat untouched at their feet.

"I doubt it," Peter said. "I mean, how would he?"

"I feel like it's spelled out across my forehead."

"You've seemed fine to me."

Looking out the little window to their right, Niklas watched the leaves shiver in the breeze and then become perfectly still.

"So are you going to get me that boat to make up for it?" Niklas asked, joking but keeping his face straight.

"You can get it with your portion of the money."

"How much is that again?"

Peter took a breath for patience. "Ten thousand."

Niklas shook his head scornfully. "We're getting robbed."

"That's just not true at all. This guy Andy Ahonen is saving my ass, snapping it up so quickly, all at once, no contract bullshit. I can't believe we got this done this quickly. You and Jakob could probably get something nice this winter when the buying's slow with twenty large between the two of you."

"Bullshit. When are we going to have a cabin and a creek on as nice a forty as that one? Twenty minutes from town? Fuck off, dude. Let what you've killed be dead." After a second he continued, like a dog with its jaws locked on a stick. "All right, so, you know, I feel like I have a bit of a right… what's the first check you write once we're back in Milwaukee? The bookie?"

In point of fact, Peter already knew the first check would be to his blow guy, but mentioning that now would put him in the hospital. "Well, I owe Tina five thousand of it, so I'll probably start there. Then I'll—"

"What? Really?" Niklas' voice was full of fresh outrage. "You didn't tell me you could borrow from her."

"Well it was mostly her asking her father, cause he thinks I'm an idiot. But he cut her off last winter right after she lent me eight. She agreed that I could just pay her five back and call it even. And now Olly's medical bills will be something like that or probably worse themselves, so."

"How much went up your nose?"

"Nik, I already told you this morning. I owe you one. A big one. The money from Jussi's place will get me through the year. I don't know how else to say it. I'm sorry dude, so, so sorry I even had to ask. But, like, what am I supposed to do? How would it look to Tina if I just sat on money while our sick child's fate depended on her angry father's forgiveness?"

"It's not just money, Pete. That's my problem, which, like I've already said, I'm looking past for your sake. But you'll have to answer to Jakob at Thanksgiving when he's out. I'm not defending you then."

"Thank you, again, Nik. I feel like my life is one big episode of riding other people's coattails and then letting them down and asking for a bailout." Peter hated this kind of ass kissing but knew that Niklas was far too earnest to see through it. Niklas smiled and nodded, not unkindly. They'd been around this block today already quite a few times.

"We gotta get Jim talking while we're here. I want to hear those stories all one last time in case he gets T-boned by a logging truck."

"You've heard more of his stories than me."

"Which do you remember?"

"Oh, the one about his dad almost chopping the barn down out of anger, the one about the burning wood stove in the truck and the cows in the garage, the one about the jealous cousin who almost stabbed his dad, the one about Jim getting more milk from his neighbor's cow than the neighbor ever could…"

They were pouring sweat now, shifting around to stay comfortable, wiping their brows at shorter and shorter intervals. Niklas tossed handfuls of water from the buckets over his forehead, then stuck his head out the door into the cool evening air for a brief rest. Peter followed suit with the water. In Jim's sauna, they never used it to dump on the rocks and steam the place up as it was intended—it was always far too hot for anything other than dumping on your neck and forehead.

They stepped out onto the grass and into the glorious evening breeze, which sent steam rising from their backs and made them shiver with the sudden drop in temperature. The sunlight filtered through the trees leaving a dappled sheen visible on their sweaty chests. They toweled off and listened to the birds chirping and flitting around in the trees above their heads. They dressed and folded their towels and walked back to the house.

* * *

"How was it?" Jim asked, looking up from his coffee and papers as they walked in.

"Wonderful," said Niklas. "Thank you, as always, Jim."

"Oh sure. Sit down. You want coffee?"

"Sure," said Niklas, and Peter too nodded and sat down at the kitchen table.

Jim poured the coffee as Cynthia came out from the hallway. She smiled bashfully at the boys and went over to the window. Jim put the steaming coffee in front of them and sat down himself. "So. Are you boys staying up for a while den?"

Niklas sipped his scalding coffee and shook his head. "I wish. We're headed home day after tomorrow."

"Mm. When's your brother get out again?"

"Thanksgiving. If he keeps his mouth shut."

"That's always da problem, ain't it? Ha!"

"I think he'll be all right. He wants to be shut of the place."

"Oh I'm sure. He thirty yet?"

"Two more years."

"Oh, wow."

Cynthia chuckled over in the living room and everyone at the table turned to look at her. She smiled with shining eyes as she launched into her story.

"Jim turned seventy da other day. I made him dinner, and afterward he goes, Hey honey, come to bed, I bet you've never

131

slept with a seventy-year old before! Ha!" And she cackled as she turned back to the countertop. Jim gave a hearty "Ha!" and his crinkly-eyed smile, warm as ever with love for a room full of friends and family sharing a joke.

Peter was amused but Niklas, zooming out a thousand feet and remembering their fate, was paralyzed with sadness. No one could replace Jim and Cynthia. He remembered his task of getting Jim rolling on his stories of the old days in the U.P.

"Jim, tell me about your dad," Niklas said. "I was telling Pete, he hasn't heard as many of the stories as me."

Jim turned to Peter. "What do ya want to hear?"

Peter looked at his hands and thought for a moment. "What was he like when Grandpa Teemu was around?"

That seemed to do the trick. "Oh, my dad could talk to anyone," he said, saying the words with the same inflection and in the same order as a hundred times before. "Big or small, loved people, loved making jokes. People'd ask him, hey Jim, how many kids you have? He'd say, I got five with spouts and tree witout!

"He was real big too, tall. Loved greasy food. We were never poor growing up, you know, we always had good meat from da cows and da chickens and pigs. You could always get a loan back den if you had a milk cow."

"Huh, really?"

"Oh, ya. In da winters when he worked at the stamp mill with your grandfather, we had a house in Freda. We kept da livestock in da garage! I remember one year when da cold came early da cows almost froze in the garage until dad got in his truck and drove over to the farm in Liminga and came back with a woodstove in the back, blazing and all! Carried it himself into the house for da cows."

"Did you work with the cows?" Niklas asked.

"Oh ya, dey always had me do it. I used to sing to 'em! I'd sing and they'd give me more milk than anyone else could ever manage. I remember we had a neighbor, he got me to take care of his cows while he was off in Detroit on business. He came back pissed 'cause his wife tells him I get more milk outta da cows than he ever did. Ha! He called me up the next time he was leaving town, dats for sure."

Peter wore an expression of polite indulgence; Niklas was lapping up every word as though it were ambrosia. Their coffees were empty and nearly full, respectively.

"He had a real temper though, my dad. One time he was walking in the barn and he hit his head on the top of da doorframe. He got so mad he went looking for an ax to chop down da barn, but by da time he found da ax he forgot why he was angry! Ha!"

The boys laughed appreciatively. Niklas could tell from Peter's expression that his patience was waning. "Did your dad grow anything?"

"Oh ya, lotsa potatoes, some blueberries. We had a vegetable garden. Mostly potatoes though. He was damn good at potatoes. Da cellar was nearly half full every winter wit da pasty potatoes aging."

"They got a different kinda potato for pasties?" Peter asked.

"You just gotta age 'em to soften 'em."

"Huh."

"Oh ya, he was damn good at potatoes. He tried to make vodka one year. My dad was never like me wit da drink, but he went on a tear every once in a while. Dats where I heard about your uncle Teemu—Dad said he woulda been a bloody pulp in somebody's parking lot if not for your grandpa fighting side by side like there was no drink in him. Dats one thing he said for sure," Jim said, unsure of whether to smile or not. "Your grandpa Teemu would outdrink my dad and then turn around and save his hide when his mouth wrote checks his ass couldn't cash." Jim shook his head. "Now here I'm da drinker, haven't had a drop since seventy-nine, and your dad's the lingonberry king!"

Niklas nodded, looking down at the table. "Any good fight stories?"

"Oh, ya, let me see. My mother, ha! One time my dad was out with a guy drinking and da guy's wife was just all over Dad. Dad didn't know she was this fella's wife, so he dances with her. They all get real drunk and he walks home at da end of da night, but this fella starts following him home, yelling and cursing, so when Dad finally gets home this guy pulls a knife on him in da yard. Upstairs my mother hears all this and she comes tearing down da stairs, eyes blazing, and tells 'em, "Gimmie that goddamned knife and go to bed." And she marched up to the fella and took his knife and sent him away and pulled Dad upstairs by the ear and into bed. Ha!"

The boys smiled appreciatively. "Damn, that's an excellent one. Not much of a fight though," Niklas noted.

"Oh ya, well here's another. One time real early in the Freda stamp mill days when our dads started running together, I remember dad telling me this one, he said it was the one time your grandpa Teemu ever started anything. Dey were at this bar and Teemu saw one of dose union busters. He picked a fight but then these huge guys got up and took 'em outside, but da bar was on da second floor, and so da guy grabbed Teemu and held him out like he was going to drop him over. Somehow Teemu talked himself off the edge and when them let him back on the balcony he knocked 'em both out before my dad knew what was going on. Oh, he would get fired up telling that one! Bam BAM, dey're lying there in da snow. Ha!"

Both boys were smiling. "That's excellent," said both at the same time, followed by a chuckle.

"What'd you do as a kid, Jim? What did your friends do, besides help out on the farm?"

"Mostly help out hauling things on da farm, chores. We fished sometimes. I remember my buddy, he taught me how everyone has their secret spots in the woods, beautiful spots, but if you want da best fish you gotta go down by da canal a hundred yards east of where they dump their sewage! Ha! I got da biggest trout and bass out by dat stinky hospital. I guess dey're like us, love the shit that makes 'em fat! Ha! When dey tore the hospital down all da kids were pissed. I should call up Donnie, guy who showed me dat spot. Probably dead."

Niklas turned to Cynthia who'd been listening by the kitchen sink. "So, Cynthia, how'd you guys meet?"

"He hung around my brothers. We couldn't stand each other."

"Not much has changed, honey. Ha!"

"We were all drinking way too much back den." They lapsed into silence, indulging nostalgia for a moment. Peter and Niklas shared a long look, one where they silently agreed to preserve the moment and put off informing Jim of the imminent sale and their departure. The silence lingered, then Niklas drained his cold coffee. Outside a dull whine grew louder and louder. Ten seconds later Niklas watched an ATV tear into the yard and skid to a stop besides Peter's car. A man with a fat belly and normal legs with a thick blond beard got out slowly and waddled up the steps.

"Huh! Dere's Randy," said Jim as the door opened.

The man, Randy, walked in, wearing the permanently bewildered look of a freshly recovering serious alcoholic. It took him a long time to recognize Niklas, who greeted him warmly.

"Randy! What's up, man!"

"Oh hey." He stuck out his hand to shake, which Niklas took. "I'm fine." He turned to Jim and waited to speak.

"What's up, bud?" Jim asked. "Sit down."

Randy stayed standing. "You take a look at that muffler yet?"

"No. Was going to do it tomorrow."

"Bob Rikkula stopped by earlier, I was talking to him, he told me, he said he got a brand new one and he don't need it, I'm doing that deck for him next week so he says he's gonna throw it in, you know, with my check. So..."

"You think we should just trow in da new one?"

Randy nodded. "Yeah."

"You're not going broke over this muffler?"

"Oh, no, it sounded like he wanted to get rid of it."

Jim looked suspicious. Randy acknowledged this look with a dismissive shrug, at which Jim shrugged as well, and both men nodded. Randy looked around as if confused.

"Sit down, Randy. You want some coffee?"

"Oh no, I better get back."

"Come on! Sit down."

Randy shook his head. "Thanks, Jim. Good to see ya fellas. Gotta get back and get working on da trailer." He stood there for another few seconds.

"Well all right, Randy."

"All right." He turned and headed out. His ATV roared out of the driveway moments later.

The boys looked long at each other, then Jim. "He OK?" Niklas ventured.

"He's fine," Jim said sternly. "He's off the piss."

"For real this time?"

"It's been almost a year. Nearly died last time. So."

"Huh," said Niklas. "So that's why we didn't see him at Schmidt's." Peter nodded in recognition.

"Dat place is a pit," Jim said scornfully.

"They've cleaned it up a bit since seventy-nine," said Peter with a defensive laugh. Jim looked doubtful.

"Randy couldn't keep away from there. Man, he really almost died. Got eight OWI's. Nine actually." Jim smiled. "You hear about his last one?"

"No, nothing. This is the first we seen or heard from him," Niklas said.

"Well after number eight, they got him in court, looking at prison time. Da judge lets him call one character witness, and he calls me. Says oh, Jim Markham's been sober and going to meetings since seventy-nine, he'll vouch for me, he'll take me to meetings and keep me in line. So I agree and talk to da judge and da judge lets him off. Two weeks later, da cops still ain't given him his car back, even though his license is suspended, and he's all pissed, so he goes and gets drunk, breaks into impound, finds his car, breaks in, hotwires it, and then falls asleep. Dey found him passed out in da driver seat of his own damn car in impound. So you bet he got number nine! HA! He's been real good since den though, boy did I yell at him. Oh man!"

Peter and Niklas were wide eyed and laughing. "That's... unbelievable, Jim."

"You literally couldn't make that up," said Peter. "Poor Randy. It's like a Greek myth."

"Oh, he's fine. A little spacey. I remember dat. At least he's got his ATV. Plenty a guys up here who can't drive no more on da roads. Dats why dey all got da ATV's. It'll wear off in a decade."

This pulled Niklas up short. A long silence hung in the air. Peter gave Niklas a pointed look and rubbed his belly. The silence lingered.

"Well, Jim, thank you so much, as always," said Niklas. "We're probably going to get going and have some dinner."

"No you're not!" Jim feigned stubbornness. The boys smiled.

"All right, Jim." They all got up and shook hands. Niklas smiled at Cynthia as they filed out.

"You're coming by before ya leave, yeah?"

"Of course," said Niklas. "Take care Jim, I'll see you soon."

"Tell your dad I say hey," Jim called out the door after them, full in the knowledge that they'd spoken on the phone the previous day. Niklas waved and followed Peter down the steps. Jim stood in the doorway watching them go. When the car had vanished down the gravel road and the dust still hung in its place, he walked back inside and sat back down at the kitchen table with his wife.

Cynthia looked up as he came in. "So what do ya suppose is eating at them two fellas?"

"We'll find out soon enough. Maybe it's nothing."

⚡ 18 ⚡

As they turned back on to Liminga Road, the speckled bits of sunlight that made it through the trees flashed across their faces and the car. Without asking Niklas figured they were headed for Schmidt's Corner. Peter pulled into the gravel lot behind the bar and they both got out stiffly.

Inside, with a Miller Lite before Niklas and a double Captain and Coke before Peter, they brooded and watched football highlights. There were two other people in the bar, each wrapped up in the TV or their drink. The guy at the end of the bar wore camo head to toe.

"So, uh," Niklas said. "Do you think it'll really go?"

Peter paused for a second as if not sure what he was referring to. "Uh, it sounds like it, yeah. I'm meeting the guy tomorrow and he sounded excited on the phone. He said he's been driving by for years and wondered. I don't know, it sounds pretty set."

Niklas nodded. "Is he paying cash?"

"Yeah."

"How are we going to split it up? You can't exactly withdraw that kind of money."

"Dammit Nik, I don't know."

"This is your fucking fault, dude. Don't forget."

Peter gave him a withering look. Niklas glowered back. "We playing pool?"

"Sure." Peter resignedly sipped his drink and followed Niklas to the pool table. Niklas rubbed chalk on a cue as Peter fed quarters into the table and racked the balls. He noticed that Niklas had put a twenty dollar bill on the table.

"Fuck that. I'm not playing for money."

"All right. Pansy."

Peter pressed his lips together and said nothing. He lined up his shot and broke.

"I'm not shooting until you put a twenty down."

Peter shook his head.

"Coward."

138

"I'm not losing all my money to you in pool right now, dude."
They'd been down this road before. Niklas was a crack shot.

They remained in their standoff for a few moments. The grizzled guy in camo and boots came down from the end of the bar and made for the door, noticing as he did the twenty on the table. He paused and looked at Niklas.

"You playing?"

"I am, yeah. You good to play for twenty?"

The guy pulled out his wallet and lay a twenty next to Niklas'. A cruel grin spread across Niklas' face. "You want to break?"

The guy nodded. In the corner Peter looked like he was trying to shrink down to invisible, both with shame and apprehension. If he had to pull this guy off Niklas in the course of the evening, or even the match at hand, he wouldn't be surprised.

* * *

On the way home, Peter lit in to Niklas. "You're going to land us in the hospital one of these days."

"That's a bullshit fucking rule and he knows it."

"Yeah, but he was huge and probably packing."

"If I get shot for enforcing this goddamn rule, then good. Martyrdom is worth the integrity of the game."

"Don't call me from the hospital when somebody puts you there."

"You are gutless, dude. I handled that fine. Absolute scumbag behavior to call eight ball last pocket when you're behind by three balls and your opponent is about to finish you off. Fuck that guy one hundred per cent."

They bickered all the short way back to the cabin. What had happened was, just as Niklas was about to cockily finish off Fred, the old plumber who was his opponent, Fred asked, "So it's eight ball last pocket, right?" Meaning the eight ball could only count if sunk in the same pocket that the shooter's last ball was. Niklas didn't mind this rule in general because it made games last much longer and favored comebacks, but to wait until the blade was at your neck and then ask for last pocket was barefaced bullshit. He'd laughed in Fred's face and told him to fuck off. Niklas was used to intimidating yuppies in Milwaukee bars with this but Fred didn't appreciate it. He asked Niklas if he wanted his ass kicked, to which Niklas replied that actually he'd just gotten his ass kicked, to which the guy said that he didn't know they were playing "kiddie pool." Niklas just laughed, turned, lined up his shot, and sank the eight ball in the pocket where his last ball went anyway. He tossed his cue on to the table, winked at Fred, gave the hip thrust motion, and said, "Ball don't lie, fat boy." All the while Peter shrunk further and further into the corner.

Fred grinned. "All right. I'm going to get a shot and see you boys out back. All right?"

"You want to get your ass kicked a second time?"

Fred almost leapt over the pool table right there, but thought the better of it and went off to the bar. As soon as he was gone Peter grabbed Niklas' sleeve.

"Let's go, Jesus, before we're paralyzed." Niklas took one last look towards the bar and ducked out the door with Peter, who comically rushed off and locked the car when he got in. Niklas laughed as he strolled the last few yards and got in leisurely.

"Holy shit you're scared."

"I have a fucking kid, Nik, and a wife. I can't be getting into fights over pool."

"That's the difference between us. You didn't fight or do shit back even when you could. Me and Jakob, if we ever get married, we won't be able to stop. Why would we? I want to die in the middle of an adventure."

"Yeah, and where did that land him?"

"At least we know that he would kill for us. Could you say that much about anyone else? There are worse things than prison."

"Like what?"

"Like being a soul starved douche bag like yourself."

Peter just laughed, though he was saddened by the gulf between them. It had always been there but when you looked at it, it always looked bigger. Before long, the headlights lit up their mailbox a hundred yards distant. Dusk had settled now, though plenty of blue was left in the sky. After the car was parked they sat for a moment and got out, sending hoppers jumping in every direction. They stood for a moment in the deep, breezy quiet.

"Let's go make a fire," Niklas said, and Peter nodded and followed him off past the cabin, past the orchard, past the berry patches and the old tires which used to hold potatoes, through the bits of spruce and chokecherry that grew where other things wouldn't, or couldn't. A wind came on and blew hard, bending trunks and setting hair aswirl, lending the evening a spooky and adventurous tinge.

* * *

Around the fire they drank slowly and didn't speak much. The light died completely around them, and the woods came alive with the sounds of night-time. Niklas prodded the fire too often and took great pains to ensure that each log burned in its entirety before too many more were added. The stars came out overhead, and besides their pinpricks above the trees, all you could see was the orange of the dancing flame on the underside of the boughs that stretched above them.

Peter just brooded. Eventually he asked Niklas if he wanted to smoke a bowl, which Niklas did, but he was glad that Peter had suggested it, leaving him the moral high ground if it came up later. Back inside the cabin, Niklas noticed his guitar case standing up in the corner. He took it back outside with him, along with his baggie and pipe.

They smoked a bowl and then the mood lightened a bit. Niklas played through his usual repertoire, a mix of contemporary American folk and older stuff like Cat Stevens, John Prine, Bob Dylan, James Taylor. Niklas got really into it, making Peter worry that he'd break a string. Jakob used to break strings all the time when he played. He was the best of the three, with Peter barely able to manage chord transitions and completely afraid of singing. The fire died down as Niklas played, and once the flame was gone he stopped and they sat watching the coals for a long while. Niklas wanted to look at the stars so they got up and walked out toward the road where you got the best view. Niklas led the way through the dark clumps of trees and tall grass near the driveway. The pale gray sheen of night lay across the shed and road; the stars splashed in their millions overhead. The great stripe of the Milky Way was clearly visible. Peter found the Big Dipper and gazed for a while, then unsuccessfully looked for Orion. He asked Niklas, who pointed out the three stars of his belt almost absentmindedly, then went back to whatever he was looking at. The world was utterly still, though they stood there long enough that the night sky must have rotated a little bit. Niklas wondered if Jakob ever got to look at the night sky in prison; wondered if he'd have to get reacquainted with the stars once released, if his window ever caught moonlight, or if any of them did in prison. How depraved must you be to take the moon and the stars away from somebody.

After an age, when the stars had surely spun in the heavens, like birds on a wire, the boys both of a sudden knew it was time, and wordlessly hucked it back through the dark woods to the cabin. They went to the fire, unzipped their flies, and pissed out the last of the glowing orange with a hiss. They lingered on the acrid smell of woodsmoke and piss which had become, against all odds, nostalgic. Peter opened a beer. Niklas bade him goodnight and went inside. Once down on the cot he remembered something with a jolt and felt for the envelope with his brother's letters, which was safely in its place, plump with its proper contents. Relieved, Niklas turned over, took a few deep breaths, and passed out.

* * *

Peter rose uncharacteristically early the next morning. The sun had yet to break through the trees, leaving the bite in a chilly morning that was a premonition of winter. Peter trudged up to the driveway fighting his usual hangover, wishing he had a bit of blow to wake himself up. The dew on the grass licked his ankles, and the cool air filled his lungs with a sweetness he did not associate with breathing. He stood by his car for a minute contemplating the morning ahead and listening to the birds conversing in the trees above his head.

He drove a mile and a half down Liminga Road, then took a right and drove down a long driveway with a semi-truck parked in the front yard. He was welcomed inside, his hand shaken warmly, a cup of coffee set in front of him. Andy Ahonen told him a bit about his operation, and about what he had in mind for the land. He would log most of it, leaving the creek alone because after the place was logged he'd chop it up into building lots and sell them off one by one. He asked Peter about his own life, but Peter was nearly mute with shame at this point. He made a few hurried excuses and left after fifteen minutes with a contract in his pocket for twenty-eight thousand five hundred dollars. While walking down the Ahonens' gravel driveway he searched his soul for joy but found only doubt. He almost threw up again as he got into his car, realizing his stomach was utterly empty—all he could do was dry heave. He decided he needed breakfast and headed for the Suomi. After part of a western omelet and two more cups of coffee he called Tina from his corner table, hoping she would remind him what a timely and important victory he'd scored. She picked up after three rings.

"Hey, Peter."

"Hey, sweetheart. I've got good news."

"Oh my God. Peter. I thought you'd be gone another week. How much?"

"Twenty-eight five, and I'll be home tonight."

Peter listened to her breathe for several moments. "Oh Peter. Oh." And her sobs were audible if thoroughly muffled.

"It's OK, shh, sweetheart, it's ok. I talked to Niklas. He signed the Quit Claim. It's all good. We're in the clear, at least for a good while."

Tina said something unintelligible. Peter could hear Olly and Josh fighting or playing in the background. Tina blew her nose.

OK. I'll see you tonight," she said. "Tell... tell Niklas he's welcome for dinner. Um, if he'd like that."

"I will. I will. All right, I love you. I'll see you tonight." And he hung up.

Peter took out the check and looked at it with deep confusion. Now that the objective was secured he was able to see at whose expense it came, regardless of how little choice he'd had. Would anyone risk not being able to afford their child's leukemia treatments? His omelet sat unfinished on the table before him. He thought about calling Uncle Hannu, but Hannu would be supportive and understanding which would surely make Peter sob like the little boy he felt like.

Poor Niklas might still be passed out in the cabin. Peter wilted at the prospect of informing Niklas of the done deal in his current state. Even last night the sale, in Nik's mind, must still have been hypothetical. Peter considered his options. He took a long sip of water and took out his phone, dialing Tina's contact.

"Hello?"

"Hey, sweetheart. I'm so sorry about this. I won't be home tonight, I'll be home tomorrow afternoon. Some issues came up that I need to be here in person to sort out."

"Peter?"

"Yes?"

"Is the deal still on? Or are you going to call me tomorrow and tell me it's fallen through?"

"No, Tina. The place is sold. I'll see you tomorrow afternoon. Maybe evening. I love you."

"... I love you. Drive safe."

Peter returned his phone to his jacket pocket, paid for his meal and left out the front door, tensely awash in the warmth of the midday autumn sun.

* * *

Niklas came awake slowly, thinking it was far earlier than it was, misjudging the light that filtered through the little windows to the east. He'd dreamed of Jakob in Chicago. It was the sort of dream or set of dreams where you have to actively reorient yourself in the real world when you wake, and throughout the morning you are continually reminded of things that you aren't sure are dream fragments or real memories.

Niklas considered the last conversation he'd had with Jakob before he went to prison. On the bus ride to Marquette, he'd wallowed in a kind of pathetic vindictive pride. Up until the end of high school nearly everything Niklas had ever done was erased by the scale of Jakob's achievements. Even a good day at hockey practice or a great game of Niklas' always paled in comparison to Jakob's, and it soon became that even the victories for Niklas were bitter. He wondered whether his taste in women was affected by this. Was he so entranced with fraternal competition that Jakob's clear advantage when it came to conventionally beautiful women made him redefine what beauty really was, just so he didn't have to lose at yet another thing to his stupid older brother? A few times, Jakob had brought Niklas around to hang out with his older friends in high school and every time, without exception, Niklas tangibly felt their disappointment. And then Jakob went off to Chicago and the tables completely turned. Ten years later, Niklas finally had a better job and was clearly far less depressed. And yet, because this victory was contingent upon his brother's suffering, he couldn't enjoy it. He was out on a snowshoe hike the week after Christmas with Peter when his phone rang and the news about Jakob's sentencing arrived. And, ludicrous though this was, for a second Niklas blamed himself and cursed his misbegotten sense of victory for bringing down this misery upon his childhood hero.

Niklas rose, feeling the stiffness of his joints and put on his boots to head outside. Peter's car was gone from its usual spot. Niklas decided not to call him for a while. He went to head inside

144

for breakfast but the motion made the world spin and then he was on his knees vomiting over the edge of the porch. This lasted several minutes. When it was over, Niklas' vision was blurry around the edges. He hadn't realized he'd gotten that drunk. Inside again, he sifted through the small pocket of his backpack in search of his toothbrush and toothpaste. He found both right next to the dirty envelope of Jakob's letters, as well as his little blue pipe and rolled up baggie of weed.

He brushed his teeth at the sink and gulped water before gathering the filthy envelope in the pocket of his hoodie and heading out for a walk. The screen door slammed behind him, and now that he was fully awake, he recognized the crisp sunny day for the specimen it was. The sky was empty of clouds and so blue it hurt to look at. The trees swayed gently now, then were still, then started up again and the grass and pine needles underfoot sparkled with dew in the sunlight. Squinting and bowing his head he headed for the aspen thicket beyond which the creek of his childhood wound ever eastward.

≈ 19 ≈

Niklas sat with his back to a birch tree and watched the light mottling as it spilled through the thickly woven spruce and hemlock boughs above. A few slivers of sparkling sunlight cast strange hieroglyphs on the quilt of fallen pine needles, mostly dead. Niklas spat on a spot of sunlight beside him, watching an ant struggle through the sludge. He watched the ant's progress for quite a while.

Looking up through the trees, he tried to count the different shades of orange but lost count at twenty-nine. He tried to take a nap but his racing thoughts kept his mind in fifth gear. He thought about his dream for a good long while. He stared at the pine standing sturdy before him and thought about all those hundreds of chairs he'd mended for shows in Chicago he'd never bothered to actually go and see. He figured they'd be gone back to Milwaukee soon by the tone of Peter's voice last night. Unconsciously his fingers closed around Jakob's letters in the pouch of his hoodie. He took out the second one and flattened it against his thigh.

> Dear Niklas,
>
> I remember going to church as a little kid and spending the entire first portion up until communion feeling sorry for myself. An hour of boredom might as well be a year; when you're on the wrong end of it, it feels like forever. I wish I could go tell those little boys that were us to relax, that an hour is nothing. All you need to do is find a nice corner of your head and the hour will be up soon. But it's been nine months and I'm tired, Nik, I'm so goddamn tired, and all the nice corners of my head are fraught with shadows, only good for retreat when the alternative is agony.
>
> I've walked the distance back to our old house in Marquette, and then some. The yard is about an eighth of a mile and I do forty laps every day. I've been walking since my third week in, so maybe I've walked to Alaska. I feel

like the last time I did any math was back when I was selling weed. My friend Tim gave me this Steinbeck novel called Cannery Row. That was one of your favorites, right? Anyway, it's the best thing I've read since we were kids.

I'm running out of words and it scares me. That's one of the things this place does to you. It's the most backwards thing—they want to reduce violence so they throw all the violent people in a cage and then let them out only after they've had literal years to nurse their resentments? There's a funny thing that happens with new guys. When you're a new guy, to yourself, you're always the exception. You walk in on day one and somebody's yelling about hating their meds or not getting their meds, or not getting a straight answer from someone official about a visit or a phone call or a parole hearing, and to you, the new guy, it's like, wow, this really is the loony bin. So you sit and enjoy it for a week or so, and then it starts to get old. You just want to work out, or read, or nap, or just sit in peace, to forget for one moment that everyone's locked up for the biggest mistakes of their lives. But the screams, the outbursts, the psychosis, it persists. Maybe you push back a little with someone—"Hey, buddy, keep it down a little, huh?" But it only gets worse. Then one day you finish cleaning out the showers and you go to make a phone call but all the phones are tied up and so you go to take a nap but your new Mexican neighbor is blasting music you've only ever heard leaking out from the back of restaurant kitchens, and the guard on yard duty is a new guy who doesn't understand that you've walked laps at this time basically every day for the last five months, that these walks constitute possibly the last shreds of your salvageable personhood, that their absence would mean a loss of such devastating proportions and now you are now a screaming sobbing mess, and, sure enough, there's a new inmate, distinguishable by the still-visible creases on his uniform, watching you with a mixture of horror and pity and telling himself that as bad as things might get on the inside, he'll never get like that. He'll never be as fucked as you are.

Jesus, Nik, I'm sorry. This probably will scare you more than reassure you. Dad told me in his last letter that spilling my guts was a good thing in moderation. It's real, he says, and keeping in honest touch with people I love will tether me to the world. But I'm so tired, Nik.

I remember asking you to pray for me last time. Well, here's the deal; whatever you've been doing, do the opposite. Stop praying, or start if you never got around to it.

Love,
Jakob

Niklas folded the letter and stuffed it back in its soiled envelope. Secondhand claustrophobia washed over him, the letter having dredged up a number of low moments in the hospital after Jakob went into the pen. Niklas remembered a story Hannu had read to him and Jakob as little boys, which offered that hell was a place without any birds. He'd taken it literally at the time but now considered that hell, without birds, was probably also devoid of fresh air and warm sun and cool breeze, that birds might just be a metaphor. That what they really meant was that hell was a place where there *couldn't* be any birds, a place with bars on the windows and uniforms of flimsy polyester, a place where the meals were, intentionally, as unrecognizably food as the inmates were people.

Niklas wept for his brother, remembering all too well the suffocation that sets in when somebody takes your freedom completely away. He felt, too, that he'd been wrong to not write back, wrong to think that the phone calls were enough. It was more acutely painful now that atonement for his silence was out of reach. Either Jakob would be paroled for Thanksgiving or he wouldn't, and surely that news would come in a phone call from Hannu when the decision was made. Niklas realized, in a new and devastatingly real way, that he'd have to tell Jakob about the sale, presuming Peter didn't drop the ball. The thought of staticky silence, of Darth Vader breath on the other end of the telephone— no, here was a chance to kill two birds with one stone. He would write to Jakob, thereby both avoiding the phone conversation and scratching the guilty itch of never having written back. There was a measure of guilt attached to avoiding the call via a letter, but

148

Niklas brushed this aside. He wiped his eyes. The wind clocked around to the north and Niklas could hear the invisible flutes sounding in snatches from the tops of the trees. A long, low note vibrated warmly in his ears, the sound like a conch shell. He got to his feet and before he knew what he was doing set a course for the tool shed out back behind the cabin.

Inside, out of the sunlight, it must've been fifteen degrees cooler. It smelled old; old wooden handles of axes and shovels and rakes, their rusting metal blades and points, a fence post driver leaning precariously on a bucket of rusting nails. A pair of ancient snowshoes hung beside the window. An assortment of chisels hung above the table, a relic of Uncle Jussi's long hours spent carving little animal figurines out of wood. Niklas remembered the Christmas when he was ten when Jussi had given one to each of them; to Jakob, a lion with a rather inflated mane; to Peter, a crow whose thin, splintery feet had broken so many times it looked like the bird was shitting glue, like it was running down the bird's legs; and to Niklas, a bear that Jussi insisted was a grizzly, poised on its haunches or maybe just sitting, it was hard to tell. Afterward they'd all gone and had a big snowball fight, which turned nasty when Peter rubbed little Niklas' face in the snow for laughing at "poopy bird," at which point Jakob rubbed Peter's face in the snow, decided he was cold, and went inside for hot chocolate before Peter could get revenge.

In the shed, Niklas' eye fell on the chisels, and dawn broke in his mind. In the corner, an old rocking chair, mostly in pieces, reminded him of his days in the shop spent mending, re-staining, repainting and reupholstering chairs for shows he never saw. He'd gotten pretty good by the time he wigged out and had to bail on Chicago and the Lyric. The light in his mind grew. He stuck his head out the door and looked into the woods. He swung around to look back in the corner where all those tools were piled up, and searched with his eyes... *there*. Behind a hoe, its rust blending nicely with the worn studs of the wall, hidden further by the shadows of similar, competing objects, was a two-man crosscut saw that appeared in working order. He managed to fish it out without knocking over the pickax or the hoe. It was lighter than he anticipated, and a little flimsier. He almost tripped over a barrel stave on his way out. He left the musty shade of the tool shed and headed back to the cabin. Peter would be back soon. Niklas set the saw on the front steps in a place it couldn't possibly be missed and went around back to stoke the fire and make himself a cup of coffee.

* * *

To Peter's surprise, Jim Markham's battered F-150 pulled into the driveway just a few seconds after he'd turned his own car off. They shook hands, Jim's calloused mitt crushing Peter's pianist hand. His stomach churned when he felt the check in his pocket.

"How are you, son?" Peter could detect a hint of something grave through Jim's stoic U.P. neighborliness.

"Oh, hanging in there. You?"

"Oh, ya, I'm fine, I'm doing just fine. Cynthia's got the kids over at her sister's so I thought I'd drop by. Got a few chores in town."

"Well, it's always good to see you."

Jim gazed at Peter out of the corner of his eye. "I spoke to your uncle Hannu on da phone yesterday, day before. He's worried about you boys. Says you guys are getting rid of the place."

"Just sold it, in fact." Peter couldn't meet his eye. "We're staying tonight and heading back to Milwaukee tomorrow."

"Say, Pete," said Jim, continuing with his own thread of the conversation. "Are you guys in some kind of trouble?"

"We lost our jobs, Jim. Or Nik's lost his, I'm on furlough which basically means I'm on deck for the chopping block."

"I thought Nik was at da lumberyard."

"Uh, yeah. He is."

"I mean, something other than that. Now you can say it's none of my business. That's OK too. Just making sure you guys aren't in some crazy debt or something."

Down the hill the screen door slammed and Niklas came out of the cabin squinting in the harsh sunlight. He waved and walked over to where they were standing astride Jim's truck. He shook Jim's hand then looked them both in the face.

"Did I interrupt?"

Peter clapped him on the shoulder. "No, you're fine, Nik. Jim was just asking about my boy. He's real sick, Jim, that's the problem. Now let's go inside and have ourselves a drink."

Jim nodded without missing a beat. He went to a corner and pulled a pint of schnapps from beneath a loose floorboard.

He winked at the boys. "Jussi and Hannu always kept one in the chamber. Have a snort." Peter took a long pull and Niklas a medium sized one. Jim recapped the bottle then replaced it beneath the floorboards.

Niklas cracked his knuckles. "So, Pete."

"Sold to Andy Ahonen for twenty-eight five. He wrote me a check which we can split once we get back home."

Jim whistled and Niklas shrugged to acknowledge that it was a comparatively vast sum of money.

"That's what, just under ten thousand per?"

Peter frowned. "It's just under fifteen. Fourteen something."

"So Jakob gets nothing?" asked Niklas coldly.

Jim looked at Peter in clear agreement with Niklas.

"Um, we'll figure that out," Peter ducked for cover. "We'll figure it out later," he said again, looking everywhere but across the table.

"Dude. We're taking nine each and giving the rest to Dad. I will die on this hill."

Jim inhaled through his nose. "I'm sure you boys will figure it out. Meantime, I should be going soon. Nik, what was that beautiful old crosscut doing lying in front of the door?"

Niklas smiled in a way that worried Peter. "Gonna make a chair, Jim. I figured we can't leave this place for good and not take a piece with us. I used to mend the chairs for the prop shop back when I worked in theatre. We're gonna cut down a nice maple and I'm gonna make it into a chair one day when it's seasoned. I can do upholstery and everything," he said proudly.

Jim nodded his approval. "Well, I'll come by and see you boys tomorrow before you take off. Good luck with that tree, Nik. Keep your head up." And he left without ceremony.

When his truck had rumbled away Peter looked at Niklas with exasperation. "You're going to cut down a fucking tree and make it into a chair?"

"No, *we're* going to cut down a tree, and then, yeah, I'm going to make a chair."

"Who is this royal *we*?"

"You and me. Don't you know how that saw works?"

"The hell I do. Jesus," said Peter. "I wanted to go home today. But I called Tina and said we were staying the night. I thought we could camp out by our old spot by the creek." He said this hoping to distract Niklas from his foolish pulp cutting impulses.

"That sounds great. There's no way I was going home without camping," Niklas said. "But seriously. After the tree."

They argued for another twenty minutes about this until Niklas pointed out that if they were sawing instead of arguing the tree would be half cut by now, and finally, Peter booted up and huffed his way out the door and into the woods.

* * *

A sort of trance had come over Niklas. He was buzzing from three cups of coffee and had spent the two hours waiting for Peter and nursing his chair idea. He was now fixated on choosing the right tree, tromping back and forth in the woods and generally mystifying Peter as to what exactly was going on. He stood in front of a great white pine, dead by all accounts, brittle of branch and naked of any bristles. Its trunk was about a foot in diameter.

"What do you think?" he demanded of Peter.

"Uh, dude. I'm not really sure what we're looking for?"

"Something I can build out of! Pine is what theaters always used, but I think that's just because it's soft and cheap. But so, I need something big enough that I can mill some of it down and carve, like, those fancy ends to armrests. You know? Sometimes they're ornate, but maybe that's just the fancy shit we used at the opera. Anyway," Niklas continued, mania in his eyes, "We need to find a dead tree that's big enough. Hence this fellow," and he gestured to the dead white pine before them.

Peter did his best to humor him. "Well, uh. Yeah, I think that's a good candidate. Definitely dead. Nice and thick. You sure you know how to do this safely?"

Niklas rolled his eyes and laughed. "It's never gonna be all the way safe. Just keep your head on a swivel and we'll be done in a minute." He looked up as if realizing for the first time just how tall this dead pine was. He coughed and looked back earthward at the crosscut saw in his hands. "Actually, fuck this."

They kept walking, crunching sticks and leaves and pine needles underfoot. Niklas found an old maple, its leaves just beginning to turn, and went to stand next to it. It was a little slimmer than the white pine. He rubbed its trunk with his hands approvingly. He looked at Peter and nodded.

152

"We need to cut a hitch first, in the direction we want it to fall. So you take one handle," he said to Peter, handing him one end of the saw, "and I'll take the other. We just work our way up to the trunk, find a comfortable spot... yeah, there it is... and then we just draw the saw back and forth, maintaining light pressure against the trunk." They took a few strokes back and forth, angling the saw to open a notch, trying to find a groove while the saw rattled in their hands. Fragrant little chips began to fall in two piles. Niklas regretted the saw's apparent dullness, wishing he'd remembered to look for a file in the shed, but now it was too late. The saw fell into the smooth, level back-and-forth of a groove. They cut a hitch on the southern side of the tree. As the two piles of chips and sawdust grew, a curious sensation spread out in Niklas' mind. He felt as though the saw were slowly biting its way, stroke by stroke, decade by decade, into the past, a past written in its concentric annual rings. And so, as they found a groove opposite the hitch and the saw scraped back and forth and sawdust piled up on the ground, Niklas felt the years he was cutting through.

* * *

In the first dozen pulls Niklas felt the recent years, the fallow years, the years after Jussi died where the land was full of ghosts and the berry bushes wilted and died untended in the summer sun. The years when the banks and the market were priming themselves to fail, flying high on Icarian thermals fueled by greed and empty from the start. He felt the paint peel on the walls of the shed, he felt the grasses and the wildflowers spring up among formerly neat rows of kale and potatoes, he felt the grass grow long in the front yard and the once proud fences trampled by vicious weather and persistent deer. No one was there to hear the flutes trickle down from the tops of the trees when the wind scraped along just right.

They paused to catch their breath. Clouds appeared and rushed quickly along to the east. Birds slowly resumed their songs as the boys' chests heaved, regaining wind. Niklas could see Peter's flushed cheeks and in them his frustration at allowing himself to get roped into this job. The day had grown chillier and Niklas was glad to be hard at work, the exertion keeping him warm. He wiggled his end of the saw to signal to Peter that he wished to resume.

They found the groove quickly and the saw bit more deeply into the tree's history. It bit into 2005, the year after Jussi's death when the snow stayed until July and no one took their coats off all summer. The frost that year killed crops all over the U.P., decimating the orchard and with Jussi gone no one had the heart to revive it the following year. He'd left the land to the boys who were all too busy trying and mostly failing to make their own way in the world.

Sawdust and chipped wood coated their forearms as they sawed into the winter of '04. Jussi and Hannu were on snowshoes, measuring a patch of ground already sparsely planted for the sake of a new fence, higher than the last one, which had failed to keep the deer out. They paced and argued about whether a hundred feet of fence was enough, or whether they'd need more. The sky was gray, and the snow fell gently: not a storm but lake effect snow, for Superior had yet to freeze over. They settled on a hundred feet of fence and walked back through the trees to the cabin. Hannu let Jussi lead their way back, knowing how he loved tromping through fresh snow, blazing a trail. They warmed up with a beer by the woodstove. It was early afternoon; they decided to take the snowshoes out to the old Freda stamp mill and make a fire in the smokestack. Jussi loved excursions to the lake and readily agreed, reminding Hannu to bring along their floorboard pint of schnapps. When they arrived they stared out long at the heaving, angry lake as the snow came lazily down. Hannu said he was cold, so they walked across the ruins and into the woods by the stack, collecting sticks and branches and then shedding their snowshoes and climbing up and in. It was a relief to be out of the wind. Quickly Hannu made a fire. They squatted over it, warming their hamstrings and butts and the backs of their legs. They talked about the football game set for that Thursday evening, the Packers versus the Saints. Jussi spoke reverently of the Packer's starstudded offense, sending Hannu off on a nostalgic tangent about Lombardi and the Packers of old.

Jussi asked Hannu if he smelled something funny. It did smell like burning rubber, but he shrugged, and continued talking about Jerry Kramer, a guard who played under Lombardi and wrote a famous book about it. A second later Jussi yelped and they both looked down to see the left cuff of his pants ablaze. He hopped around while Hannu scrambled, eventually nearly dumping the pint of schnapps they'd brought along on to the flaming pant leg, actually pitching a thick handful of fire-quenching snow. The fire went out. Jussi began to laugh about it. Hannu told him to roll up his charred pant leg, which revealed a nasty burn. Jussi didn't care. He was shocked and a little bit delighted to have been "fully on fire" as he kept saying. Eventually, Hannu relaxed, and it wasn't until later that evening after dinner that Jussi mentioned it again. The size of the burn seemed to have increased, the redness and swelling angrier and beginning to fill with a kind of pus. They got some burn cream in town and went to bed, but the next day it looked much worse.

Hannu drove Jussi to the Portage Emergency Room, where they blanched at the severity of Jussi's burn and told Hannu to take him to Marquette for treatment. Driving east with Jussi in the passenger seat, Hannu felt black dread beginning to rise in the pit of his stomach. He wasn't sure why. It was a burn on the lower calf. A hell of a long way from the heart. At the hospital in Marquette, Jussi was whisked away down a long white hallway. Hannu sat and waited. An hour or so later Jussi was led back out, walking with a slight limp, yet breathing heavily and unable to focus on Hannu's greeting and inquiries. His grip when Hannu hugged him was surprisingly weak. On the highway headed home, he said he was just tired. But his breathing speeded up, and he kept looking one way, then the other. He babbled in response to a question from Hannu. That was when Hannu turned the car around. They almost made it back to the hospital. Hannu was carrying Jussi like a baby in his arms when the spittle stopped bubbling, when the breath went from his chest and the life from his eyes. He was twenty yards from the hospital's sliding front doors.

Much later, Hannu learned it was sepsis and, therefore, totally the hospital's fault. But that didn't matter, really. What mattered was that Hannu had been too in love with the sound of his own takes about the Packers in the seventies to recognize the smell of burning rubber in his nose. A week later, after the funeral, knee-deep in grief and desperately grasping for something solid, he accepted Jim Markham's invitation to stay a while. They drank coffee and prayed and worked on the house. Jim had a busted radiator he was looking to fix, so one day the two of them went at it. They figured out the issue and Hannu got to work on it while

Jim took a dump. It was then that the radiator exploded. Shock kept the pain at bay for a few minutes. Jim came barreling out of the bathroom right away, hearing Hannu's roar and then seeing the dinner-plate-sized red gashes, the burns that streaked his whole torso. The man on the other end of 911 said it would be an hour at least until an emergency vehicle could reach them out in Liminga. Stay on the phone, the operator said. Yell and swear at me if you have to. I don't care. Scream loud as you want. Just stay with me.

Then the saw bit into '03 when Jussi was still alive and well. The lingonberry patch was thoroughly weeded and crotch spreaders kept the fruit trees properly erect. The fences were flush to the ground and any spots where thieving rabbits had burrowed under were promptly filled in. A neat yet massive pile of firewood sat beside the cabin, covered by two weather-beaten sheets of plywood. The front porch was tidy and the wildflowers from the western corner of the property were in a vase where Hannu had set them during a visit some months prior. Jakob and Niklas visited relatively often and always together, clutching their fly rods and duffel bags full of camping gear. They'd stumble hungover back to the cabin after an early morning of fishing, and sweat it out all afternoon with Hannu and Jussi in the orchard. The flutes in the trees, forever though they are, were the loudest and clearest during this time. Or perhaps everyone was merely happy enough to hear them. In any case it was the happiest of times, golden days that were only ever real when they were actually happening and now that they're gone feel a bit like a dream everyone had together that's mostly similar but a little different. This was the time when Niklas and Jakob, and Peter to a lesser extent, had come to really love this land and their Uncle and all it stood for. It was a time when the cries of little boys becoming men could be heard along with snapping sticks and rushing water and the wind in the trees. It was a time when the snowshoes in the shed were covered in fresh snow five months a year, when the gully at the corner of the property was littered with empty beer cans, the cans themselves torn to shreds with bullet holes, and at night the cabin lit up with candles and righteous voices clustered around a euchre game. It was a time when the maple they were cutting had green, pungent branches and sap that dripped slowly earthward. If the most recent years were defined by death, this era was defined by robust life.

Then came the early years when Jussi was learning to tend the land. Hannu, much younger then and paunchless, was around like clockwork on the weekends. He taught Jussi many things about tools and carpentry and tending an orchard, often teaching himself simultaneously. Sometimes he had his little boys along, grabbing his huge hands with their own tiny ones, occasionally taking turns riding on his shoulders as he surveyed the property and marked off locations for berry patches, scouted for mothership chokecherry clumps to raze with the chainsaw, tallied up yards of fencing to be purchased at the Tractor Supply in town. Slowly the place came together, the outhouse was built, the lingonberry bushes spread with purpose, fences were put up and mended, the chokecherry clumps receded, and in their place Hannu planted pines and birches galore. Often when the wind picked up the two men would stop their work and listen to the flutes in the tops of the trees, hearing it more and more every day. This was the era of the land coming to life once again.

* * *

Peter paused and slumped over in a sweaty huff. He held up his hand for a moment while his breath billowed in clouds and filtered up into the trees. Niklas wiped his brow. The saw was doing good work and the piles of temporal sawdust were growing steadily. In spite of this, they were barely a quarter of the way through. Niklas wiggled the saw and they got back to work.

Next came the years before Jussi; the years of Bruce Gregson and ATVs and bullets tearing into the sides of hills after passing through old beer cans arranged on sawhorses. Not Bruce's, of course—just the local kids who figured out that nobody cared what they did on the property. It was a place where music was blasted, virginities were lost, new drugs were tried, where younger siblings tentatively sipped warm beers and tried not to look nervous as their older brothers tore up the ground with vehicles and guns. Around this time there was far too much noise to ever hear the music in the trees.

The saw bit more deeply with their renewed fervor, cutting through the eighties when Hannu was studying to be a teacher at Northern and Olli Jr. was off in New York chasing profit, doing spreadsheets. Teemu was still alive these days though Violetta sadly wasn't. She'd gotten lung cancer after almost forty years of hosting parties and chain-smoking cigarettes. Her death had been a blow to the whole community in Hancock, and her parties were sorely missed long after she was gone. Her death aged Teemu two decades overnight. He grew weak and had to stop fishing and hunting with his dogs, and if you asked any of his friends that's what killed him. He'd long since sold the mill and made enough to comfortably rot and leave his children a decent chunk of change. Without Violetta, he was never entirely happy again, though his son Jussi had always been able to make him laugh.

They were nearly halfway way through the tree. Niklas felt strong as sweat gathered on his brow. Peter was heaving but laboring. They were making good progress.

Niklas drew the saw back and forth, pulling with new energy. Now the saw bit into the first half of the midcentury, when the land was occupied by a mill and its associated furnishings. The mill and surrounding area were populated by tough, calloused men who worked hard and earned just enough but not very much. Some of them drank, and if anyone ever ran across the site of the old workers' outhouse, beside it they would find buried a pile of whiskey and beer bottles. American greed was in its infancy and just beginning to show its ugly temper; men still fished and hunted and loved the land but people were beginning to worry if their sons would be able to do as they had done. Things were like this for many years, years when people acknowledged the threat of robber barons but didn't fuss enough to do anything about them, and so "business" and "progress" ate away at wild places uninhibited. The saw bit through these years hungrily, eager to get beyond them, eager to dig more deeply into the past.

They'd found a deadly rhythm. The sawdust piles were growing quickly now, the saw blade nearly two thirds of the way through the maple's thick trunk.

Peter raised a hand. "One more break then we finish her off?"

Niklas nodded his assent. They caught their breath, wiped their brows, and once again found the groove for the last stretch of sawing. Niklas gave the tree an experimental push to see if it would buckle. It didn't and they redoubled their efforts, heaving the blade back and forth.

The saw bit past the war and into the thirties and twenties, the years when Teemu brawled in taverns and before that when he brawled on the ice at hockey games. The saw bit further backward into Teemu's childhood when he and his sister Sofia were sick and saved their parents' lives from the Italian Hall disaster in 1913. It bit into the years before Teemu and his sister, the years when Olli Sr. and Ana were newlyweds and back, and back, to when Olli would go out with his dear friend Jussi fishing, brawling, hunting, drinking. These were the wild years, the years when much of the Great North was still relatively untouched, when the grandest of white pines hadn't been pilfered by the profiteers out east, when the streams burst with trout and the deer romped aplenty through the swampy hills. These were years suited for men like Jussi and Olli, young men who loved the woods and drinking and fighting and each other. These were men who would have fought bears if they could have, and probably would have won, too. These years were very hard but nobody remembers them as hard; they merely remember the demigods that lived through them. The saw bit through these joyful years with ease, the final few strokes of the rusted blade, and then finally the tree began to crack and topple over and Niklas barked "Timber!" and it fell backward with a crash, breaking the spell.

* * *

They dragged the felled maple about ten feet before Peter gave up. The tree was proving nearly impossible to drag out. They needed one of those log skidders that they used to drag huge trunks out of the woods. Niklas realized he hadn't limbed the tree either; that was what was making the dragging so difficult. He straightened up abruptly.

"Look, why don't I just wait till we get the chainsaw from Jim?"

"I thought he was just swinging by to see us off."

"Yeah, I know. Can I take your car and go ask him to borrow his chainsaw?"

Peter took a deep breath. "Sure. We need to be out by noon, though. One at the latest."

"All right. I'll get beer."

They walked back up the hill through the woods toward the cabin. The sun was seconds away from falling behind the trees in the southwest. At the front porch, Peter took his keys from his pocket and tossed them to Niklas.

"Don't fucking crash it."

"Thanks. I won't."

Peter watched from the porch as Niklas sauntered over to the car, hopped in, and tore off in reverse a little too quickly for Peter's comfort. The poor kid was a bit out of his head but securely in the center of his own heart.

* * *

Niklas called his father on the short drive out to Liminga.

"Hey, bud."

"Hey, Dad. What's up?"

"Oh, I'm just in the kitchen chopping vegetables. Mom's out with her friend, Lena. What's up with you? I got a call from Don Klingberg."

"Oh, yeah. Yeah, uh. Peter and I are at Jussi's cabin."

"How are things?"

"Good. Beautiful. The same mostly, though the orchard's gone to hell."

"I'm sorry to hear that."

"Yeah, uh…" Niklas began to choke up. "Look, please don't be angry, I didn't mean to…" Niklas was blubbering now.

"Shh, bud. Buddy. Hey. What's going on?"

"Peter, uh. It's all fucked, dad. I don't know where to begin."

"Begin where you want. I'm sure you'll get there."

Niklas took a breath as he stopped at the stop sign by Schmidt's Corner, then accelerated again through the empty crossroads. "Well, so Peter's kid has leukemia. And he's in some serious money trouble. I don't know exactly what, but he lost his job last year, and apparently almost did time. You know he worked for Wells Fargo… right. So he got me to agree to come up and sell the place. I don't even know how. It just didn't feel like saying no was a choice, sitting there with him and hearing about, like, real debts and his sick kid. I don't know. There's just so much going on here. You know? I'm sorry, Dad."

Hannu paused for a moment in case Niklas had more to say. His tone was exceedingly gentle. "Well, bud, you don't have to apologize to me. That's your place, and I think Jussi would be happy to hear that you're helping Peter out of trouble. I'm… I don't doubt it's been hard on you."

"It's just bullshit, though. He made choices. I feel bad about his kid but, like, his bar tab from last year would probably cover the treatment. It's fucking bullshit. We put so much work—you put so much work into it. And it's all we have left of Jussi." He started to sob again.

"I know, bud. I know. It's… Try to be easy on yourself, here. I know that's easier said than done. But don't beat yourself up for being generous."

"But we're also selling the place without Jakob's permission."

"I know, bud. And I'm sure that's hard. But if I were you, I might have done the same thing." This stopped Niklas dead in his tracks.

"Huh?"

"Taking care of your people is more important than that piece of land, bud. As much as I'm sure you'll miss it. It's never wrong to take care of your people."

These seemed to be the words Niklas needed to hear. Once again, he was astounded at his father's ability to diagnose what was sticking in his craw, even over the phone. He turned right down the gravel Superior Shores Road, a hundred yards from Jim's driveway.

"Thanks, Dad. I'm nearly at Jim's."

"Give him my love."

"I will. Bye, Dad."

"Take care, bud."

It wasn't until Niklas was out of the car, goosebumps on his bare arms from the evening breeze that set the trees astir, that it occurred to him his dad had known about everything before he'd even answered the phone.

* * *

Niklas drove up right as Jim was giving it an extra shake behind his truck after pissing. He made a show of wiping his hand off on his jeans and laughed. Once seated at the kitchen table, a steaming cup of coffee before him, Niklas got straight to the point.

"Could I borrow your chainsaw for an afternoon? I'll drop it back off tomorrow on our way out."

"Oh sure. I didn't think you were going to leave, though."

Niklas looked confused. "How do you mean?"

"Oh, I seen this before. When it comes time to up and leave, some guys just can't. My brother, Floyd, was like dat. Dats why he's da one still living on da family place."

"If I'd a known that was an option…" Niklas shook his head. "I'm in too deep, Jim. I feel like a little boy. You know? Like a boy too little."

"Ha! That goes away a bit when ya get old but never all da way. I felt like dat when your dad had his accident working on my radiator. Completely helpless. Oh, it was bad." He looked grave as he fell silent. Niklas sipped his coffee. Gene Wilder made some quiet crack on the TV.

"What you need da saw for?"

"I gotta limb the tree Pete and I cut for that chair I'm going to make. I tried to drag it outta the woods and couldn't."

"You guys really went and did that? Ha! Dats great. You'll have to chop up da trunk too if it's gonna fit in Peter's little car. You good for all that?"

"Oh, I'm fine," said Niklas, shaking his head for emphasis.

"All right. If you lose an arm, your dad'll come for my ass."

"I'll be careful."

Jim and Niklas sat for a while talking about the Lions and the Packers, about how Jim thought they were in for a cold winter, about how to mill down the lumber Niklas would need in order to build a halfway decent, sittable chair. There was a long silence, then they both rose almost simultaneously. Cynthia walked in from the bedroom hallway. She smiled at Niklas. He smiled back.

"When are ya leaving?" she asked.

"Tomorrow's the plan. I would make a fuss about staying longer, but I got work and Peter's wife'll kill him if he pushes it back another night. We were gonna go back today, but…" he shook his head. Cynthia nodded and shook hers too.

"You want to take a sauna before you head out?" Jim asked.

"Oh, I wish. Peter and I need to see some people tonight. I'll come by tomorrow before we get on the road."

"All right. Lemme get that chainsaw for you." Jim got up and went outside. His footsteps receded after thumping down the front steps.

"You guys gonna be back soon den?" Cynthia asked from her spot in the living room.

"Oh, I'm sure. Least I will be. I'll try to bring my brother this winter, too, once he's free."

"Oh, dat'll be good," she said, nodding.

Niklas shook his head. "I know this isn't how it ever works, but I wish I lived here. I mean, imagine never having to leave. But would it change, then? Would it make a difference, or would it feel the same as now, just less special?"

Cynthia looked at him quizzically, then smiled. "You know, my whole damn life I been waiting for tomorrow. But den I wake up, and it's always today!" She shook her head, then went to the sink to rinse Jim's coffee cup. "You be safe wit dat chainsaw," she said with her back to him. "Come back before you leave." Jim thumped back up the steps and the front door opened.

"Oh we will. Bye, Cynthia."

Jim had set the chainsaw on the ground next to the trunk of Peter's car. He beckoned Niklas out the door.

"Gave the chain some oil just the other day. Tank should be nearly full. Now I know you know, but lemme just show ya," he said. "So I can tell your dad I did when you lop off a couple a fingers."

* * *

Niklas tore into town for beer and sausages, hustling back to the property in a race against the falling sun. In his mind, he collected all the necessary items for an evening: the four-man Coleman tent plus its rain fly for what little heat retention it would offer, to be found in the corner of the cabin; the iron skillet from the stove; warm clothes, food, and pot, all from his backpack and shopping bags; sleeping bags, balled up inside the tent; and some paper, a pencil, and a headlamp to write to Jakob. Niklas left the chainsaw in Peter's trunk and made for the porch, where Peter was reading a novel in a rocking chair. As Niklas got closer, he could see it was the copy of Steinbeck's *Cannery Row* he'd brought in the other morning from the shitter, unable to abandon Doc and Mack and the boys mid-chapter on the dusty shelf of the outhouse.

"I wasn't sure you remembered how," Niklas shot acidly as he went by. Several seconds later, Peter looked up.

"Huh?"

Niklas considered whether the insult was worth repeating. "How is it?" he asked, nodding toward the slim volume.

"Makes me wanna bring back a stack so I can start reading at home. We all used to read so much, remember?"

"I remember."

"You get the chainsaw from Jim?"

"It's in the car."

"You doing that tonight?"

"I'll do it in the morning. I'll be up early. It'll be your alarm."

Peter nodded and the two young men considered the night ahead, trying to forget about the rest of their lives. Peter opened his mouth to begin a thought but checked his swing several times before speaking.

"It occurred to me. We've got a fair bit of packing to do," he said. "There's… there's a lot of stuff I don't want to leave." Peter's voice grew panicky and he squinted off into the husky west.

Niklas considered for a moment. "I'm sure the Ahonens will sit on anything we ask them to set aside. I mean, right? You talked to them."

"Oh. Yeah, sure, we can ask. I guess so."

Niklas offered Peter a hand up even though the rocking chair wasn't at all shallow. Peter looked up at him, eyes brimming, and took the offered hand, rising gently. For a moment, they were unnaturally close and stiff as boards. Then each choked and leaped toward the other in a tight, wobbly hug that felt to both of them impossible to survive without. Niklas felt Peter's ribs and shoulder bones pressing into the muscle surrounding his own. They held each other until the tears went from a flow to a trickle and then came apart slowly. They shared a long, oblique look where each was looking about twenty degrees across the other. Peter's arm went around Niklas' shoulders, then Niklas' around Peter's. Niklas clapped Peter on the back.

"What say we make a fire and cook us some brats and have a couple?"

Peter smiled. "Bad night to be beer in the Keweenaw."

And they went inside to gather things for the night ahead.

* * *

Twenty minutes later, they were laden like sherpas and ready to hit the woods. Peter was dithering so Niklas waited on the porch. The first prickle of stars blinked on. Niklas found Mars and lingered on it overlong.

He felt good about the clear night—if the moon came out unimpeded they could hike out to a six-square-foot field of agate quartz that sparkled brilliantly in the moonlight. The quartz was so dense that if you stood around it with your buddies you could see their faces. It was deep in the woods over a few steep ridges. It

164

occurred to Niklas that Peter might be a hard sell. Aside from the difficulty of the hike, things seemed to be hitting Peter rather suddenly and returning to favored childhood spots in the woods might just pour salt in the wound. But returning to the sacred spot had roosted in Niklas' mind, which meant he would go, come hell or high water. It would be a crime not to pay it one last visit. Jussi had discovered the spot before Niklas was born. He'd taken great pleasure in showing it to Hannu and the boys, who'd haunted the spot ever since.

Behind him, the screen door swung open with a squeak and Peter emerged, looking a shade foolish all bundled up and overladen with gear. They'd always differed in that respect. Niklas and Jakob always packed light and were content to do without almost anything in a pinch. Niklas wasn't much bothered by this. It was fine with him to sit on porches or in living rooms alone with his thoughts, waiting for Peter to remember some item he didn't need.

They set off east into the dense woods. It was a chilly night, destined for the low forties, and the last of the day lit up their breath as it blew from their chapped lips and red noses. The property line was unmarked but for a fence post haphazardly driven every ten yards—surely, thought Niklas, a job that Hannu left to Jussi while he was off elsewhere. Peter turned on a flashlight but Niklas told him to turn it off. The moon was not out yet, or at least not yet visible to them. As they fought through a dense grove of cedars, Niklas kept his eyes peeled for the head-high pile of field stones obscured by thick bramble. He wondered where the field had been, now surely overgrown with second and third-growth forest. At the stones, he turned slaunchways to the right, and in ten paces, the world brightened ever so slightly thanks to the stand of aspen. And there was the creek, rushing over the rocks in time with a breeze, the sweet music of the woods that left the boys to stand motionless for a full minute. Then slowly, wordlessly, they got to work.

Peter set immediately to amassing a thick bed of dead pine needles in a mostly flat stretch between two huge pines. Niklas sorted out the pieces of the tent, his head "on a swivel" like the hockey coaches used to say for wildlife and the moon. He'd intentionally left the two fly-rods on their shelf in the cabin, against everything in his nature, for fear he would just get drunk and fish all night in the moonlight and be faced with penning the awful letter to Jakob in the car tomorrow on the way home.

Now as he sorted the poles, snapping each hollow piece into the adjacent pieces, Niklas considered the logistics of a dawn "fishing huck" as Jakob used to say. Accounting for limbing and sectioning the maple, he'd have to be up before first light, fish for an hour, then get to work on the lumber. He could sleep when they got back to Milwaukee, surely exhausted enough emotionally to sleep for several days. Niklas remembered his father's words on the way home from the hospital in Chicago a million years ago, words that rang true here and now: "He rides the roller coaster. High highs, low lows, and terrifying intervals careening between the two. I talked to an Ojibwe man who was a friend of my father's once about it. He said we have a kind of 'bear medicine.' We can eat and sleep for a week straight then go out in the woods or to the bars for a week without sleeping. At best, we can mitigate the worst of the roller coaster. Obviously, there are worse things than sleeping too much." Frankly, for Niklas tonight, a little bit of manic bear energy might not be the worst thing. The letter, he'd sworn to himself, must be absolutely perfect.

Peter called out when the site was padded and tent-worthy. They could have assembled the tent together blindfolded, and as it was, Niklas realized with delight, the moon had just come out. It peeked through the trees behind them and cast the world in blue and silver.

Once the tent was up, they each went off into the woods and returned with an armload of firewood, Niklas' rather larger and more diverse in thickness than Peter's. Niklas looked around, then retraced his steps back to the pile of field stones and loaded up an armful. After three trips, he had enough to make a good-sized ring, inside of which he began to build the fire. He structured and nursed the fire in his practiced way. After sitting for a minute to warm his hands, he rose and went to Peter.

Peter, meanwhile, was inspecting dinner and slugging a beer. The pack of four cheap thick Polish sausages was slit open on one side, and an onion and a potato sat chopped in the pan with a tablespoon of butter waiting to be fried. He looked up at Niklas.

"Wanna throw that on?" He gestured to the pan of onions and potatoes.

"Dude."

"What?"

Niklas shook his head. "We've camped together our whole lives and you want to cook over a fresh fire?"

"What's the problem?"

"You let it get real hot and then scrape coals over to the side."

Peter mulled this over. "Oh. Yeah. Well you guys never let me cook."

"Because of shit like that, dude. Don't blame me for your shitty instincts."

Peter looked surprised at this escalation in tone but held his tongue. Niklas sat down with his back to one of the pines. He leapt up after half a second and went rummaging through his backpack, coming up with a pen and the legal pad he'd snagged from the cabin. The head lamp was elusive, but eventually he found it in a side pocket. He'd barely sat down again when Peter spoke up.

"What's up?"

"We can't keep putting off Jakob, dude. I don't want to write this tomorrow."

"Can't we at least eat first?"

Niklas thought for a second. "Ok, sure. But don't pull some bullshit after dinner."

"I won't." But the defensiveness that bled through Peter's promise was tangible.

Niklas went back to the fire and poked at it for a few minutes, adding little but making sure any partially burned logs got turned around so their unspent side was centered above the hot coals. He went back to the tent and retrieved his water bottle, filling it at a fast clear bend fifty paces upstream. His tread was all but silent in the moonlight. The moon itself had risen, now clearly a waxing gibbous, nearly full. The fire cast flickering orange on the trees, creating a sort of half room around Peter and the tent. For a brilliant moment, Niklas caught the moon glittering off the water and shadows dancing on the trees around the tent all in the same sweep of the eye. And then he was back beside the fire.

The fire had burned bright and hot and had settled into the prolonged burn sponsored by only its largest logs, smoldering orange and gray and black, peeling and flickering, ever restless, presenting a bird's eye view of the sea. Niklas found a good poking stick and shuffled the hottest coals into a little pile between two rocks. He retrieved the pan of butter and onions and potatoes and placed it on the rocks above the hot coals. Peter was on to his second beer. Niklas asked for his first and was tossed a cold Miller Lite. He cracked it, drinking deeply and swallowing, taking a deep breath and trying his best to brake his racing mind. When the butter was sizzling, he spoke his mind.

"How about we hike on out to the quartz field later, huh?"

Peter thought about it as he swallowed. "See how I'm feeling later."

"Come on."

"It's not the only quartz field in existence, dude."

"Yeah, but it's the only one we're intimately acquainted with. It's ours. Like the prince's rose."

"I guess I'm just not sentimental like you, Nik," Peter said in earnest, missing the reference. "We'll see. Maybe if I get drunk enough."

"Then drink up."

"I gotta drive us tomorrow home, too."

"Don't look at me. You're the one who's gotta rush back."

"And you know I have a good reason. Whatever. Just please let me punt on the quartz field for the time being."

"All right," said Niklas, satisfied. "Did you grab the spatula?"

"Should be hanging out of the side pocket. Blue with white zippers."

Niklas retrieved the spatula and flipped the potatoes and onions as best he could. He fed a few twigs into the coals beneath the pan. The wind picked up and his heart raced along with it, cantering anxiously, trees whipping by as he clung with both hands to the horn of his emotional saddle. It died a second later, then picked up again, though at more of a dull roar. The fire whipped around like a compass gone haywire. The moon had risen high now, pale and bright against the blues and blacks of the forest at night. Peter found himself a suitable skewer, whittled one end to a point, and commenced roasting a sausage. Niklas did the same but soon the stuff in the pan was ready.

"Hold my sausage?"

"Har," said Peter, accepting the skewer from Niklas.

Niklas went back to the tent to get plates and silverware from Peter's backpack. Back at the fire he plated even portions of fried potatoes and onions, steam and scent wafting splendidly.

"How long on the franks?"

"They're not franks," said Peter.

"You ever hear the one about the Southern girl who goes to college in the north?"

Peter looked up, confused. "Rings a bell. Tell me anyway."

"She gets there, first day, wants to do some reading. Goes to a neighbor in the dorms and says, "'Scuse me, miss, but could ya tell me where the library's at?' and the neighbor says, 'Sure I can, but here in the north, we don't end our sentences with prepositions.' And the Southern gal thinks for a second and asks, 'Could ya tell me where the library's at, bitch?'"

Peter smiled. "Nice. What was the point?"

"How long on the franks, bitch?"

Peter looked down at the scorched black ends of the sausages. "Looks done to me."

Niklas rolled his eyes and traded Peter a plate for a sausage. He cut his sausage up and mixed it all together. They both scarfed wordlessly, worn from the day behind them and anticipating the taxing night ahead. Niklas moved on to his second beer, Peter moved on to his fourth. The fire hissed and popped, only a few logs truly aflame anymore. An owl sounded far too close for comfort, given the food in their hands. Though the wind was not as fierce as in recent minutes, the woods felt more alive, animals accustomed maybe to the campers and the fire or perhaps just able to see, now that the moon was nearing its zenith. In the winter after a fresh snowfall, one of Jussi's favorite activities was to hike around on snowshoes and look for different types of animal tracks in the snow. A family of rabbits stuck to the same natural trails through the pines as the humans did; a deer had dragged a wounded leg to a grove of trees, where numerous coyote tracks surrounded the rotting carcass; from the woodpile, though no one bothered to ever research this, a snakelike slither meandered out and around to the cherry trees and then back under the woodpile. It's a snake, Jussi said. Do snakes slither in the snow? asked Jakob. I'm not sure, said Hannu. What else could it be? asked Jussi, incredulous. Bullshit, said Peter, who'd just learned the term. Snakes don't go in the snow. Niklas leaned on his memory after a long pause and realized, dismayed, that he'd forgotten the rest of the conversation.

When the plates were wiped clean, Niklas finished his second beer and took the dishes down to the creek for washing. Something pretty big scampered behind him and he looked around but all he saw was trees and bramble. The beer sloshed around in his stomach and he took a drink to try to level things out. He tripped over a root hidden in the shadow of a trunk on his way back. He set the dishes in the corner of the tent by Peter's bag.

"Toss me another beer," Peter said, crushing his fourth. Or was it his fifth? Niklas took one from the thirty rack and tossed it to Peter, whose catching hand missed the can entirely. "Fuck," he exclaimed as he picked up the beer and brushed dirt and pine needles from the top rim. Niklas grabbed what would have been his third beer, but immediately stooped back over to put it back. The first two had set his head abuzz, which was rare. He went back to his backpack and grabbed the pen and paper, then returned to the tree trunk opposite Peter's that was his seat. He took a long drag from his water bottle and cleared his throat.

"Let's get going on this before we get too belligerent."

Peter looked over, askance. "I'm fine, sure." And he drank deeply.

Niklas used their copy of *Cannery Row* as a surface to write on. He started *Dear Jakob,* then looked up. "OK, so how should we do this?"

"'Dear Jakob,'" Peter said. "Hope you're doing OK. We had to sell Jussi's farm or else we'd starve and my sick kid would die. We're sorry. Rest assured we feel at least as shitty about it as you do, if not more. Get home for Thanksgiving. Love, Us.'"

Brevity was certainly an issue, Niklas thought, but that would make a decent summary of what they needed to say. He wrote It's Niklas. I'm here with Pete around the campfire at our old spot by the creek. Hope you're taking care of yourself in there. We're sure eager to see you. He thought for a second then looked up.

"OK but look, Pete, he's gonna read this in a fucking jail cell. We need to be appropriately contrite."

"Why do we have to be contrite?"

"'Cause we're selling this shit out from under him. He deserves a say, one that we're not giving him."

"He waved that right when he beat a guy to death, Nik."

"Are you fucking serious?"

Peter hesitated, then waved a hand. "I just don't think this letter needs to be a weepy apology. Or a masterpiece. Or anything, other than the information we owe him."

"But we owe him more than information! He's *our* older brother, remember? You said those words, and you said them right here."

"We were in high school, Nik."

"Maybe so, and maybe you were right. We owe Jakob the sum total of everything he taught us or showed us here on this farm. We owe him the benefit of the doubt. He'll be out by Thanksgiving..." here Niklas and Peter both reflexively rapped their knuckles on the trees supporting them "...and devastated that we can't come straight here. No, we're staying up and working until we have that."

Peter crushed and threw his current empty on the pile by the fire and grabbed another from the case. "Look dude. I did all the work to actually fucking sell the place. Can't you handle this?"

"What, so you can do the easy shit that gets us out of here and I'm left with writing the letter to the person I love most in the world about why we lied by omission and sold the most important family heirloom that was also our safety net? Completely without him? He's gonna be furious, dude, and if it's obviously my letter, he's gonna blame shit on me!"

"Tell him about Olly's treatment. He wouldn't be mad at that."

"It's not about the thing itself. It's just that we didn't even give him any kind of heads up. And we fucked that up. We totally should have."

"All right, dude, if you won't tell him I will. About Olly. I know you think I'm an asshole who doesn't get it like he does. I know I'm not tough like either of you. But I fucking hate this, too, Nik, and I'm really not trying to throw you under the bus."

The creek rushed over the rocks, louder than it should be in the space of silence. A breath of breeze tossed the page and left it folded over in Niklas' lap. He set it down and placed the book and the pen on top so it wouldn't blow away. He got up slowly and grabbed himself another beer. He looked back at Peter, who was draining the last drops of his current beer. Niklas thought about trying to get Peter to slow down. He quickly dismissed the idea and grabbed another beer for him.

"'Anks," said Peter, now audibly slurring his words. "Shit!" he cried as foam burst out from the tab as he popped it. He felt around in his hair for foam and, finding none, he scratched his head.

"Aren't you gonna drink any more?" Peter asked rather aggressively as Niklas swigged from his water bottle.

"Sure, dude. Not right now."

"Whatever."

"Really, though. We owe Jakob a decent letter."

Peter merely tipped back his head, chugging for several long seconds. "I think I'll save my explaining for a face to face chat. You've heard what I think we should say."

"That's so pathetic, dude," spat Niklas venomously.

"Well, fuck you! Who's to say which will hurt him worse? Did it occur to you that he might be even more devastated getting this news in the fucking clink than among the guys who've been in it with him from the start?"

"I'd say springing on a guy that his family sold something out from under him, something that was just as much his as it is ours, telling him at the last minute, in person, when we know he has a fucking gasket to blow? I'd say that's fucking stupid, Peter."

Peter looked hard at Niklas and finished his beer in four angry swallows. He lurched over to the case and fell back down against his tree. The fire was merely embers now. The moon was on its way back down. In an hour it would be gone.

"Hey," Niklas said. "Let's go huck some wood and get warm." He hoped Peter had picked up the conspiratorial note he'd tried to drop in. But as he watched Peter struggle to his feet, he figured that subtle messages would have to wait for daylight.

Peter, finally on his feet, was looking wild eyed at Niklas. He raised a hand and pointed a finger. "Only if you shotgun with me."

Niklas returned his gaze. "Fine. What number is this?"

Peter screwed up his face and thought hard. "Seven? Or eight?"

Niklas shook his head.

Peter had only one thing on his mind. "Shotgun. Now." Niklas tossed him a beer and began pressing one of his keys into the lower abdomen of the can, gently poking a hole so that none was wasted spurting out. He worked his fingers around the edges to make the hole in the can about the size of a nickel. He held the can sideways so none spilled and he worked his fingernail under the tab. He looked up at Peter.

"You ready?" Niklas asked.

Peter had spurted all over himself again, but he held his can sideways at the ready. He frowned and nodded deliberately. Niklas began the countdown. "Three, two, one..." and they twisted, eyes skyward, and sucked the prickly beer down their straining throats. After six pumps of his gullet Niklas, felt the can begin to crumple, and so he threw it at his feet and stomped on it. He looked over at Peter who was struggling. Halfway through his beer, Peter had to come up for air. Niklas felt a bitter satisfaction in watching Peter be the lightweight he'd always been.

"Finish it," Niklas taunted. "Come on." After a moment's rest, Peter suffered through till the final drops, which he poured at his feet.

"All right," Niklas said, looking around in the near dark to get his bearings. He started into the thicker woods but Peter called after him.

"Hey. Hey. I'm spinning. I'll be there in a second."

"All right." Niklas shook his head as Peter crumpled to the ground and began to retch. He hurried off to get away from the scene, eager for a moment alone in the moonlight.

Niklas walked for several hundred yards, much longer than he had to. He shook whatever trance was upon him then, realizing how far he was from their camp. He spun around carefully but couldn't make out any trace of orange or even jumping shadow to give him a clue. Knowing the general direction would be enough, which he did. He set to work gathering wood, mostly tearing the limbs off a downed birch and making sure to peel some of the remaining bark off for kindling. An owl hooted overhead and above him Niklas could hear the beating and flapping of large wings. His eyes went to the ground, but they found no mouse tracks in his vicinity. He went back and grabbed a few last shards of birch bark, then turned to head back. Something stopped him just before he set to walking. He stood stock still and listened acutely to the night. There was nothing for a long while. But then a rustling, short, quick little bursts, and then silence, came from directly behind him. Niklas waited with held breath as the rustling resumed more slowly around his right side and ahead of him.

It's a rabbit, he thought just before the tall ears became visible through the foliage. He'd tracked many rabbits through the woods before. The sound of their hopping stride on dead leaves and branches is unmistakable. Niklas was almost ashamed it had taken him as long as it did. The rabbit had his head on a swivel and Niklas tried to melt into the darkness. A moment later, the rabbit decided it was safe to proceed, continuing to hop with a burst of speed off toward Peter and the campfire. Niklas decided to stay on its trail.

The rabbit slalomed through the woods towards where Niklas supposed the creek should be. Niklas did his best to stay back and quiet but was sure he was doing a terrible job. He wondered what a rabbit was doing out this late and alone. Rabbit tracks were easy to spot in the snow, but they always stuck together, and, to Hannu's delight, they also stuck to the same paths through the trees that the humans did. So who was this rogue agent? Who was this nocturnal adventurer? He led Niklas quickly to the creek's edge, where he stopped briefly to drink and look frantically around. He continued along the west edge of the creek for quite a while. Every seven or eight hops, he stopped, and Niklas ducked quickly behind a tree or bush while the rabbit sniffed the air and twitched his ears in apprehension. The wind clocked around to the south and a warm breeze lifted Niklas spirit for the slightest moment. Ten paces ahead were Peter and the campfire. The coals barely glowed enough to reach Niklas several paces out. He'd intended to continue on the rabbit's track, but the breeze and arriving home had distracted him just enough. The little beast had scampered away, maybe back to his family, maybe not.

Niklas was so intent on getting the fire going that it was only when he looked up, a minute and a half later, a ten-inch blaze dancing beneath his chin, that he saw and heard Peter at the same time, chin on his breast, snoring, well and fast asleep.

He should have seen this coming. Niklas racked his brains, trying to remember which was the pivotal seventh beer that always sent Peter into a drunken spiral. Niklas was inclined to sympathize, given his recent escapade and given that it was a rare bout of drinking that didn't send Peter to bed early. Also, total authorial control of the letter was probably for the best. He wondered about the rabbit for a little while. Then, when his cheeks were hot and his eyes bored of staring, he gathered up the paper and pen and book to write on. He sat down heavily with his back to the tree. He shifted around and took a deep breath. And then he began to write.

The first page he threw on the fire after *Dear Jakob* and only two sentences. The second lasted nearly a paragraph. The third he kept and copied onto a clean fourth page, adding a little here, changing a word there. The fourth he copied onto a fifth, clean page. He read it over, and over, and over. And then he folded it up and put the letter in his backpack. He finished the last of his last beer ever at this sacred spot. Then he got up to rouse Peter.

"Hey, Pete. Hey."

"Huh." His eyes fluttered and drooped.

"Pete, it's late. Come on, let's hit the tent."

"Wha?"

"You wanna sleep with your back to a tree trunk?"

"Un unhh."

"Then get up. Come on, bud. Come with me. There you go. Let's get you to bed. Right in here. There you go. Isn't that better?"

In ten minutes, Peter was fast asleep, splayed like a starfish across the entire floor of the tent.

* * *

It took Niklas a few minutes to dig through Peter's pockets and find his keys. He checked that he had his wallet and zipped up the tent. The breeze still blew, bending chokecherry saplings which straightened with a wobble when it died. Niklas raised his feet as he walked through the dark, a trick Hannu had taught his children to avoid tripping on roots and other things unseen in the night. He came out from under the trees at the driveway and tipped his head back to look at the stars. A few dark clouds scudded across the stripe of the Milky Way. Niklas found Orion and the dippers, then spun around looking for planets. He tore himself away as the whine of an ATV approached from a distance then went dead all of a sudden.

On the short drive to Schmidt's, Niklas' head was tense but empty. He was exhausted from the ups and downs of the weekend and knew this was the proper way to finish things off, the way he would want to remember it later. He was drunk enough to know he didn't need much more. The parking lot was almost at capacity when he arrived. He felt a tingle in his belly as he wondered if his pool opponent from the other afternoon would be waiting for him.

It was two deep along the bar with the juke box blaring Johnny Cash and the pool table crowded with guys in boots and camo. Niklas shouldered his way to the front and ordered a High Life.

He drank three beers and stood at the corner of the bar, casting around for a friendly face or a conversation where he might fit in. He watched the same set of college football highlights three times before deciding to check out the pool table. There were two sets of guys waiting in line, and the current game had just begun. Niklas eavesdropped on a man telling his buddy about their other friend, who drank too much.

"...which, whaddam I supposta do? I'd only had two 'cause I hadta do that deck out in Painsdale da next day, and he was out, like, all da way out, so I take him home and put him on my couch. A banging on my door wakes me up about two, tree hours later and I go to the door and there's Nancy, screaming about how I'm encouraging him, it's all my fault, blah blah blah. Poor guy, Nancy took him home right there and then at three a.m. He was slobbering all over everywhere."

His friend, with compassion and real sympathy for his buddy's plight, screwed up his face all serious-like and replied with a heartfelt, "Fuck. That blows."

Niklas soon found himself outside in the cigarette cluster. It occurred to him that out of all the places in a bar where you were expected to socialize, outside with a cigarette between your lips was the only place where other people could really hear you, and the only place where they really took the time to respond. Along the bar inside you pounded away at your story or point with a battering ram, hoping to balance your force with that of your counterpart's, so that each of you can finish whatever you were saying before the other jumps in and goes off on a tangent. Outside, when someone else is speaking, everyone is happy to listen and drag on their cigarettes, and nobody has to yell over the music. Niklas was greatly relieved to be out in the fresh fall air.

Before him were two rather ripe girls, each talking animatedly over each other to a tall man with a massive red beard and a belly barely contained by his Carhartt work pants. Next to him was a smaller fellow in a blue hoodie and jeans. It was he who bummed Niklas the cig that he'd dragged twice, and, remembering that he actually hated the headache that nicotine gave him, allowed to slowly go out in his hand as he watched the conversation bounce between the two big girls and the bearded fellow they were after.

His friend in the hoodie rolled his eyes and said to Niklas quietly, "I'd have left an hour ago if not for this horny motherfucker." He gestured to his large friend and rolled his eyes. Niklas chucked and smiled in sympathy.

"This happen before?"

"Oh, all the fucking time, dude. It's excruciating. I thought I knew all the fat girls in town, but here they come out of the woodwork…"

"I'm sorry, man. I'm probably headed out soon, too."

"All right, man. Hey, did you hear about that Angolan kid? That was fucked."

"What?"

"Oh, shit." The man's eyes lit up. From the way he spoke, it sounded like he'd relayed this anecdote numerous times already tonight. "So this news story comes on this morning about this kid in Angola, whose mom died recently. The kid says that on her deathbed she confessed to him that his father was an orangutan."

"What the fuck?"

"I know, dude. Apparently she was a zookeeper or a vet or something, and worked really closely with this one male until his death, and she had all kinds of intimate tokens of their relationship. But so, of course everyone calls bullshit, but here comes the Angolan government who praise her and are celebrating this kid, who, frankly, resembles an orangutan—not in the racist sense—I mean his face makes the story seem plausible. So, but the government are calling it a miracle. Like, as if he's some example of, like, God making the impossible happen, or whatever."

Niklas was shaking his head. "Can they, like, paternity test or something?"

"The father is dead, if it's in fact that orangutan."

Niklas thought for a second. "So, like… can he talk? How are his language skills?"

The guy looked at him funny. "I don't know, the story didn't say."

"I guess that's just my question. Did he get a human brain or an orangutan brain? Does he have opposable toes?"

"I don't think orangutans have opposable toes, dude."

"Are you sure?"

The man burst out laughing. "How the fuck should I know?"

"Do you think this is legit?"

"Like, is his mom telling the truth?"

"Yeah."

"I don't know. I guess so."

Niklas laughed and shook his head. "Wouldn't your friend have better luck at the Downtowner?"

"Probably. He knows a few of the bartenders here. The Downtowner gets expensive." His tone was uncharacteristically acidic. The Downtowner was beloved in Houghton, and Niklas only favored Schmidt's because of the memories, and they'd only gone to Schmidt's on accident one day and then Jakob had hooked up with Hayley the bartender, and so they'd kept coming back. The randomness of it all began to boggle Niklas' mind. Vertigo washed over him. How easily they could've spent all these years drinking at the Downtowner, but they didn't.

"You a local?" The man looked at him with intensity.

"Marquette. My family's got some land in Liminga, or, well, used to. Me and my cousin just sold the place."

"Well, shit," said the man, breaking into a smile. "Congratulations. You're free."

Niklas looked at him quizzically. "You don't like it here?"

"I was born here, bro. I grew up in Chassell. I tried to go to college in Florida and quit after a semester 'cause I wanted to work." He shook his head and looked at Niklas. "Get away while you can. I keep trying to get away but the farthest I've gotten is Flint. It's always something, man, a girl or a job or a favor for a buddy or some shit." He shook his head. "I'm never gonna leave, man. And that changes a place."

"How come?"

"How come I'm never leaving, or how come it makes a difference?"

"Either. Both."

"I don't mind it all that much, most of the time. I had buddies who are in Chicago now, Detroit, you know, cities. I just can't seem to... I can't make it happen. There's too much keeping me here. My mom's sick now, so there's that, and once she dies, my older brother'll need someone to take care of him, you know, he's got Down Syndrome and lives with Mom now. You know, man. Just shit."

Niklas nodded.

"And how come it makes a difference? 'Cause anywhere you can't leave is prison."

"But you have left."

"And look where it's got me."

Niklas considered this. "All right, sure. But I just got screwed over by my own goddamn cousin over a piece of land we inherited from our dead uncle. My great-grandpa worked in the mines, and my grandpa did too, and I feel like I'm stomping all over their graves for a bullshit reason."

"Yeah, maybe. But at least you won't get sucked in, happened to him," he jerked his head at his friend. "We cut brush together down in Escanaba, we both work at the lumberyard now." (Here it took all of Niklas not to butt in and exclaim that he worked at a lumberyard, too.) "We said we were moving to Minneapolis after a year. Guy's got a cousin there who does concrete. We were going to work for him and his buddy. Way more than what we make now."

"What happened?"

"He met a girl, and by the time they'd broken up. I'd met a girl, and after we broke up, we just never really talked about it. He told me his cousin is moving to California, so." He shrugged. "You need another cigarette?"

"No, man, I'm good."

"OK."

They listened to the girls chattering for a few seconds. Niklas looked back at his friend. "But I don't want to leave. This place... at least the land that my family has, well, had in Liminga, it's the only place I've ever been truly certain I wanted to live. There aren't many places in Milwaukee where you can walk into the woods and only hear the sounds of the woods. Plus, I feel like I grew up there, or at least did the best parts of my growing up with my dad and uncle and brother and cousin. I love it so much, and I've always loved it so much, even when I was little. And now somebody other than me decided we had to sell the place. It's not so different than having to stay against your will. It's not like either of us has a choice. I'm gonna start crying if I talk anymore."

The hoodied man regarded him. "Except that I'm right. This place sucks and the rest of the world is huge. Any sane person who can should get the fuck away." He paused. "It's in your head, man. You may think you're in heaven, but then you wake up twenty years later and the walls are the walls of a prison. But if you leave now? You might have a shot at remembering this place as heaven. Be grateful that no one's spoiled it yet. Don't think I don't love the woods and the lake and the snow in the winter—of course I do. It's just everything else. Get out while you still have happy memories that make this seem like a happy place. Because it isn't."

Niklas looked around. Suddenly, the night seemed desolate, the streetlights blotting out the stars and casting light in unnatural places in the weedy grass sticking up through the gravel parking lot. The babble of conversation from inside had increased in volume, and the shrieking girls made it hard to focus.

"I'm taking off, man. Hope you get out. I want some answers about that Angolan kid."

The guy looked at him and shrugged. "Ah, well. Who knows. Better an ape for a dad than this man," he said as he followed his friend inside, who was being dragged back to the bar by the two giggling girls.

* * *

The drive home passed in a blink. Niklas' head spun as he took one last long look at the stars and walked past the cabin into the woods. He tried to step lightly, but in his drunkenness broke twigs and careened off the path and gently into trees. He found the creek quickly and thought about a final trip to the rock pile but decided to do it in the morning. Peter surely would take a while to rouse.

At the tent, Niklas pissed one more time on the fire and decided to sleep outside. He dragged his sleeping bag from the tent, part of which was under Peter and had to be yanked. He kicked a lump of pine needles into a bed. He lay down, spinning, and listened to the rustling of the night, and all of a sudden, it was morning.

Tuesday, 5:31 a.m.

Niklas was up before the first of the birds. A gray so faint he might have been imagining it creeped in from the southeast. But he wasn't imagining it. Soon nearly half the sky was gray enough to notice and Niklas, going down the list of tasks in his head, laced his dirty boots and stoked the fire for coffee.

After coffee, he hiked out to the quartz field and immediately wished he'd done it while the moon was out the previous night. He cried a little then. He stayed at the quartz field for almost an hour, until the sky was mostly light and only a bit of blue hung around in the northwest.

He hiked back, gathered his fly rod and bait (Peter's unfinished dinner scraps) and fished for an hour and a half. It was a tough morning. He miscast over and over, to the extent that he wondered if it was a displeased Uncle Jussi cursing him from beyond the grave. Finally he recaptured his touch and his casts landed where they were intended to. He only kept two small trout, which were frying in butter over the fire fifteen minutes after he caught them. He thought about waking Peter up for breakfast but decided he couldn't bear the thought of one of his two hard-earned trout making a second appearance alongside last night's beers and sausages. He wolfed his fish and then set out for the cabin to retrieve the chainsaw and get to work on his felled maple.

It was a horribly beautiful day. The birds chirped as if from every branch, a chorus to accompany the flutes in the trees. It was good to sweat and to feel his muscles strain after a dissolute evening. Soon the sky was a brilliant blue, the trees dancing in the wind, no sound but the roar of the chainsaw and occasional whine of an ATV or a car stereo when he rested. The labor felt so regular that the dread lifted from atop his aching heart for the duration of it.

The lumber was limbed and cut and loaded in Peter's car before nine. Peter was staring groggily at the dying fire when Niklas stumbled, out of breath from his work, back to the campsite.

"How you feeling?"

"About as good as I deserve."

"I already got the wood in your car."

Peter looked bewildered but nodded.

"I'm all packed."

"All right. Give me a second."

He took a few steps away from the tent and then vomited violently. Niklas watched him retch until he was finished. It took them fifteen minutes to break down the tent and clear up the campsite. They walked back to the cabin and gathered their bags, each lingering inside until there was no longer any reason at all to be there. Peter announced that he was ready to roll. He waited by the car as Niklas took one last lap around the cabin and surrounding area, then the campsite, and at last the outhouse and the shed. This took twenty minutes; Peter nearly called out to him in a yell, nearly walked back down to one of the three or four places he would surely be to drag Niklas away like he feared he would have to in the end. But then Niklas came back. He was red-eyed when he came up to the car.

"You got everything?" Peter asked gently. His head was pounding out a rhythm he didn't recognize.

"No."

"What'd you forget?"

"Everything."

They hit the road at 9:01, stopping off at Jim's to return the chainsaw. Waiting in his driveway, Jim said he had something for Niklas and ran inside. When he returned, he pressed a small bit of float copper with little bits of silver around one edge. He said it used to be a half breed, originally belonging to their great-grandpa, Olli. Somewhere along the line, the silver had been chiseled off. It had been given to Jim's father by Teemu, albeit with the silver still attached. He felt Niklas should have it, seeing as he was leaving for now. That's how he said it, bless him, thought Niklas: "Oh, just for now."

"You boys drive safe," he said as they shook hands. "Say hey to your dad for me." He went back inside, and they drove away, Cynthia waving from the kitchen window. Halfway between Houghton and Baraga, Niklas noticed a cluster of little wooden crosses in a patch of dead wildflowers on the outside edge of a tight curve. For a second, he wondered why. And then, a second later, seeing winter and icy roads in his mind, he remembered why.

He began to cry again, and then Peter began to cry too. And then they were gone.

* * *

When they got back to Milwaukee, the first thing Niklas did was pore over the letter he'd drafted the previous night. He added three sentences to the end of one of the middle paragraphs. Then he went to the post office, sealed it up, and sent it to Jakob's southern Illinois prison. The letter read thus:

> Dear Jakob,
>
> Now that I'm sitting down to write to you I feel like an idiot for not doing this before. It's hard, and I keep having to scrap what I have and start again. I know what Dad would say—the same thing as when I would get all rattled in hockey. "Stop thinking. Just play." So I'll give that a shot.
>
> I know I said this on the phone the last couple of times, but Peter and I are on the ropes money-wise. Work is scarce and since Pete got furloughed he stuck around a while thinking his job might come back, but it didn't, and so all that extra time waiting ate up all his family's savings. And now apparently Olly has leukemia. Basically we are thoroughly fucked.
>
> I am writing to you by the fire at our old spot by the creek on Uncle Jussi's farm. Peter got drunk too quickly and passed out early like always. At least he didn't throw up the dinner I made him. The moon burns bright and lights my way through the woods—remember all those midnights at the quartz field with Peter? If it sounds like I'm mourning it's 'cause I am. We had to sell the place, Jakob. I am so sorry. It's done, and we're leaving for good tomorrow. Andy Ahonen bought it, which is better than nothing, but believe me, we have torn ourselves to emotional shreds over this. We were looking for a way out right up until the papers were signed. I realize now that I should have let you know beforehand. I guess I thought I'd find some last minute way out of this. But I didn't. And I will suffer for it.
>
> There was this play called The Cherry Orchard that I worked on during my first few weeks in Chicago. I think I

183

even told you about it. Do you remember? It's about a wealthy provincial family that gets complacent and, over the course of four acts, loses their gorgeous country estate to a businessman, who, in the final moments, begins to cut down their beloved cherry orchard. I remembered this as I was gathering firewood from the pile of old chokecherry. Maybe I was paralyzed in the same way as that family. Just as they do in the play, I plugged my ears and proceeded as though it was business as usual, and now the place is sold and there's nothing I can do about it. Christ, I even cut down a tree. A maple. I was thinking about all that work on chairs in Chicago and I decided to take a piece of the place with me. I'm going to make us a nice chair from the wood of one of Uncle Jussi's trees.

The hardest thing about this, and I know it'll be doubly hard for you, is that there are so many things I won't be able to consciously do for the last time. When was the last time we strapped on snowshoes and tracked every animal we could find evidence of through the snow? When was the last time we shot at last night's empty beer cans, and whoever took the longest to knock all five off Dad's old sawhorse had to pay for dinner? When was the last time we explored an abandoned mine outbuilding and wondered if Grandpa Teemu or Olli Sr. had been inside? When was the last time you ate a fish you caught yourself, from a creek whose babble you know as intimately as your father's voice? Parting for good can only be sweet when it is acknowledged as such. I remember lots, Jakob, but I can barely remember our last time here. Every day I wake up and remember less and less about Jussi. And it all conspires to break my heart.

I'm sorry if this is all too soppy and miserable, but that's how things are. Who's to say what's oversensitive, considering all there is to be thought and felt? Again, I'm sorrier than all hell. I know I should wait until the financial clouds pass, but I want to look at listings for land up here so we can start fresh as soon as we can. Not sure why I'm telling you now except to let you know I fully intend to be back up here on land we own as soon as I can justify it.

Stay out of trouble so we can see you at Thanksgiving. I'll send some money for a bus ticket to Milwaukee. Peter is hosting at his super-ritzy condo on Water Street which he's gonna have to get rid of. He's pissed, but I would be way more pissed if he managed to keep the place for some reason. Anyway. Call me when you're out. Or if you're not. Just call me.

Love,
Niklas

❧ 21 ❧

Thanksgiving Day

Jakob was paroled, as planned, on the sixteenth of September and obtained special permission for his Thanksgiving visit to Milwaukee. The process took forever: it was incredibly draining to be so close and yet unsure of exactly which moment he would be free. By the time he boarded a Greyhound bus in Edwardsville, early on Thanksgiving Day, he was dead tired. He'd spoken briefly with Niklas on the phone and had written down Peter's address, as well as directions from the Milwaukee station.

Jakob felt a panic rise in his throat as he realized, watching the driver shut and secure the door, that he was, once again trapped in a tiny space, barred from fresh air for an undetermined amount of time. Thankfully, he was as tired as he'd ever been, and repeated deep breaths did the trick. His eyes closed before they were even on the highway, and he slept the whole way to Chicago. He woke with a jolt as the bus turned off the highway and over the Chicago River to the Harrison Street terminal. Brake lights washed the pavement red. The sky was a husky dark pale orange reflection of the streetlights below. All around him buildings towered and the lights from their windows shone on the hoods of cars and on the shimmering surface of the river. The heart of the city made Jakob feel like a ten-year-old on Christmas Eve.

His luggage was just a backpack and an extra set of clothes. Niklas had sent along some money for the ticket and food on the journey home with his letter, which was stuffed in a brand new dollar store faux leather wallet. His clothes were similar— Goodwill, and Walmart for the shoes, which were new. His hair was buzzed, head covered in a cheap black beanie. He looked of a piece with the haggard faces that filed out in front and behind him off the bus and into the brightly lit terminal. Jakob distinctly remembered a time when he'd been offered cocaine on the very steps he was descending. A million years ago.

He boarded the Milwaukee-bound bus for the last leg of his trip after an hour layover spent watching the small TV in the corner of the terminal without really paying attention. When the boarding announcement came over the PA, he waited until everyone else had lined up before taking his place at the back. He was eager to suck as much fresh air as they'd let him. As the driver punched his ticket, he swore to himself that his next apartment would have lots of open windows. The driver delivered his memorized spiel, which everyone ignored as they got settled in. Jakob balled up a shirt in another shirt and wedged the makeshift pillow between his shoulder and his head. He closed his eyes but couldn't fall asleep. He'd slept the whole way from Edwardsville, and in two hours, he'd be sitting down to Thanksgiving dinner with Niklas and Peter and Peter's family.

As he stared at the passing lights, Jakob was steamrolled by the enormity of the evening ahead. Niklas had called him in prison the week after the letter arrived. They talked about it, but there wasn't much to talk about. Niklas went ahead and mentioned that Peter's kid was sick, that that was the main catalytic component of the whole thing. It made sense to Jakob when he said it. He knew Niklas as well as Niklas knew him, and Jakob knew the kid had probably kicked and screamed and made it as hard for Peter as possible. Jakob was nervous about seeing Peter. Actually, he was more nervous about Tina, but he did his best to put that out of his mind. The shock he'd felt in himself upon inhabiting the outside world for the first time made him question the rate of change in others. He knew he'd have to get used to the shame of having done what he did. But that didn't make it any more inviting. He wondered if Olly, Peter's little boy, knew he was a bad guy. He thought hard about it intermittently for the rest of the bus ride and realized he hadn't the slightest clue whether the kid knew or not. Frankly, the soaring joy of freedom would not allow many other emotions besides a dash of apprehension about the first ten minutes back with his family.

Jakob was so wrapped up in the evening ahead that when the interior lights of the bus blinked on and the passengers in front of him began to file out into Milwaukee, he had to scramble to gather his things, which were few. He was still zipping his backpack as he hopped off the bottom step of the bus and felt the blast of a November gale bite his cheeks. He pulled out the crumpled envelope where he had recorded Niklas' directions for taking the bus to Peter's house. Four blocks north to Water Street. Catch the Green line or the 15, Pete's place is like three stops after that. Buzz up when you get to his building. Fourth floor, take a right out the elevator, fifth door on the left.

Jakob fought his way north against a stiff wind that watered his squinting eyes. He kept looking over his shoulder for an assailant on the prowl or a guard who'd chased him down this whole way to tell him there'd been a mistake, his parole had been denied, he'd be going back for another year. At the bus stop, he counted his change over and over and over again despite the fact that his fingers froze each time. He waited. A homeless man with a huge garbage bag full of aluminum cans joined him at the stop. Seemingly every other bus in the area came and went. The man turned and regarded him.

"Man, iss a cold one tonight."

"Yes it is."

"You got a woman you rushin' home to?"

"No sir. You?"

"Oh, she left me a long time ago." He laughed. "It's all right though. It's Thanksgiving. You got people to eat with?"

"Headed there right now."

"Well, shit. I'll be seeing some people too. Real good people."

Jakob knew he was lying. "That's good."

"Ain't it? Man. Once I drop this load off, imma get right back to 'em."

Jakob started to say something, but the words caught in his throat. The man looked off down the road in the direction the bus would come from. Then the first tears came, a trickle and then a gush, Jakob looking off in the other direction to spare his lonesome fellow passenger the sight of him.

* * *

The bus came ten minutes later. Jakob nearly missed the transfer but was able to pull the cord only one stop beyond his intended destination. The Green line came quickly, and soon enough, he was buzzing Peter's apartment from just inside his building's foyer. The front door clicked open a dozen seconds later, allowing Jakob into the lobby. He felt the blood roaring in his ears as he pressed the UP button beside the elevator.

The elevator doors opened to reveal a heavily chrome hallway with brutally tacky wallpaper and orange carpeting, tacky in the way only folks who wish to appear rich can manage. He counted out five doors on the left side of the hallway. Behind the fifth came children's playful cries and bursting laughter that sounded uncannily like Peter's. Jakob took five deep breaths, then another five, then another five, then knocked on the door.

"Holy shit, I got it, I got it, that must be him." Jakob heard Niklas' muffled voice through the door. He heard footsteps pound the floor growing ever closer. He saw the prick of light through the peephole disappear along with a shifting shadow blotting out the crack beneath the door. He smiled as the door opened and his brother tackled him out onto the ghastly carpet in the hallway.

Acknowledgements

The author would like to express his boundless gratitude to the following people for their help with the novel; to Allan Bates, Ben Schneider, Trevor Taylor, Casey Oberto, Frank Mayfield, Peter Meyers, Sam Greene, Grant Papastefan, Charlie Stelnicki, Will Lund, Ryan Deweerdt, Rein Tael, Jacob Bartz, Wendy and Joe Taylor, Bob Rich, PhD, Victor Volkman, Tyler Tichelaar, Joseph D. Haske, and most of all John Austin.

About the Author

J. D. Austin was raised in St. Louis, Missouri and has been moving gradually north since the age of fourteen. After dropping out of college in November of 2019, he worked as a kayak guide, a wedding server, bar security, lighting designer, stage carpenter, ski technician, and in the nursery department at a Home Depot. His fiction has appeared in *The Incandescent Review* and *U.P. Reader Volume Seven*. *The Last Huck* is his first novel. You can learn more about him at JDAustinStories.com.

Printed in the USA
CPSIA information can be obtained
at www.ICGtesting.com
CBHW031255010424
6163CB00003B/9